TH BRIDGE

LEO PETRACCI

Thank you to everyone who helped with the production of this novel- to the beta readers, my editor, my illustrators Caterina Kalymniou and CM Dugan, fellow authors, and my fans.

And thank you to my teachers, my parents and grandparents, and everyone else who helped me reach this point.

Table of Contents

Part 1: Horatius

A starship is struck by an asteroid on its way to colonize a distant planet. Now, hundreds of years later, the inhabitants must learn to survive deep space without technology or perish.

Chapter 1

The asteroid was called the Hand of God when it hit.

Not that we know much about God, of course. There are plenty of books that survived the destruction, though the readers far more sparse. And those that could spouted nonsense after a few pages, about things called suns and moons being created, about talking beings called "animals," about oceans. About legends of old, myths, wishful thinking. But what I do know about God is, if his hand caused the damage to the ship, I don't want to know much more.

The stories say that the ship used to be one before it hit. That the asteroid split the ship right down the center, making the way to the other side dangerous, impossible. But we can still see it, entangled in cord and moving alongside us, and we can see in their windows. We can see the faces far more gaunt than our own, the cheeks near bone, the eyes hollow and staring hungrily back at us. And we can see them fighting, using knives stashed from the kitchen along with strange flashing devices, and though we cannot hear, we know they scream.

There is a third part of the ship as well, this one with no faces in the windows, all dark and barely held to the main two parts. But no one has ever seen movement there, and it is far smaller than the halves.

There are one thousand of us on our side, a census conducted each year by scratching marks into the cold wall, making sure we have enough to eat. Any number over eleven hundred has led to shortages of food, and more importantly, water. As one of the gardeners, I know this too well, planning out the ship's rations and crops, utilizing the few rooms remaining with glowing ceilings. Deciding if I plant only those seeds specified for meals, or if we could splurge on space for the herbs demanded by our doctors or the spices requested by our cooks.

We worked together on the ship, each of us with our task for survival, none of us expendable. At ten, a child was assigned their task, from chief to scourer, based upon the skills they possessed. That first year, they were evaluated, deciding if a change was necessary, and I had been applying for the coveted historian. For keeping the tales and the knowledge from long before, from where the recovered books on ship census marked twenty-five thousand.

In the stories of old, it is said that God could speak even if he couldn't be seen. That he could be heard as a voice alone, sending commandments down to his people.

And today, in the year 984, I, Horatius, heard him.

"Systems rebooting," said the voice, jolting me out of my duty of watering the plants. "Ship damage assessed. Reuniting the two halves of the ship and restoring airlock, approximately twenty-four hours until complete."

Staring out the window, I saw the cables holding the halves of the ships tighten. I saw the eyes of the hungry faces widen as they were dragged closer.

And I wondered if the hand of God was striking again.

Chapter 2

At age four, I started schooling.

Out of the thousand inhabitants of the ship, one hundred and fifty attended schooling, going to one of the three locations near the center of the ship. There was Hippoc, the school for doctors and chefs due to the similarities in their trades, the mixing and application of plant herbs, of which approximately twenty students attended, their parents typically from those positions. Next was Empri, where students were taught to read, their futures as the historians, leaders, and other educated members of the ship and admissions set for a maximum of ten total seats. For the rest of us, a hundred and thirty in all, there was Vertae, the school for gardeners, porters, and the occasional chief guard or assistant.

I still remember the year before my first day, when my father held my hand and whispered bedtime stories to me.

"Once," he would say, as I resisted sleep with wide-open eyes. "Once, it is said that the ship was so large that you could walk for days without touching a wall. That the potatoes you see me farming used to grow as tall as me, perhaps even taller, and had stems as thick as my arm. Instead of the glow lights above, there was only one glow light, and somehow it split into the many that we have today. And in the floor of the ship, there were rushes of water, hallways so to speak, that entire men could float down."

"Float down water?" I asked, at three, even back then my brows crossed in confusion, "They must have been very rich, to have that much water."

"Indeed, they must have been. But these are only stories, Horatius, stories that my father told me, and his father told him."

"But where from?" I asked. "Where did the stories come from?"

"The historians, of course," my father answered. "They have all sorts of stories, some so ridiculous it makes me think that they are crazy, not full of common sense like ourselves."

"The historians," I had repeated, the cogs in my young mind spinning. "I want more stories, Papa. I want to be a historian."

A frown creased my father's face, and he sighed, "Well, Horatius, I don't know—"

"But I do!" I protested, and regret crossed his face.

"Look, Horatius," he said, "we gardeners, we keep the ship alive. Without us, there would be no food. There would be no one to carry water. Everyone would starve and thirst. But without the historians, well, we would lose stories. And we could do without that, Horatius. Food provides, stories do not."

Then he tucked me into bed, using the patched blanket he had mended from his own youth and still bore his scent, and departed.

"A historian," I had whispered before falling asleep, disregarding his last words. "A *historian*."

One year later, my father dropped me off at general assembly, where the twenty-five children of my year awaited their school assignments, each with a pack of vegetables for lunch and shy expressions. We had seen each other throughout the ship before, and Mitch, my best friend, was there next to me, but today was different. Never before had I been with that many people my age at the same time.

"Welcome," said an adult at the center of the auditorium. High above him was a single large glow light, surrounded by eight other lights that had appeared to have gone out, or perhaps were never installed, but were rather painted over with various colors. I remember being impressed with one that was swirls of green, white, and blue, and had situated myself underneath it.

"Today, you will receive assignments to your schools," continued the adult. "One of you to go to Empri, two of you to Hippoc, and twenty-two to Vertae. While these placements are permanent, I encourage you to work hard, as your final assignments will be conducted at the end of your schooling. It is not unheard of for a farmer to seek to become a chef, or a doctor a chief, but it comes only with hard work."

I remember nodding and waiting, my arms crossed over my chest. I was ready to learn stories, and I was ready to learn letters. I knew I could do both.

"Elliott and Hannah," said the adult, "both of you will be attending Hippoc, so please exit through the door on your left, where you will be escorted to the school's chambers. As for Empri," he said, scanning the crowd, his eyes landing on me as I burst into a smile. "Ah, yes, for Empri, Segni, if you'll come with me."

I froze as another boy pushed past me, heading to the front of the crowd, his hair recently cut and his white smile reflecting the glow of the light above. I knew him from passing in the hall, when my father had pulled me to the side to allow the chief to pass with Segni following.

"But—" I said, though the adult cut me off.

"But the rest of you will be attending Vertae," he finished. "Remember, Vertae is the strength of the ship. Without Vertae, none of us could survive."

My father repeated those words when I came home with tears on my cheeks. And he repeated the same thing he had for the past year, assuring me of its truth.

"Without food, we starve," he said. "But stories, stories are not sustenance. We can manage without them."

And for two years, I nearly believed him. Until age six, when Vertae started training us in gardening the fields, and two stories of my own began.

Chapter 3

"What are you doing, Horatius? Trying to *read* again?" said Nean, shoving me into the wall as he walked past, sneering. "Go on, pick up your shovel, before I pick it up with your head."

I regained my balance, staring upwards at the squiggles that had held my attention, focusing on what I knew to be letters. On what those at Empri would be learning, and I, as a six year old in Vertae, would not.

It was the second year of schooling, our first year spent learning about subjects such as roots, stems, leaves, and the other components of plants. We learned of the water reservoirs and how to use just the minimum amount of liquid in growth. And we learned of the sewer and compost troughs, which had to be distributed among the crops every few months or else the plants would not grow as well.

"Why do we have to switch out the dirt?" I remember asking after following Nean into class, as Skip, our adolescent instructor, showed us how to spread the compost. "Why don't we just use the old dirt?"

"What do you mean *why?*" Skip had retorted, his expression accusing me of stupidity while Nean snorted behind him. "You just *do.*"

"I get that, but why?"

"It's just what you do. You take the dirt, and you spread it. Plants grow, you pick them, you repeat. 'Why' doesn't matter. Stop wasting our time with these questions. There is food to grow and work to do."

And by the end of our sixth year of age, Skip trusted us enough to start preparing our own patches of garden, practicing with the easiest of seeds, the ones that could suffer the most abuse yet still have some yield. By now, he had grown accustomed to my questions, positioning me at the far end of the practice field near the wall, far away from the rest of the class where I could not interrupt him as he inspected their gardens.

"No, no, no, you're doing it wrong again, Horatius," Skip had said, watching me as I planted seeds in a neat line. "Use the blade of your shovel to open up the dirt, not the handle."

"Seems faster to use the handle to poke a hole, see?" I said, showing him how I could indent the earth and place a seed inside, without actually scooping earth out.

"It's *wrong*. Just do things the right way. If you don't improve soon, I'm going to have to reduce your marks. Just do it right."

"But it's faster!" I complained, trying to show him again, though he had already moved on to the next student.

With time, I discovered that so long as Skip's back was turned, it didn't matter *how* I planted the seeds. Mine grew just as well as anyone else's, and I could plant that at about twice the pace, especially without him distracting me at the edge of the field. And more importantly, as my practice field moved farther away from the others, I discovered something that never would have occurred had I remained with the rest of the class.

That if I gardened quietly, and stuck towards the edge of my field, I could hear voices. Voices that carried over to me from the other side of the wall, and though muffled, were intelligible.

"Now, Segni," said the voice, "we're going to go over this again. In order to become chief one day, you'll have to read. And to read, you'll need to know your alphabet. Can you recite it for me?"

"Why do I have to read to be chief? I can just talk," replied the young boy's voice.

"No, you must read. Let's go over it again. Here, listen, this is how you recite the alphabet. Start with A."

Each day, I listened in, paying close attention to Segni's lessons, reciting the letters in my head. Learning the difference between vowels and consonants, and how to spell without knowing how the letters actually looked. Even with the wall between, I absorbed the lessons, eagerly accepting what Segni resisted as I planted my seeds.

Within the next month, another instructed called Angie taught us at night when Skip's morning classes ended, taking us to another learning patch and showing us how to plant slightly more difficult seeds. Skip had already warned her of my slowness to learn, so Angie had followed his example and placed me on the outskirts of the group, this time near the window that peered out into the starry expanse outside the ship.

And as I planted, the rules that Angie reiterated to the rest of the group time and time again had already rooted and been improved upon in my brain, and I found myself practicing the lessons from the mornings in my thoughts. Finishing quicker than the others in planting, there were times my gaze flickered out through the window and to the other half of the ship, where figures moved in the distance.

But each time I let my stare wonder, I always came to rest on a window to my left, near the end of the other half. Where a face constantly filled the glass, a face of a girl around my age, with red hair and her palms on the glass.

A face whose eyes met mine, and who stared at me while I worked.

Chapter 4

"S-H-I-P," said the teacher through the wall as I walked through the potatoes I had planted, administering carefully measured water to each. "What's that spell?"

"Sheep," said Segni, his voice exasperated.

Ship, you little shit. I thought, nearly spilling my watering apparatus in frustration. *Ship!*

It had been two years since I'd discovered my listening spot, and in those two years, Segni had slowly and painfully progressed through the alphabet to the separation of vowels and consonants to spelling. I gritted my teeth each time his teacher sighed, each time Segni came in to lessons and had not practiced the night before, each time he asked for a break after five minutes.

"Close," came the teacher's voice. "We learned about sheep last week in the readings. Try again."

"I don't feel like it," said Segni, and I heard a thump as he put his foot on the desk. "Close enough."

"No, it's not close enough," said the teacher. "I'm going to need you to try again."

"Look, I don't have to do anything that I don't want to. I'm the chief's son, and he's the one that gives you your rations. He's not even sure why you're making me learn reading, said he thinks it's a waste. So I'd be careful or maybe I'll tell him you're not doing your job, and you'll go to the fields."

There was silence inside the classroom for a moment, then the instructor spoke, his voice bitter.

"As you wish," he said. "If you shall refuse to read, I shall read to you. Today, we study the history of the ship prior to the Hand of God. Prior to when the ship was split, and our brothers and sisters were separated from us, perhaps forever. Segni, are you listening? Quit drawing."

"Go on, I'm listening," said Segni with a yawn as the teacher continued. I suppose I should be thankful for Segni's general attitude, for without it, I never would have heard the stories. Instead, Segni would have read them to himself, and I would be no better off.

"As I was saying," continued his teacher, "the ship was once one, one people. From their census, we know that food and water used to be in higher abundance, that they used to be able to sustain a population far greater than our own. *Listen* to this, Segni. This is the reason why our numbers cannot exceed one thousand now, because we do not have the resources. When the asteroid hit, it took with it much of our capabilities, much of our ways to provide."

"Yeah, the asteroid hit and killed a ton of people. That happened forever ago."

"It wasn't the *asteroid* that killed those people, Segni. From records, we can see that only two hundred people died in the actual collision. The rest died after. From starvation, from famine, from thirst. Segni, as chief one day, you will have to understand this, that we must be prepared for famine again."

"If the asteroid hits again, we'll probably all die, so it doesn't even matter."

"There's plenty more than just an asteroid that can go wrong, Segni."

"Whatever," he said. "We'll make it through. We always do."

"Because we are *prepared*. Three hundred years ago, our ship panicked when the water stopped flowing. Our numbers were at three thousand then, and when the flow stopped, they plummeted. It is said that a great historian, Archim, was able to discover how to start the flow again. But even he could not bring it up to normal levels, and so we persist today weaker than ever. One hundred years ago, half our crops died, for an explanation that we cannot identify. *Half*, and we are barely able to sustain as is. Without food stores, we likely would have followed. This *will* happen again, Segni, and unless you are prepared, we will not, as you put it, make it through."

Segni huffed, and I continued gardening, heart pumping as I listened. I had heard of the *Great Thirst*, but that was supposed to be false, something my father said to me when I felt like complaining.

"Segni, you must listen to me," said the teacher. "Our lives will be in your hands. History repeats itself, and there are precious few who we can dedicate to leading the ship, precious few that know the purpose of our existence. You will be one of them and you must use that knowledge wisely, in the case of another disaster. In case the Hand of God strikes again."

Chapter 5

At age ten, we gathered in the general assembly, the rest of the ship together for the announcement of our positions. Extra rations were available to all that attended, so not a single person was missing from the crowd.

"Welcome," boomed the chief from the podium at the front, his eyes bright. "Welcome to the selection ceremony. We are proud to receive the next wave of students into our citizenship, into our community. Only through work do we persist, and only together we survive." He gestured at us, wearing the blue graduation robes that spent most of their lives locked in a closet, and as such had far brighter colors than any other garment. Then he continued his gesture to a table, where there were twenty-five items resting on the surface. One pen, two mounds of dried herbs, and twenty-two cherry tomatoes.

"Today, we accept our graduates with open arms. We have full faith in them and bestow upon them the responsibility of future generations to come. But first," he said, and held up a waiting finger, "they must pass their tests."

Three people stepped forward from behind the chief, each in different-colored robes. One I recognized as Skip, his hair plastered down for the occasion. The other was Sage, the lead cook of the kitchens, who sometimes gave me an extra portion when I gave her my best smile. And the third was a man that I did not recognize, with a beard that spilled over his chin, and a volume under one arm.

"I shall administer the first test," claimed Sage. "will the interested individuals please step forward?"

Elliott and Hannah moved as one from our crowd, their chins high, their parents in the crowd with beaming smiles.

"For the past six years, you have studied, and you have persevered," said Sage. "And now, we must know if you have succeeded. Three questions I have for you, three questions that either a doctor or chef can answer. First, what is the proper herb to administer to those complaining of aches and sores?"

"Ginseng!" they said together, and Sage nodded as the crowd applauded.

"Next, demonstrate the correct way to prepare the following herbs for cooking," said Sage as two people rushed forward from the crowd with trays, knives, and several green leaves. Both Elliott and Hannah took the knives and separated the herbs accordingly, dicing or rolling them into the correct shapes as Sage nodded.

"And lastly," said Sage, with a smile, "what is the oath of the school of Hippoc?"

"To preserve, to sustain, to nourish, and to aid, for the good of the ship."

And with a final nod, the crowd erupted, Elliott and Hannah returning to their seats with the piles of herbs from the table clutched in their hands.

"As we all know, no test is required for students of Vertae, so the next test shall be administered to the sole student of Empri, my very son, whose progress has made me most proud," said the chief, and the bearded man stepped forward, a frown on his face.

"It is known," said the man, and I recognized his voice from Segni's lessons, "that the direction of our future is held in the hands of our leaders. That those graduating from Empri are of the highest caliber, are of the brightest minds, and of astute moral righteousness. Will the interested individuals please step forward for this year's opening of historian, so that I, Pliny the historian, may extend my blessing?"

Segni strode to before the podium, his father towering above him as he prepared for the first question. I bit my lip as I looked ahead and pushed my way to the front of the student crowd, Nean pushing my shoulder as I walked past so I staggered behind Segni.

The chief's eyes widened as I stared up at Pliny, my shoulders thrown back, and my fists clenched to hide the dirt under my nails. Behind me, I heard the crowd start to whisper, and looked back to see my father among them, shaking his head as his eyes met mine.

"A *gardener*," laughed one from the front. "A gardener. Go back to the fields, boy. Don't embarrass yourself."

"Indeed," said the chief, looking down at me. "Do you presume that you can pass a test designed for the students of Empri? This is for intellectuals, boy, absolutely unheard of. Go on back."

Skip stepped forward, his face red, pointing at me. "Out of all my class, he has the lowest marks!" he spat. "Can't even make a hole correctly after four years! Slowest learner I've ever seen. I apologize, chief, for my student's ignorance. Get, Horatius."

Pliny stared down at me, his eyebrows raised, and spoke as well, addressing the audience in his deep voice. "It is written that anyone may take the test, and it is wrong to bar them entry. As such, we cannot deny him, regardless of our opinion if he will pass or fail. Let us begin."

Chapter 6

"That's not fair!" shouted Segni, "I've spent hours enduring lectures, years putting up with work, and now you're going to let *him* have a shot at it?"

My jaw stiffened as Pliny smiled and replied, "Of course, young chief-to-be. With all those hours of study, you should have nothing to worry about, should you? This should be easy for you."

Pliny cleared his throat and addressed us both.

"There are three main qualities that Empri instills in its students. First is the ability to learn, or reading. With reading comes the second quality, which is knowledge. And only through those comes stewardship, which is the only quality that truly matters. The first two are but tools to attain the third. As such, there will be three questions for this test, three questions that must be answered correctly, one for each of the qualities. Do you understand?"

Together, Segni and I nodded, and the chief's eyes narrowed.

"Question one will be on reading. I will spell a word, and you will tell me what it is, which should be simple for anyone accomplished in the field. For you, Segni, what does L-E-S-S-O-N spell?"

Segni thought for a minute, his eyes closed and mouth working to sound out the letters.

"Less!" he shouted, and a wry smile formed across Pliny's mouth.

"Close, but not quite," he said. "Lesson, Segni. It spells lesson."

"Close enough to count," said the chief in a low voice, and Pliny continued.

"Now you, Horatius, I believe. Here is your word: O-P-P-O-R-T-U-N-I-T-Y."

From behind in the crowd, I heard Nean shout out, his voice nearly cutting off Pliny's.

"It spells *stupid gardener!*"

Chuckles sounded from the crowd, the vast majority of which did not have the means to tell if he was correct, and I waited for them to quiet down to whispers.

"Opportunity!" I said, my voice near a shout. "It spells opportunity!"

"Indeed," said Pliny and tilted his head as he looked into my eyes, his expression as curious as the chief's was red, the whispers in the crowd dying to surprised silence. "Precisely. Next, a question regarding history and knowledge. Segni, I shall allow you to go first due to your hard work in schooling. Before *The Hand of God*, how many people inhabited the ship?"

Segni smiled and stuck his chest out, speaking the answer, "More!"

"Is that your answer?" asked Pliny.

"Yes, my answer is more!"

"Technically, I suppose," replied Pliny, "though I was looking for something more precise. Horatius?"

"Twenty-five thousand," I answered, and the curiosity in Pliny's eyes increased as his pupils dilated.

"Precisely again," he said, studying me, though I held his gaze and did not move, "How strange, how curious. Now for the final question, on stewardship, should the Hand of God strike again, how should we be prepared for it?"

"It *won't* strike again," spat Segni, and his father nodded.

"Food and water stores," I answered. "Enough to get us through disaster and to recover. Spread around the ship in case one area is impacted."

"Correct," said Pliny. "Three for three, with no marks off."

"For both candidates," said the chief, and a frown formed on Pliny's face.

"Well," he said, turning to face the chief, "based upon the integrity of both answers—"

"Three out of three for *both*," repeated the chief, his voice rising. "*Both*. My son and this, this *imposter*. Integrity, Pliny? You want integrity? I'll show you *integrity*. One last test, one more to determine the true winner, and to out the obvious cheating that is occurring. A pen and paper, now."

From the crowd, one of the attendants to the chief rushed forward, carrying the materials. And the chief marked the paper, writing letters big enough for the crowd to see, and displaying it.

"Horatius, it is enough that you have embarrassed my family. It is enough that you have mocked our rituals and tests. Should you admit that you are cheating now, should you admit guilt, I will spare you any punishment."

"I'm not cheating!" I answered, the fists at my side tightening.

"Then what does this spell?" asked the chief, brandishing the sheet.

The letters danced in front of me, letters that I had never studied by sight but only heard. Blood rushed to my cheeks as I stared, praying for a revelation, praying for a miracle.

"Go on," said the chief. "Show us how you are worthy to be historian. What does it spell?"

"I- I don't know," I answered, tears forming near my eyes. "I can't read it, I can only—"

"By his *own* admission, then, he can't read," said the chief, and turned to where Segni already bounced on the balls of his feet with anticipation. "Now, Segni, what does this spell?"

"Sheep!" his son cried out, his voice echoing.

"*Ship*. Precisely," said his father, and walked to the table that held the awards for each of the vocations, picking up a pen and cherry tomato. He placed the pen in his son's hand, holding it high.

"Welcome," he said, and the crowd cheered. "Welcome, to our new historian."

And walking to me, he took the cherry tomato, and crushed it above my head such that the pulp fell into my hair, and the juice dripped down my face.

"And *welcome*," he hissed. "Welcome to our new gardener, whose position will start in one year. Until then, he will be punished for cheating, and will be obligated to fulfill any of the ship's hauling and porter needs. Now go, Horatius. Your job has begun."

His finger extended to the door, and I left, Nean's voice trailing behind me as drops of tomato juice dripped to the floor.

"Thought he could be a historian. Not even fit for a gardener." And turning back, I saw Skip nodding, the crowd laughing, and my father turned away.

Chapter 7

Each morning, I started with an hour of exercise, which was required of porters.

I would arrive in the heavy room slightly after breakfast, feeling my spine compress as I walked across the threshold, adjusting my posture slightly as I walked inside. Waiting was weight lifting machinery—an arrangement of dumbbells and plates designed to help increase muscle capacity, all at twice the weight they would be outside the heavy room.

There I would pair up with the others who had been assigned to be porters, many of them for life, their chests bulging from under their shirts and the veins in their necks popping. Most of them were those who could not succeed at gardening, though some were placed there for punishments like myself, for crimes such as hoarding water or striking their neighbors, though violent crimes were so rare, I had not heard of any in my lifetime.

"Tom want first breakfast," said my partner as I watched his form. As usual, it was impeccable, near robotic, not a single mistake as the weights were cycled through lifts and rests. But for all his skill with strength conditioning, Tom had troubles outside the heavy room, where his difficulty in grasping the intricacies of planting seeds and grammar had dragged him down the societal ladder to porter.

"Fine," I answered. "I'll take second, then."

We ate in shifts, as porters. It meant that there were always some of us available to cart away waste, or move bundles of vegetables, or shift furniture around living spaces. But there was a perk to being a porter, one that was required by the sheer physical requirements of the position— we were rationed portions and a half, of both food and water.

"Good," answered Tom, dropping his weights so that the heavy room shook. "Tom done, then."

And he lumbered away, sweat staining the back of his shirt, his physical stature larger than any on the ship. In his absence, I racked the weights, then retrieved a cart at the end of the hall, one that was to be transported to the kitchens and was filled with potatoes.

At first, the going was hard, since being so near the heavy room made the cart difficult to push. But after my first week of being a porter, I had learned the inner layout of the ship, hidden from the main corridors, where the light halls were and how to connect them.

I'd been in light halls before, of course. Before being required to work, I'd often played in them, running up the sides of the walls and jumping from end to end of the corridor in a single bound, much to the annoyance of any traversing porters at the time. For just as the heavy room added weight to my frame, the light hall removed it, making transporting overfilled carts as easy as those that were empty in the normal, more occupied areas.

The light hall I used that morning was dark, the glow lights much lower than in other areas of the ship, and ran behind a row of living spaces that emptied their waste into the hall for porters to collect. As soon as I finished crossing the hall, there would be hardly another hundred feet before reaching the kitchens, and I could switch duties with Tom as he finished breakfast. The thought had my stomach growling, especially since the new chef Elliott was already known for his skill in dish preparation.

And that morning, I was so hungry, and so focused upon completing my task, that I never heard the footsteps behind me.

"Stupid *porter!*" said Nean's voice as an oversized hand gripped the back of my neck, pinning me to the wall. "Think you're smarter than all of us; look where you are now. If it was my decision, you'd stay here."

"Get off!" I shouted, my muscles sore from the heavy room, adding to the agony of Nean cheese-grating my nose against the rough metal.

"All I want to do is make sure you've learned your lesson. Help the chief out. He asked me, you know. Well, not him particularly; just the future chief."

"Stop it!" I shouted, but Nean ripped me away from the wall, driving my forehead into the hard edge of the cart so hard that the room flashed. I fell, feeling his shoe contact my ribs on the way down, and once more as I curled on the cold floor, struggling to draw in breaths. Then Nean leaned over, his face so close to mine that I could smell his breath.

"Segni says if you try to humiliate him again, you won't just be a porter. He says I can hit you hard enough that you think like them too. Right here."

Then he spat, his phlegm mixing with the blood on the side of my head, before his running footsteps receded down the light hallway, and he was gone.

Ahead, I heard a door open, spilling more light into the space as a tall figure walked out, his voice angry.

"I swear by the hand, if you kids are playing this early in the morning, I'll have your rations personally cut so much that they'll stunt any form of development," he hissed, coming closer. "I'll—Oh God, God, boy, what happened to you?"

Above, a face materialized, a face surrounded by a beard, one that I could now match to the voice when the anger left it.

"Fell," I answered as Pliny reached a hand downward, pulling me to my feet.

"Bullshit," he answered before leaning inside the door that he had come through, "Clea, we're going to need a doctor. Please fetch one. Yes, right now, hurry!" Then he turned back to me, his voice low. "Boy, what happened to you? Who did this?"

"I fell," I repeated, gritting my teeth as pain started to set in.

"Like I said, bullshit. God, son, you look awful."

I turned away from him and started pushing the cart, limping towards the exit before his hand caught my shoulder. "No you don't, boy. The doctors are already on their way. They'll be here in under a minute."

And he looked into my face, studying it again, with the same curious expression as he had during the test.

"Tell me, boy, can you think straight?"

I nodded, though my vision blurred, and heard footsteps down the hall, doctors that had nearly arrived.

"Then if you understand this," he said and started to spell, "M-E-E-T-space-M-E-space-H-E-R-E-space-T-O-M-O-R-R-O-W-space-N-I-G-H-T."

"Why?"

"Because the ship needs a historian," he answered as the doctors arrived, carrying me with them to their designated rooms, where herbs and bandages awaited.

Chapter 8

Pliny held up the sheet of paper, the word imbued upon it in his thin handwriting, and waited.

"*Stu—*" I said. "Stud... *Student.*"

"Correct!" he said, a smile playing across his face. "*Student.* Four weeks of lessons, Horatius, and you're already sounding out complex words. Not to mention that you already have most the history absorbed, which takes up the bulk of the lessons. I suppose you did have somewhat of an advantage, though, what with all the gardening."

We were in Pliny's apartment, his wife Clea listening from the other room as she finished daily chores and prepared for bed, and Pliny sitting with me in their living room. It was bigger than I was accustomed to—my father's apartment had been only three rooms, consisting of his, mine, and a closet. There were plenty of vacant rooms about the ship, but very few with space, and Pliny's was one of them.

Since my incident with Nean, I had come to a near full recovery, all that remained of the accident being a small circular scar in the center of my forehead just above my nose and between my eyes. I'd spent a few days in the doctor's care, though remembering them was difficult as I tried to focus.

"Look here, son," the head doctor had said while Hannah pressed a combination of ice and freshly cut herbs to my swollen face. I'd likely helped grow the herbs, and the ice was from the edge of the ship, near where the Hand of God had struck and could be collected off of the walls.

"Look here," he repeated when my eyes failed to focus. "This is no falling injury. Bruises like that don't show up on your ribs from a small tumble, neither does spit end up in your hair, nor a head injury to this degree. I'm going to need you to tell me what happened, so I can properly report it in. As a member of the council, I can ensure the punishment will be swift."

"Was walking, decided to jump around in the light hall just like when I was younger, and I tripped on the cart," I answered.

"And I became a doctor by drinking piss," he answered. "I need you to report the name, or else this could happen again, to someone else. He will know justice."

For a moment, I believed him. For a moment, I almost let *Nean* slip out of my mouth, and put the matter in his hands. But then he spoke again.

"Trust me, son, an act like this deserves at least a year of being a porter."

The thought of spending every day with Nean for the next year was so unbearable, I was only able to say two more words: "I fell."

But that was a month ago, and in the space of that month, I'd had my lessons with Pliny to take my mind off my injuries. He'd started with an interrogation, demanding to know how my father had taught me to spell, or where I had picked up the art. And he had laughed when I sheepishly told him the answer, his eyes smiling, and asking if I could return each day at eight. I nodded, and he spoke again.

"There's work ahead of you, Horatius, and you're still behind Segni in many areas. But I'd rather have an eager student than a more experienced one. For now, though, let's keep this between us. I will teach you only for the sake of you learning—what you do with the knowledge is your decision. I cannot guarantee that you will become a historian in name. However, I can make you one at heart, and better yet, mind."

So I learned the letters that I had become so familiar with, understanding how to pick them off the paper and transform them into the auditory format that I was so accustomed with using. And soon, Pliny lent me a small book, one that I was to read every night before bed in my quarters.

"It's for learning," he said, handing it to me. "It won't always make sense, but it will help you adjust to sight reading. Go on, read me the title, get started."

"*One Fish, Two Fish*. What exactly is a *fish*?" I asked.

"We have some idea but believe that they must have existed in the past, before the *Hand of God*. Most the books, especially this one," he thumped a larger one, one I later would know as the Bible, "seem to mention them. Apparently, they are for catching, so pay attention, Horatius. For many of the greatest learners were fishermen, and I will teach you to fish."

So I rehearsed *One Fish, Two Fish*. And soon I moved on to other books, books slightly more complex, with more words that I couldn't understand. Sometimes it took my entire concentration to follow the storyline, so when we moved on to other books, books that Pliny called *manuals*, I was far more interested.

"This," he said, after two years of lessons, "this is the *Guide to Gardening*, which lists many of the techniques we employ today to ensure that we are able to feed the ship. Perhaps it could use a good read-through from someone like yourself who knows more on the subject, and could see if there is anything else we have missed. It's been quite some time since anyone has cracked it open."

So I read, and I learned. I found out that it was light that made plants bear fruit, not just water and soil, which explained why some students had better success than others in different areas of the gardening fields closer to the lights. I learned other things, descriptions of how to rub plants together in ways to make bigger yields, that planting the seeds from bigger vegetables instead of eating them would lead to better yields.

As I studied under Pliny, my body began to change. From my year as a porter, my muscles had grown tighter, able to lift more than before. With more food, I'd grown, just as plants grew more with more light. When I returned to gardening, they'd treated me as an outcast, giving me grunt labor for the first three years, essentially working as a porter again in the fields. So by fourteen years of age, Nean no longer made as many comments when I walked past, my shoulders broader than his. And by fifteen, Skip decided to give me ownership over a small portion of the garden.

"Horatius, it's been years since you've been in my class," he said, calling me to the side of the fields where he monitored activity, "and I am a forgiving man. I believe in second chances, and now I am offering you one. A chance to own your own piece of land. A chance to be a respectable gardener. Are you ready to take this responsibility?"

"Why are you doing this, Skip?" I asked, my voice considerably deeper than the last time we had talked at length, and his face turned red.

"Are you not excited for the opportunity, Horatius? I believe that you've had time to reflect on your past transgressions and poor marks, and—"

"Cut it, Skip," I answered. "I know you're not doing this because you want to. Why are you doing this?"

Skip sighed. "Look, Ann is getting old. She works in the center of the garden and complains that the bright lights hurt her eyes there, and she's never able to carry enough water there to properly water the plants. No one else wants the spot."

"I'll accept under one condition, then, Skip."

"You'll *what*? Accept? I'm giving you the chance to turn your life around. You should take it gladly!"

"No, I'll take it under one circumstance. That I manage my garden on my own, with none of your supervision, and none of your intervention."

"Ridiculous! I won't have you ruining a perfect square of soil because you can't garden. I won't leave you unattended, Horatius, I absolutely *won't*."

"Fine, then I don't want it."

"You *have* to take it. No one else will."

"Then agree to my conditions. I'll even make you a bet, Skip. If my plot of land does not produce three times as much as when Ann worked it, then for a full month, you can have half of my rations. *Half*, and you choose first."

Skip looked at me, his eyes narrowed, chewing on his lip.

"Fine," he spat. "Fine, be difficult. But when you fail, I'll be taking those rations. And you'll be doing *exactly* as I say from then on, Horatius. You hear me? You—"

But I was already walking away, reviewing the *Guide to Gardening* in my mind. For twenty years, Ann had worked that spot, and for twenty years, it had likely been neglected. I'd seen her work, not taking care that every drop of water found its home, spacing her plants too far apart, walking slowly from a combination of old bones and general apathy.

Which meant for twenty years, the spot with the brightest lights in the room had been mismanaged.

And now it was mine.

Chapter 9

"This was a mistake," said Skip from the edge of my plot. "I never should have agreed to this, and now you're *ruining* perfectly good seeds."

It had been three weeks since Skip had agreed to the deal, and though he was true to his word to never set foot within my plot, his comments still came frequently.

"Skip, what did we agree on?" I asked, rehearsing passages from the guide as I ripped out sprouts that had just broken soil, leaving only the largest behind.

After seedlings have developed two leaves, remove approximately one out of every two, selecting those that are the smallest and leaving the largest behind, allowing the healthiest germinations to persist. Doing such frees up root systems, allocates space for air and light, and will provide greater yield.

"But I won't stand by for you to throw away perfectly good crops! I let you change what you wanted to plant, Horatius, after Ann planted the same thing there for twenty years! Twenty years, and you wanted to change it! Just do your gardening like you're supposed to!"

"I am," I muttered, ignoring him and the growing crowd of gardeners as I pulled plants up by the roots, tossing them away. Every step along the way, Skip had balked—from changing the soil to manure composition, to using the guide to determine which plants would fare best with increased light, to making my holes in the fashion I had devised years before.

"Yeah," shouted Nean from the growing circle. "*Stupid—*"

But his voice cut off as I turned to face him, the sweat beading around my eyes, gripping the shovel tight enough that my biceps showed through my shirt. A few nervous chuckles sounded as I stared at him, though far fewer than there would have been two years before, and sounding thinner.

"What was that, Nean?" I asked. "I seem to remember when you said it the first time. I remember *everything* that you've said, Nean. *Everything.* I haven't forgotten a word, and it would be best for you to stop reminding me. You may rather I forget."

Nean swallowed and broke his gaze away as I touched the scar I still bore and straightened my back now taller than he.

"We'll see," he said, turning away. "We'll see what happens when the chief hears about this, when your crops fail."

But the chief never did find out. He never had the chance.

Two days after the incident, he died in his sleep, a cluster of confused doctors surrounding his bed the next morning, wondering how someone so healthy could perish in the night. According to them, he seemed even healthier than anyone else on the ship, due to his rapid weight gain and the bump that had been growing larger on his right shoulder each year, now nearly the size of his head.

"A sign of the chief's ruling power, the arm of his law, and the power of his hand," the head doctor had said after discovering it, and the chief had taken to wearing tighter shirts to display its presence.

After his death, Pliny's apprentice had taken command, one the chief had assured the ship for years would provide a future brighter than they could imagine. Segni had smiled at the ceremony, the crowd cheering, and had declared a feast be administered in his and his father's honor.

But one week after the chief's death, Pliny made an announcement during my lesson.

"Horatius," he said, "there is something that I wish to show you. Something that precious few know about on the ship, something that Segni should know if he attended his lessons, and that his father neglected to tell him before his death. Something that I do not trust Segni with, and, should you ever become historian, you must know."

"What is it?" I asked, placing a strawberry on the counter for Clea. It was her favorite food, and I had grown it just for her, sneaking the largest one out of my field.

"Come, follow me," he had answered and led me from his apartment, "Keep your distance, though. We have done well in keeping our interactions secret, and now that Segni is chief, more caution may be necessary."

He led me through the corridors of the ship, to where the rooms grew colder and we approached the center, near where the ice grew on the walls. Typically, this area was deserted, the rooms too frigid for living and the fields unable to support life, and hallways turning unpredictably to behave like light and heavy rooms. It was quiet, our footsteps the sole source of noise, and our dim shadows the sole source of movement.

And after nearly a half hour of walking, Pliny opened a small side door into a stairwell, and we descended.

"Long ago, before the Hand of God," Pliny said, his voice echoing, "it is said that the ship was one. But not only was it one, Horatius, but it was *different*. According to records, the area we now walk was once habitable. The lights above you could once change in brightness as you desired, or the air temperature be adjusted. We know this among many other things, many other ways that we could control the ship, rather than the ship controlling us."

"Why does it matter, though, Pliny?"

"Think to gardening, Horatius. Think to how much more you could produce if you could change the lights as you wished, or even the temperature. But beyond that, think if you could decide which of the corridors were light halls. Or if you would heat this portion of the ship again, and use these fields now thick with frost."

"But how? How would we do that?"

"That is the question, Horatius. And rather than *how*, is *should* we."

We had come to a door, a door that was nearly encapsulated in ice, and Pliny removed a screwdriver from his pocket. Aiming for the cracks, he chipped around the edge of the door, until it shifted in the frame and he could open it.

The room we entered was caked in dust, and so cold that my breath formed in front of me, colder than I had ever experienced in my life. It jutted out beneath the ship, such that windows extended in every direction, allowing for a full view of the surrounding empty space. A table was in the center, nearly a hundred books piled up on its surface, all bearing a resemblance with the *Guide to Gardening* given to me by Pliny. Behind them, there were shelves of lights—tiny lights that flashed amid rows of buttons and levers, accompanied by countless knobs and switches.

Above, on the ceiling, I read words that had long been forgotten, but were etched into the metal.

Command Center: The beacon in the darkness, the hope of humanity.

"What is this place?" I whispered, afraid even to break the silence, my eyes wide.

"It's how the ship used to be controlled," answered Pliny, "It's where our greatest strength used to be."

"Then why don't we use it?" I asked, walking over to the table. "Why don't we take advantage of it?"

"Do you remember the story of the *Great Thirst*, Horatius?" Pliny asked, and I nodded. "Before the *Great Thirst*, our numbers were at three thousand. Now they are but a third. I told you that the *Great Thirst* was resolved when the historian Archim discovered how to restart the flow of the water reservoirs, and that much is true."

Then Pliny leaned forward and pointed to a row of controls at the far end of the room.

"What I never told you is that Archim is the reason why the Great Thirst occurred. That he killed two thousand people by pressing one of those buttons, because he thought he could double the reservoir production and just barely managed to partially correct his error after several days of frantic research before the entire ship died. As I said, Horatius, we have an inkling of *how* to control the ship. But *should* we?"

Chapter 10

I was eighteen when Pliny died, in the *Year of Feasts.*

Just two years prior, I had been added to the chief's council, Pliny taking me to one of their meetings and addressing Segni.

"Your Honor," Pliny said, bowing low, "I come to you today with a petition that will succeed only in strengthening the continued success of the ship."

"Yes?" Segni said, lounging in his chair and chewing on a strawberry. He had decreed the last year that the chief be provided with triple rations, such that he not be distracted by hunger or lack of energy when making decisions. And since that decision, his face had grown slightly more round, and his shirts slightly tighter.

"Within your council, you have representation from the doctors, from the historians, from the cooks," said Pliny, "But what you do not have is representation from the farmers, from those who provide your food. It would be wise, chief, to include them in order to predict crop yields and set the desired crops for the year."

"I do agree," said Segni. "Such as strawberries, which have been smaller this month than usual."

"Exactly, your Honor. Exactly. So it is with your acceptance that I propose to appoint a gardening relations, to make your wishes more clear in the fields."

"Oh?" said Segni and cast his eyes on me. "Sure, go on, then. I'm sure Horatius will fetch him from the gardeners."

"Your Honor," interrupted Pliny before I could speak. "Actually, I have elected Horatius to fill this role."

Segni's eyes widened and he coughed, a cough that spread into laughter as bits of fruit flew from his mouth.

"*Him?*" he said, struggling to catch his breath. "*Him?* Oh, Pliny, what a joke, he can hardly keep his place in the fields, let alone the council. I nominate Skip."

Beside Pliny, I gritted my teeth, keeping my gaze straight. Word had started circulating the ship after I won my bet with Skip about my methods of farming. Few seemed to mention the success I'd seen, focusing rather on how I'd thrown out seeds, or changed from the methods of the past, and had simply been lucky.

"Oh, but that is precisely why we need him, chief," said Pliny with a smile. "You see, I would hesitate before pulling Skip from the fields to attend meetings, in case the crops falter in his absence. And Skip is smarter than most the gardeners—no, we need someone that the average gardener can relate to, someone who they see as an equal or else they will not listen to him. Plus, with Horatius, your yields will not be disrupted, and he will have less time to cause issues in the fields if he is in meetings. Furthermore, he is able to represent the porters after the time he spent in their ranks. Chief, I advise Horatius not because he is the best, but rather because his skills are replaceable, and he will not be missed in his absence."

"Hmm," said Segni, narrowing his eyes at me, "I suppose that is true. But will you keep your word and tell my wishes to the other gardeners? What if they do not listen to you, what then?"

"Your Honor," I said, bowing lower than Pliny, "all my life, I have faced adversity and dissent. I will relay your word even if it means damage to my reputation, which is already marred, or loss of the few friends that I have. I am but your servant, and have no other ties."

Segni eyes gleamed as I bowed a second time, and he nodded.

"Then I consent," he said, his arms stretching wide, "servant."

***

Council meetings occurred once per week, consisting of Segni relating his wishes to his leadership team.

"Today is the anniversary of my father's death and my coronation," Segni said, smiling, a year after I had been on the council. "And as such, I call for a celebration."

"A feast, your Honor?" asked Elliott, who was on the council after quickly rising through the ranks as chef.

"Not *a* feast, Elliott. Feasts! A year of them, to signify the bountiful years to come."

Pliny cleared his throat and I spoke, keeping my voice level.

"We cannot accommodate that much food from our gardens, Segni. With the limited water supply, we cannot afford such waste."

"Dare call it waste again and you will be a porter again!" Segni shouted, pointing a finger at me. "I have decreed it, and thus shall it be. I will have extra workers delivered to the fields."

"From where?" asked Elliott, shaking his head.

"From where they are idle in other departments," said Segni. "But in the far future, we will need more workers. Which is why I am commanding that each family strive to become larger as well, so that we can grow as a society."

"But the water," I said. "Even with more workers, we will not have the water to grow, even if we harvest ice from the far reaches of the ship."

"We haven't tried it yet, so we don't know," countered Segni, ""But until then, we will dedicate one hundred percent of the fields to growing food. Elliott, the feasts will start next week."

"But what about the herbs!" cried a doctor representative. "We cannot apply medicine without our herbs!"

"Last I checked, you had a year's supply," said Segni, "And I said we were having a *year* of feasts. They'll last."

"But that's for emergencies," protested the doctor. "Emergencies only!"

"And this is one. Is the honoring of your chief not a top priority? Is not the remembrance of his father an emergency in itself?"

"But—" said the head doctor, but Segni raised his eyebrows.

"Do you wish to be a porter, doctor? Do you really wish to speak against me?"

So the meeting concluded, and the feasts began the next week.

The first was successful, as was the second, and even the third. But by the fourth, chefs were cutting rations from the other meals to ensure there was enough to cover for the feast. Water was lower than it had ever been, the reservoirs often dry, rows of plants that required greater amounts dying off.

With the frenzied production and cooking, there were more burns, cuts, and other injuries, causing the doctors to fly through their supplies faster than typical. Stored herbs were not as potent as fresh ones either, so they found themselves using more to treat smaller injuries.

It was halfway through the *Year of Feasts* when Pliny cut himself falling down a flight of stairs, the bloody laceration stretching from his shoulder to forearm. Typically, on a younger man, the cut would have healed quickly. And even at Pliny's age, with the help of doctors, it was nothing to be concerned about.

If there was medicine to treat it.

"Horatius," gasped Pliny, coughing on his bed, green pus oozing from an arm that had steadily lost function. "Horatius, I want you to know, I regret years ago not declaring you historian. I regret not standing up to the chief."

"You still taught me," I said, wiping the sweat off his forehead with a rag. "You did everything you could, Pliny. I can never thank you enough for that."

"No, I didn't," he said. "You can see the state of the ship. It is not enough to know the stories as historian, Horatius. You must *use* them too. And I should have prevented this. I should have seen it coming more clearly."

"You *did*," I answered, my eyes watering as his turned glassy. "And you took measures against it."

"There are other measures," said Pliny. "Actions that I was too much of a coward to do. And other things, darker things that I could have done. I put you on the council to bring you closer to Segni, to intervene when you can, so promise me something, Horatius. Promise me that if the time comes, you'll take action. Promise me that the stories remember me one day as the man who prevented the disaster of the ship, not the one who caused it. Promise me that."

"I promise, Pliny," I said as Clea started sobbing again at the edge of the bed from where she held his hand.

"Stories are just stories," Pliny mumbled, the spirit fleeing his body. "Stories cannot feed people. Stories cannot give water. But one who knows the stories can, and he must."

I cried that day, tears falling down my cheeks as the doctors collected Pliny's body. More of them than when my own father passed away in his sleep the year before.

And staring outside the window of my room, long after sleeping hours had begun, I saw a familiar face on the other side of the ship. One who had grown older with me, who now had her hand against the glass, and watched as I broke out in sobs once more.

When dawn was still several hours away and sleep still impossible, I made my way to the room that Pliny had showed me. And as I opened the books and began to study, I remembered his final words.

Promise me that if the time comes, you'll take action.

Chapter 11

Three years had passed since Pliny's death, three years that I spent on the council, watching Segni's stomach expand while others contracted. I had fought to remain on that council, biting down my pride and common sense to satiate him, learning to choose which arguments were crucial to the ship's survival and which were simply principle.

Part of me grew bitter during those years, part of me that grew just as lost as the ship. For when Pliny was alive, we shared a common knowledge, a common understanding of how to preserve the ship. An appreciation of the stories, a regard of the wisdom they held. With Pliny, we were a team of silent guardians, protecting that which we knew to be true and right.

But without Pliny, there was no one to share the burden. And I alone stood between the ship and destruction.

But as *gardener*, nobody knew.

"I have opened the position of historian," said Segni, two weeks after the death of Pliny. "And I have filled it, with my younger brother, Vaca. Like myself, he was trained by Pliny in the esteemed school of Empri. Like myself, he is *most* suitable for the task."

Scowls circled the council, but no one spoke, all eyeing the two figures on the left and right of Segni, long knives from the kitchen tucked into their belts. Nean was one of them, staring at each of us in turn and daring us to object, his fingers twitching about the handle of the knife. Tom the porter was the other, his size alone performing the necessary intimidation, his gaze off in the distance unless prompted by Segni.

"I have created their positions for my personal safety," Segni had said when he introduced them, "for without a chief, the ship would have no leader and would surely fall into chaos. I do this for the good of the ship."

So Vaca joined the council, on the days he decided to attend, often choosing instead to study in his room. Considering he took no books with him and rubbed his eyes whenever he returned, I suspected that the true purpose of his absence had little to do with learning his letters. And though my jaw clenched when he shirked his duties, I was thankful that Vaca did not attend nor have the ambition or capacity to push an agenda, else the situation on the council would have been even worse.

But from what I had failed to accumulate in those two years in terms of political power, I had gained in knowledge and control of the gardens.

"Skip," I had said shortly after Pliny's death, "you lost the bet I set and I have proved that my methods are successful. By next week, I want four apprentices, four new gardeners to teach how to attain higher yields."

"Ridiculous!" spat Skip. "I won't have you tampering with the rest of the gardens, Horatius. I simply *will not* have it. I can bear that you do not follow directions, but it would be a disaster if others did too."

"Four, Skip!" I said, raising four fingers. "Four out of your class, a mere twenty percent. I'll take them off your hands, and they will not be your responsibility. I'll take them by force if I have to."

"*Absolutely not,*" he responded. "That's final, Horatius."

"How about we make a bet, then, and if mine produce more—"

"No more of your bets!" said Skip and muttered to himself, "Nonsense, chaos and nonsense. I won't have it."

"Then a quarter of my rations," I answered. "A quarter until I have finished teaching them. You look hungry, Skip— What's wrong? I thought this was the *Year of Feasts.*"

Skip grimaced and turned towards me, pausing.

"Fine," he answered. "Fine. But they shall not be my responsibility in the future, Horatius, if you mislead them."

"Of course," I answered. "Of course, Skip. I will ensure that their actions are in no way attributed to your reputation."

Skip was lucky that day, that he accepted a quarter of my rations. He would need them.

When the new gardeners arrived, he selected the four smallest, those that could barely lift a shovel, and he pushed them in my direction.

"I sincerely apologize," he said to them as their faces fell, "for assigning you to Horatius. He was last of his year when he went through my program and still cannot plant properly. However, I cannot handle all of you myself and must call upon his aid."

"But, but—" one said as relief flooded across the students that remained in the larger group, and Skip interrupted.

"I'm sorry, but it cannot be helped. It's for the good of the ship. What's done is done."

Then Skip assigned us to a plot of fields that had traditionally had lower yields, an area I had noted had dimmer lights above it than the rest of the gardens. And he returned to the rest of his class, leaving four dismayed ten year old children behind.

"As Skip mentioned," I said, my voice loud enough to carry across the garden to his group and cause his face to turn red, "what is done is done. It is most unfortunate that some of you were selected to be part of the lesser group. But that group is not ours. Listen to me now and listen closely. The four of you are the smallest, but your plants will grow taller than anyone else's. And they will bear more food than the rest of the class combined."

The four students grimaced, and one spoke, his voice low and his foot kicking the dirt.

"It's okay, Mr. Horatius," he said. "You don't have to pretend. You don't have to make up stories about what will happen."

"What's your name?" I asked.

"Matthew," he muttered.

"You're right, Matthew," I said, leaning over and looking him in the eye. "I don't make up stories; I tell them. It's time to make a story worth telling."

So we began, and I taught them how to dig quick holes and gave them the tricks I had learned from the *Guide to Gardening*.

But that wasn't all I did.

At night, I walked to the room Pliny had showed me, and I studied the books laid out on the table. Most of them were manuals, thick volumes filled with instructions and procedures about processes and objects that I could not understand, about things called engines and oxygen regulators and generators. But the rest were journals, journals that were marked off by year, fifteen in all, all signed at the bottom with the same name.

Archim.

Each was titled by its subject, with names ranging from "Temperature Modification" to "Gravity Enhancement," the last of which only half filled out and named "Water Controls."

Each of the books had Archim's handwriting in them, showing his every step in touching the ship's controls and the resulting observations. And after a week of reading, I found what I was looking for, in a journal titled "Luminosity" from his seventh year of experimentation.

Chapter 12

Controls to the lighting arrangements of the gardens, read the notebook on luminosity at the top of page one hundred and forty-four, in flowing handwriting. *I have determined that the array of knobs marked 1152-1280 control the brightness of garden lights, as well as the light composition. After several weeks of study, I have determined that altering the state of the lights has no noticeable effect on the remainder of the ship. Additionally, I have inferred that different combinations of light settings affect plant growth and seek in the future to determine the optimal settings by enlisting the help of a gardener, as I have little knowledge on the subject. At present, however, all that can be determined is the settings that must be avoided else the plants should deteriorate, as listed below.*

I smiled, reading the combination, knowing from the *Guide to Gardening* that certain types of light were better than others, and remembering a passage that stated that too high percentages ultraviolet could be detrimental to growth. I never knew what "ultraviolet" was, so I tended to skip over that section in the past. But there, drawn in Archim's notes, there was a knob labeled "ultraviolet," with a warning not to set it to high.

It took three days of checking before I was confident enough to approach the array of controls that related to the gardens. Three days of poring through the *Luminosity* notebook, searching for areas where Archim's experiments might have gone awry. Looking for inconsistencies among his wording, or anything that might dissuade me, or support the voice in my head that screamed at me to *stop* as I looked at the array.

Even when I did approach, my palms started to sweat, and I cast a nervous eye towards the last notebook on the desk, the one labeled "Water Control." I found a section far away from the center of the garden, and my fingertips brushed against the knobs, feeling the cold in the metal sear my skin. Hearing the knobs call out to me, demanding to be altered, to be changed for the first time in generations.

I shook, remembering Pliny's story of the Great Thirst. And I wondered what might occur if turning the knob resulted in the ship losing light, light that was crucial for the plants to grow.

What if I would be known by historians as the man to cause the Great Hunger? But according to Archim's journal, nothing of that sort would happen.

Closing my eyes, I turned the first knob, holding my breath as I waited, listening closely to silence. I moved it barely a quarter of a rotation, gliding with too little resistance, too eager to move.

But nothing happened when I finished—no screams echoed down the hall from the interior of the ship, no drastic change in light levels occurred. Then I ran, sprinting through the twisting hallways to the gardens, and inspected the lights above, where one had taken on a slight purple tinge, my heart racing as I waited for two hours to ensure no other changes had occurred.

So I returned to the control room. To start my plan.

Identifying which knobs were above Skip's student gardeners, I turned those knobs to high during each night before returning to medium each morning. Then, with my own sections, I raised each of the knobs slightly, returning back each time until I was satisfied with how they appeared overhead.

I never said a word as I watched Skip screaming at his students, demanding to know what they were doing wrong, even accusing them of being worse students than me. But as the weeks passed, Skip's plants shriveled, often dying before they could yield crops, all while my students' vegetation took root and grew faster than even the most experienced of gardeners, something unheard of in a beginners' class.

Soon the slumped shoulders that had arrived with my students were replaced by straight, proud backs. Their hands worked quickly, their minds absorbing the information I gave them, until all that was left for them to succeed was practicing.

And when that happened, I started teaching them something other than gardening. I told them stories, emulating the education I had received from an unknowing Pliny many years before.

"Matthew," I said, addressing the student that had spoken to me on the first day, "why must we always grow more food than we eat?"

"We must store it!" he piped up as he watered his row of plants. "In case we have a bad year of crops. To be prepared."

"Correct," I said and turned to address another student.

"Mary, what happens if we do not have stores?"

"We cannot feed the ship," the tiny girl answered, wiping sweat from her brow. "And if we cannot feed the ship, it will be disaster."

"John, what happened one of the last times we ran out of a resource?"

"The great thirst!" said my third student, his arms spread wide. "And a lot of people died. Two-thirds."

"Yes, well done, well done. You all are learning so quickly—the best gardeners, and the most educated. You should be proud, and your parents should be as well. Ruth," I said, and addressed the last student, the quietest of the bunch but who absorbed information faster than the rest. "What is S-H-I-P?"

"Ship," she said, her voice barely above a whisper, and I smiled.

"Yes," I responded, looking over my garden, a garden of mind and earth, while Skip shouted behind me. Over the course of the weeks, I noticed his students had steadily migrated their gardening activities towards my side of the fields, their heads cocked when I told my class stories, their eyes squinting when I demonstrated techniques.

Until one morning, when my group gathered for class, a fifth face joined us.

"Mark," said the voice as a tiny hand extended outwards.

"Good to meet you, Mark," I said, shaking it. "How can I help you?"

"I want to be in your class," he answered. "I want you to teach me."

"Of course," I said, while Skip turned his eyes away from where he scowled on the far side of the garden. And a fifth student learned to garden.

Then the next week, a sixth. Then a seventh after the following. And by the end of the class, the entirety of Skip's program were clustered around me before returning to their fields, ignoring Skip's shouts as they found results in their new methods. I helped them, of course, fixing the light levels on every student that came to me for advice, such that their plants grew tall.

The next year, Skip gave no objection as I taught his entire class, instead choosing to recede to a corner of the garden and focus on his crops, banding together with the more experienced gardeners who held their noses high as they practiced the old methods. As we had agreed, Skip was enjoying a quarter of my rations, enough of a bribe to force him to turn a blind eye after his class deserted him. What Skip did not know was I had struck a deal with the doctors and chefs of the council after a particularly frustrating argument with Segni, agreeing to supply them with their most dire herbs in secret from the garden despite Segni's wishes, and that I would receive a quarter rations from the kitchen in return for my efforts.

I caught the occasional glimpse of experienced gardeners watching as my students' plants grew faster and stronger than their own. I never spoke a word to them about the superiority of my methods, instead waiting until forty of my students were fully trained, forty students that I was confident could outgrow the rest of the workers.

I knew forty to be the perfect number for my plans, that after convincing Segni to save a humble store of crops, they would produce just enough food to keep the ship alive without starvation. That forty could just barely put us through a fasting period.

As soon as I was convinced that the ship could survive, I returned to the control room, reviewing the prior two years in my mind. In the past, the only way I had convinced students to join my class was through their personal failure, when they came to me for help. As a historian, I knew the future would be no different.

So I set the lights to ultraviolet for every gardener that did not follow my system.

Chapter 13

"It happened before, a hundred years ago," I said to Segni at the council, the other members white in the face as I spoke. "We survived then when half our crops died, and we will survive now. With our stores, we should have enough that no one will go hungry."

"*Survive?*" said Segni, his voice rising. "*Survive?* How could you let this happen? How in the Hand of God itself could over half the crops die overnight, for no explicable reason? There was a feast to be next week, to celebrate *my birthday.*"

He slammed a fist down on the table, the carton where he typically held his fresh strawberries bouncing upwards, then toppling over to show only nubs of green within.

"Simply put, we don't know," I said with a bow, keeping my face somber. "We are simply fortunate enough that you had the foresight to prepare for such an event, your Honor. And with the humblest of intentions, I remind your Honor that I am but a messenger, with no control over the state of the gardens. As Pliny stated when introducing me to the council, I am average at best at gardening, and thus not suited for leadership."

"Messenger be damned!" shouted Segni, raising a fist. "I've heard about your methods in the garden from Skip. I know what you've been up to, meddling with the way of things, stealing his students! And now half the garden dies! Nean, seize him, and let us make him an example of what happens when you act against the will of the chief!"

"Your Honor," I said, speaking quickly as Nean advanced, Tom's face creasing in a slow frown behind him, "I have practiced my methods for years. Never before has there been a problem or decrease in yields. In fact, your Honor, not one of my own plants or my students' plants have died – they seem to have survived this disaster. Without them, the ship would be in far greater trouble than a few hungry weeks."

Segni watched as Nean seized me by the elbow, dragging me towards the door. Tom grunted as his face tracked me from across the room.

"You Honor!" I shouted, red in the face. "In four weeks, we can have a feast! Four weeks, if you let me revive the gardens. If not, it will be at least twelve before we reach a full recovery, let alone a surplus."

"A feast?" said Segni. "We have had many feasts, Horatius, and had more planned before you brought this news."

"Not just a feast," I said, "but I have found that we can convert an entire field to growing strawberries if we increase our yields. Pliny said that fruit used to be sweeter in the stories, in the old days. Give me four weeks to bring you the sweetest strawberries of your life, and more of them than you have ever seen, to prove myself as your loyal servant!"

"Lies," said Segni as Nean's grip intensified and Tom's eyes narrowed, a vein showing in his forehead. "Just as you tried to lie your way into historian long ago. Don't think I am a fool, Horatius, and trick me like you tricked Skip."

"But I came prepared! With proof!" I said, reaching into my pocket to pull out a small box and open it, revealing a small lump of red within. "A gift for you, your Honor. I had planned to give it to you on a more celebratory occasion, but here it is now. The *sweetest* strawberry you have *ever* tasted, and the largest. Take it, and know that I can make one twice as tasty in the future. It took me years to discover this secret, but with the rest of the gardeners working with me, we can prepare the best for you. And not just strawberries, but the other foods as well!"

"Wait," said Segni, gesturing to Nean, and leaned forward, removing the berry from the box and raising it to eye level. Then he bit into it, chewing slowly, the red juice dripping down a chin that was on the verge of doubling. His eyes closed, lips puckering after he took another bite, and another, until all that remained was the stem on the table, curved like a scar with crimson juice puddled about it.

"Four weeks," he said without opening his eyes and holding up his fingers. "Four until I want a feast, a feast of strawberries. A *birthday* feast to make up for the one I'll miss."

Then Nean shoved me from the room, Tom exhaled from behind Segni as his shoulders relaxed, and I walked towards my apartment, a smile tugging at my lips as I prepared for the next day.

I scoured the *Guide to Gardening*, reviewing everything I would need to teach, reading over each of the sections carefully, particularly those on growing speed.

Four weeks on average is required for maturation, the passage stated, *made possible through genetically enhanced seed stock as well as the controlled conditions and light sources aboard the ship. In natural environments, such as New Earth, growth rates will be slower as anticipated by the solar studies performed prior to departure. A separate seed stock to be used in those conditions, as provided by the preparatory drops.*

I read the first sentence again, filtering away all the extraneous information. According to the guide, as well as my experience, preparing the feast was possible. Not only possible, but I'd only need half of the experienced gardeners to comply.

"Disaster has struck," I shouted from the front of the gardens the next morning as my forty students rounded up the other gardeners, bringing them in a mob before me, "but we have known disaster before. We have known hardship before. And we will prevail."

"Word is that you told Segni we could have a feast in four weeks!" shouted Skip from the back. "Word is that you said it would be possible!"

I raised my hands as the rest of the experienced gardeners began to shout, thumping the weathered handles of their shovels into the earth, where dead plants crackled under their feet.

"I did," I said, my voice level. "And we will. We have enough to survive between our stores and the surviving plants, enough to *just get by*. All we have to do is grow enough to provide a surplus. It is possible, and I can teach you how. Together, we can do it – look at the plants that did survive, look at their health, look at their yields! And if we cannot, then I promise you that I alone will be held accountable. I promise you that I will leave the gardens and become a porter, and that you may forget that I ever partook in this."

"How about we forget you ever partook in it now!" shouted a man from the back, wrinkles cut deep into his face, and several nodded in agreement. "How about we return to the ways that have worked for generations in the past and will work for generations to come?"

"Because not only can I offer you a feast," I said, "but by eight weeks, I can offer you double rations. Not just you, but everyone on the ship! More food than you have had in your lives."

"Nonsense, all of it," replied the man, and turned on his heel to return to his plot, brown with fallen stems and leaves as several others followed him. "Absolute nonsense."

I bit my lip as more left, counting the numbers in my head as I felt two small hands wrap around mine, from two children that had separated from the crowd.

"When our plants died under Skip, and he called us slow," shouted Mark's voice, "Horatius taught us, and he taught us how to garden the plants that are still alive today!"

"And he took the smallest of us, the weakest," shouted Ruth, "and made us greater than the strongest! Don't leave without giving him a chance!"

The crowd paused, looking at the numbers of children growing at my sides, several shaking their heads. Many continued to trudge away until just under half remained, just barely under the calculated threshold that we would need. But those that remained were younger, some of them from my own class ten years before, with enthusiasm still in their eyes and muscle still on their bones.

"We start today," I said to them. "Each of you pairs with one of my students, which will help in teaching you. The methods are largely similar, only slight differences exist, and the work is easier than before."

But as we started class, and the experienced gardeners attempted to salvage their crops, Skip walked across the fields until we were face to face, spitting into the soil at my feet.

"When everything starts to go wrong, when tradition crashes down around us," he hissed, pointing a finger into my chest, "we'll know who to blame."

***

After the first day of gardening, I returned to the control room, ensuring that the ultraviolet was lowered down to normal levels and optimizing the light of the entire garden, even for those who refused to follow my methods. There would be time to teach them again in the future, but now that stores would soon be running out, we needed food. Already stomachs had started to growl from the reduced rations arriving from the kitchens.

Day one had been successful, the gardeners far more receptive to my methods than I had anticipated. Most likely this was due to them being younger, to being less trapped in the ways of tradition. But I had also handed out strawberries before the lesson, three to each new gardener, the type that I had perfected for Segni.

"Taste these," I had said. "Taste how much better these are, and know within a few weeks you will be growing your own. Know that you not only will be giving the ship more food, but you will be giving them better quality food. When this disaster is remembered a hundred years from now, you will be in the stories. You will be the heroes."

By the end of the first week, their planting speed had doubled, their hands moving through the technique as if they had practiced it their entire lives. And I saw hope on their faces as the first of the greens began to sprout, poking defiantly through the soil far quicker than they were accustomed to in the past.

I think I'll always remember that first week fondly. That I'll remember my intentions were good, that I had set the ship on the path towards not just survival, but improvement.

That when I stared outside the window each night, and I saw the face staring back at me from the other side of the half of the ship, her spindly fingers forming gestures across the glass, I imagined that even she somehow knew that brighter times should be ahead.

That maybe one day even Segni would recognize that I deserved to be historian, and I could head our food stores. That I could prepare us for times to come, seeking the other secrets long forgotten in stories trapped in written books. And maybe that a few students of my own, gardeners like their teacher, might read them one day. And might bring good to the ship after my passing.

Yes, I'll always remember it that way.

Until I think upon the seventh day.

When the voice spoke from above.

Chapter 14

"Systems rebooting, ship damage assessed. Reuniting the two halves of the ship and restoring airlock, approximately twenty-four hours until complete."

The voice repeated three times, gasps echoing around the fields with each start, faces tilted upward and searching for the source. And though I knew the source from my studies, it was no less disconcerting.

Shrieks erupted around the garden as the floor lurched, knocking gardeners off their feet and into the mud as the cables holding the ship snapped taut. Above, the lights flickered and dimmed as the ship lurched again, the visuals accompanied by the sound of screeching metal in the distance.

"First the chief died," shouted Skip, raising to his knees, his face white, "then the crops died. Now this; now *we* die! The Hand of God is upon us again and no doubt in *punishment*!"

Glancing around, the gardeners stared at me from every direction, many of their expressions accusing. But in greater numbers were the children I had taught and the group of gardeners that had recently adopted my methods, a different expression on their faces. A mix of confusion and of expectation. Faces searching for hope.

"Listen up," I shouted to them, planting the blade of my shovel deep into the soil for a post to hold on to as the ship shifted again. "There is no reason yet to be frightened! There is no reason to panic! We are the gardeners, the backbone of the ship. We are the lifeblood. Stay put, and continue working on the crops—show the rest of the ship your example and your grit."

"But what if—" shouted Skip, and I turned towards him, my nostrils flaring and voice commanding.

"There is no time for *what ifs*. Skip, it is now your time to lead. Now more than ever, we must enforce your mantra and *do as we have always done*. We must garden, we must provide for the ship. And I promise you that while you protect the crops, I will speak with the chief himself, and determine what action needs to be taken for your safety and the safety of your families. Do you understand?"

Wide-eyed from across the field, Skip nodded as there was another tremor and the color flooded again from his face. Then he was standing, barking out orders to his gardeners, his voice slightly higher pitched than normal. Not because I had given him the order, but because it is easier to face a disaster while staring at work than staring at it head on.

Once my gardeners were organized, I walked calmly from the gardens, then broke into a sprint as soon as I was out of eyesight, zigzagging through the hallways to the council room. Even with Segni in charge, there would be an emergency meeting – and though he might not be present, which was likely to be the preferable option, the rest of the council members would still convene.

As I neared the council room, my path brought me parallel to the windows of the ship, where I could watch as the second half pivoted in the distance. It was slow, so slow I had to stop my running and compare it against the background of stars to be able to tell, watching as it eclipsed a peculiar grouping of seven stars shaped like a ring. And within the windows of the other side, there was a flurry of movement, dark shapes that hustled through corridors, followed by bursts of the strange blue light that had occasionally flashed through the windows in the past.

"You!" shouted Segni, pointing at me as I burst through the doors of the council room, breathing heavily. "Just who we were waiting for. Now we can begin!"

"Segni, as I was saying, our situation is dire," said the head doctor, his top apprentice Hannah shaking by his side, "The lurch has caused dozens of injuries in the kitchens, from burns to cuts, and already we are stretched thin on herbs to treat infections—and that is just for the kitchens! The number of reports of lacerations alone I expect in the next few hours is surely to be astronomical."

"Then grow more herbs, Horatius," said Segni with a shrug, "so that we don't face a shortage."

"The bare minimum time I need to grow medicinal herbs, depending upon the varieties you require, is three weeks," I answered, and my muscles in my shoulders tightened as I thought how the overhead lights had started to dim when the ship moved. "Make that four weeks."

"Fine. In four weeks, you'll have your herbs, then," said Segni.

"But the infections will have set by then! We need them now, Segni!" exclaimed the head doctor as Hannah put her face in her hands.

"Then maybe," snarled Segni, "you shouldn't have used so much in the past!"

"And refuse treatment to those who needed it?"

"You could have stretched it," said Segni, "instead of using them for everyone who came crawling for aid. Obviously, they need it more now."

"There's more," said Elliott, his voice quiet from the other end of the table. The council turned to face him, a vein on his neck throbbing as he spoke and his eyes hard. "More news, after I took stock of the injuries in my kitchens."

"Go on, then," said Segni, waving a hand.

"As you know, we rely upon porters for the transportation of food to the kitchens. During the lurch..." Elliott swallowed, then continued. "During the lurch, the majority of the porters were in the heavy room."

My breath caught in my chest as Segni waited, his expression blank. After all the hours I had spent in the heavy room, I knew the caution required when handling the equipment, how anyone who endangered others by using it inappropriately was swiftly punished.

"And?" Segni said, his voice impatient.

"And I've already called for the doctors," said Elliott, shaking his head and staring at the table. "It's... It's a mess."

"We'll send the porters back to clean up the weights then," responded Segni. "The doctors wouldn't be much help in lifting them."

"No!" shouted Eliot, and I saw tears threatening to spill onto his cheeks. "No! It's a mess because at least half the porters are dead, Segni! It's a mess because the entire room is painted crimson and those who are not dead are severely injured, with little to no herbs to help them! A wall of weights fell when the ship lurched – I'd like to think it killed them mercifully had I not heard the screams when I approached, but I did. Oh, I did. And now they're gone, half our labor force, but also our shipmates, our friends!"

"We can replace them with gardeners," countered Segni, "They're just porters, so their job can easily be learned. As well as the chefs who can help—hey, where do you think you are going? What are you doing?"

"I'm going somewhere I can be of use!" shouted Elliott as he reached the door, "Because that place *obviously* is not here!" He slammed the door, the sound echoing throughout the chamber as Hannah stood and followed him, not saying a word as she departed.

"Half the porters dead," I muttered. "The kitchens injured. The doctors short on medicine. The food stores low and half the gardens dead."

"I know," hissed Segni, "Don't you think I know that?"

"But what about what happens next, Segni? Look, out the windows. The ship is coming together where the Hand of God smashed it apart. The voice said the two halves of the ship are reuniting in a day, which means that everyone on *that* side will be able to come to *this* side. Watch, through the window. See their half moving?"

"By the Hand of God," whispered the head doctor. "He's right. We need to call Elliott and Hannah back! As well as the historian! We'll need full council to determine how to meet them. It will be the first time in centuries."

Segni squinted as he stared out of the window, then he leaned over the table, his nostrils flared and jaw clenched as he looked towards me, one of his hands resting inside the box that normally kept his strawberries.

"Like he said, someone will have to meet with them. But this," he said, waving his other hand in the air, "all of *this*; how will this affect the birthday feast?"

Chapter 15

The council met in secret, just before midnight when the rest of the ship was asleep.

Elliott had returned with Hannah, and they took their seats at the far side of the table, their hands clasped together. Of our class, they had been the first to marry, and often I forgot their relation during council meetings. The head doctor, Disci, sat across from them with another one of his apprentices at his right side, who had delivered each of us the messages to attend.

"Everybody but Segni," Disci had told him, just after a heavily rationed dinner consisting of uncooked vegetables due to the low number of chefs on hand. "This must be a secret from him, for the good of the ship. He must not know."

So his apprentice delivered the message to each of us, and we waited until the bustling of the halls turned to silence before stealing away, careful not to make noise ourselves.

"It is evident," said Elliott, his voice low from his side of the table, "that the condition of the ship has reached a dire low. Do we have body counts?"

"None from the gardeners," I said. "Some minor injuries, but the doctors have already seen to those. The soil broke most of their falls."

"Four burns from the kitchens," said Elliott. "Six deep lacerations from knives. The rest is manageable. As you know, nearly everyone in there was injured in some fashion or another."

"And the porters?" I asked Elliott, who turned to Disci.

"We saved who we could and cleaned out the heavy room as best we could, but not all the stains could be removed. But of the original porters, I would say only ten percent are fit to work, thirty percent injured, and ten more percent crippled for the long term. And the rest—you know the rest."

"We do," said Hannah, somber. "With the blight in the fields, this could not have come at a worse time. Already we are short staffed just to provide food and herbs. Horatius, we need both of those; can you provide them?"

I frowned as she mentioned the blight, then responded, "Yes, I can. If we can do away with the feast, we can devote half of the gardens to herbs and the other half to high yielding crops as opposed to strawberries. As I said to Segni, four weeks for each, assuming that nothing changes."

"The feast is cancelled," hissed Elliott. "Damn the feast. There is no such time for such trivialities. Priority number one is those herbs, Horatius."

"Agreed," I answered. "But what about when Segni intervenes?"

"Prepare a feast for one," responded Elliott. "It will suffice, and with the rest of the council on your side, he should listen to the majorities. Damn strawberries at a time like this."

"Done. But now, we need to speak about a more important issue," I said.

"Yes, yes we do," murmured Disci and turned to the window, the rest of our eyes following.

Outside, the other half of the ship had turned, righting itself to be perfectly parallel with our end. Its flank was illuminated by a strobing white light that emanated from just behind the corner of the window, where the two halves of the ship came together. Only a few hours ago, it had originated, too bright to look directly into and mimicking the color of stars far away, accompanied by a hissing and a vibration that I could feel through my shoes.

"What caused this?" Disci whispered. "And why now? Do you think they know that this is our weakest moment? Do you think they did it on purpose, as a strike against us?"

"Why should they?" Elliott answered, arms folded across his chest. "The Hand of God struck hundreds of years ago. If this was an act of aggression, then it makes no sense why they would have waited this long to perform it. Besides, we were once one people before the Hand of God split us, and if the stories are to be true, we lived in even greater peace back then than we enjoy now. They're probably just like us."

"Probably," said Disci, but his eyes narrowed.

"Probably," I repeated, but continued staring across to where the gaunt faces scattered throughout the distant windows stared back, where there was the occasional flash of blue light, and where I had seen the glinting of brandished cooking knives in the past. "But I wouldn't put much faith in it."

"I agree with Horatius," said Elliott slowly. "We can never be too careful. Where the ship is coming together, where it is joining, has anyone actually *been* there?"

"I have," I responded, and the other faces turned towards me, their eyebrows raised, and I quickly shut my mouth. The control room was just underneath and a three-minute walk to where the halves were coming together, close enough that Pliny had shown me the door that had once led to the other half.

"Here," Pliny had said, pointing to the door that was as wide as two men, with frost encrusted around its edges. "Here is where the ships used to connect. In fact, it was the *only* spot where they connected, the logic being if one side of the ship contracted disease or underwent disaster, it could be sealed off. Based upon our current situation, I suppose the logic was sound."

He traced the outline of the frame with his index finger, feeling the crease between door and wall. I remembered studying the door, a solid metal slab with handholds inlaid near the center, though there was no knob or opening mechanisms. The metal was smooth, so smooth I could see my own reflection peering back, as though another version of me was waiting right behind the door. All except for above it, where a single word had been scratched into the metal at the top of the frame, chiseled with a heart dug into material around it.

Necti

"Necti?" I remember having asked. "What's that?"

"Likely some form of graffiti, committed far from where the rest of the ship would see to avoid punishment. To be honest, I don't know, but it's been here since I was first shown the door."

And above, where the top of the door reached the ceiling, something else was written. Something small, that I had to stand back to see on my tiptoes, and had to squint to read.

Separate we fly. Together we land.

Back in the council room, Elliott snapped his fingers, bringing my attention back to the meeting.

"Horatius, pay attention. Why in the Hand of God have you been there?" he asked, tilting his head slightly.

"There, ah, I had to fetch ice when I was a porter," I lied, keeping my voice steady. "Tom strained himself in the heavy room, and he claimed his mother always said ice was a remedy. But the ice grows too thin on this end of the ship, where hardly any frost forms on the walls, and a decent-sized piece is difficult to find. So I had to travel deep within the ship, all the way to the back."

"And? What did you see?" inquired Hannah, leaning forward.

"There's only one entrance, and the door can be shut," I answered. "But there is no lock, so it will need to be held in place, if need be."

"Alright," said Elliott. "Here's the plan, then. Together, we will go to greet them, assuming this door actually does open. None of us will go to their side of the ship unless they trade with an equal number of their own people, and it will remain that way until we are absolutely certain that it is safe. Unless there are objections, Disci and I will be the spokesmen to negotiate peace and give an impression of strength. Horatius, prepare a small basket of a variety of crops to present as a token of our goodwill. We'll want the remaining porters there as well, in case we have to force the door shut."

"I'll have it ready by tomorrow morning. According to the voice, we should expect the door to open around noon. Plus I can lead you there."

"Good," said Elliott and smiled. "Now see, *that's* how you have a council meeting. Without this feast nonsense that's not going to happen anyways."

"Not for you it won't," shouted a voice from the door, and the council jumped, turning to see Segni with his finger pointed at Elliott. His face was flushed bright red, spittle flying from his mouth with each word, his eyes so wide that the blood vessels were visible among the white. Nean and Tom stood at attention behind him, accompanied by two other porters, all with kitchen knives. And his younger brother waited at his side, his own stomach starting to approach the size of Segni's, such that both could not fit within the entrance at the same time.

"You *traitor*! You dare plan a mutiny, you dare defy me as your chief?"

"How, how did you find out about this?" stammered Elliott, his face turning white. "No, your Honor, we—"

"Lies! Lies and flattery. Nean, Tom, take him and lock him in one of the unused apartments. No food for three days so he can experience the food shortage first hand! His wife too! And I knew because you invited my brother, my own flesh and blood, to betray me as well!"

"We what?" exclaimed Disci, turning his head to his apprentice.

"You said everyone but Segni!" he squeaked, "His brother is the historian, and on the council, so—"

"Here, he admits it!" shouted Segni, "I want them both locked away as well!"

"Segni, you can't do this!" I shouted as Nean led the porters into the room, seizing the accused. "We have to prepare to meet the others, to set our first impression!"

"And as chief, I obviously would be most suitable for the job. Who else would they desire to meet, besides the leader?"

"You don't understand, Segni, it could be dangerous. We don't know anything about them. We don't know what they'll do."

"You're right, Horatius, which is why you'll be there, right by my side, to make sure that that nothing happens. You said you knew the way to the door, and tomorrow you will lead me to it."

Chapter 16

"At eleven, you're to appear at my apartment," Segni had said with a smile. "With your gift of vegetables ready, which you will present after carrying it to the other half of the ship. As a past porter, you should be used to that. What a treat tomorrow will be, a moment in history, set by a previous historian. Set by myself. And I cannot think of a better time for it to happen, can you?"

"No," I answered, the muscles in my arms tight.

"Of course not, because as you know, tomorrow is my birthday. And what an *excellent* gift this shall be before the feast you shall prepare next week."

I grit my teeth as he spoke, as I watched Nean dig his knife into Elliott's back and push him from the room while Tom led Hannah out with a hand on her elbow.

"My daughter," Hannah said. "I know you have to do this, but see that she is cared for."

Tom nodded before they disappeared down the hallway, with Segni following, and leaving me alone in the room, sitting in the darkness as my fists clenched as I saw the council crumble with a few simple commands.

Pliny's voice spoke in the darkness then, reminding me of his final words. Reminding me of my duty.

There are other measures, actions that I was too much of a coward to do. And other things, darker things that I could have done.

My palms started to bleed as my fingernails pushed into the skin and I closed my eyes, forcing my heartbeat to slow, thinking about what needed to happen next. And with Segni, what needed to happen afterwards. Darker things.

I never spoke out when the council was taken because I knew that I could not let Segni go alone. I knew that whatever the danger, I had to accompany him. Not because of what might happen to him.

But because what might happen to the ship.

***

I did not retire to my apartment that night as the meeting broke apart. Instead, I waited for them to disperse, and walked down the length of the ship, following corridors that had long grown familiar since Pliny's death. I listened to the chatter of my teeth grow louder and louder as frost accumulated on the walls as I neared the control room.

Once in the control room, I flipped through the books left on the table from ages past, reading Archim's handwriting. I reviewed both the capabilities that I could and that I could not understand, running scenarios in my mind for the next day, bookmarking pages for each, and ranking them in terms of priority.

Then, at just after six in the morning, I found what I was looking for, deep within one of the thickest journals. Journal number six, three hundred and seventy-one pages in. I read it twice before placing two different-sized paperweights on top, applying a constant to keep the page number from changing.

And carefully, I walked to the knobs at the far end of the room that controlled what I had found. My fingers brushed them, sending adrenaline through me as I hesitated, biting my lip.

All I needed was a test, a test to find out if it would work. Just for a few moments, no more, unless required by events the next day.

Holding my breath, I then turned a specific one just slightly to the right, watching my theory become reality just as I had done with the lights in the garden. And I smiled.

Segni might not be willing to defend the ship.

But I would be.

Chapter 17

Segni's apartment was at the very back of the ship, near where the wall curved in upon itself and turned back towards the front. As tradition, that room had always belonged to the chief, being by far the largest, having a steady temperature gradient from warm to cool from the back to the front, and having all the best furniture from the other apartments brought in. It was shaped like a wide hall, ending abruptly at a thick sealed door at the back, where the metal of the frame had been physically fused together in several spots to make it eternally impossible to open. A red "C" was plastered off center on that door, for "Chief," and a few old wires that dangled from holes in the walls had been utilized to hang picture frames.

Segni was still wiping away sleep when he exited, his brother Vaca following behind. Nean joined us with six porters as we walked down the length of the ship.

That morning, after two hours of quick sleep, I had collected a basket of produce from the gardens as Elliott, then later Segni, had instructed. I took three of everything, the best specimens that I could find, arranging them together to display our agricultural capabilities. As I worked, the other gardeners gathered around me, some of the children asking me questions.

"What's going on?" demanded Mark. "Where are you going? Are you going to meet the others?"

"I am," I had answered, leaning over to liberate a green bean. "We're going to impress them with all the fine gardening that you've been doing. Maybe they'll want us to teach them too!"

"Will they be new friends?" asked Matthew, and I smiled, biting my lip.

"We can only hope!" I responded and repeated the sentence in my own thoughts, trying to convince myself as well. But it was the last question that caught me off guard as I walked out of the gardens and felt a small hand tugging on my shirt. I looked down to see the face of a young girl, tears spilling down her cheeks.

"When will my parents be back?" Ruth said, and buried her face in my shirt.

"What happened?" I asked, stunned. "Where did they go?"

"Uncle Tom said they were with you," she answered, "when they were taken away. He said that you saw it!"

I took a sharp breath inward, remembering the night before, and bent down to speak with Ruth.

"Hannah and Elliott?"

"Y- Yes," she stuttered.

"Soon, Ruth. Listen to me, soon. Nothing like this will *ever* happen again, do you understand? You have my promise, and they will be back soon. But I have to go now, Ruth. As soon as I come back, I will help you, okay?"

She nodded, then turned and walked back to the gardens, whispering before she left.

"Okay, Horatius. You've always been able to do it before."

I then left Ruth and the other gardeners, their gazes following me as I departed. And as I met up with Segni, his eye wandered to the basket I carried as we walked. Reaching a hand over, he rooted through the arrangement of food until he found the three strawberries at the center and tucked them into his shirt pocket.

"What are you doing?" I demanded, and he laughed through his heavy breathing from the exertion of walking.

"It's not like they're going to know," he said. "It's not going to make a difference either way." Then he popped one into his mouth, discarding the stem on the ground behind him, where the four leaves were promptly trampled on by Nean's foot. And his hand returned to the basket, removing a green bean, then a tomato, and other produce until only two of everything remained.

"We're getting close," I said as Segni started to shiver and his shoes scuffed across the frost-encrusted floor, cutting out arced streaks among the white. Nean dragged his knife along the wall, leaving a long scratch behind him as metal grated against metal, absentmindedly flicking the edge from time to time to scatter ice on the ground.

"Cut it out, will you?" I said, the noise reverberating in my ears.

"Figure I'll leave a trail, in case you try to get us lost here," he said and dug the knife in with a sharp *squeak.*

Then, minutes later, we arrived at the door, and placing my hand against it, I could feel it humming, vibrating from something behind it.

"The four of us will enter," said Segni, looking at the narrow width and gesturing to me, Tom, and Nean. "Horatius and I in front, Nean and Tom behind with your knives ready in case I am in danger. I will present the gift and accept theirs in return. Other porters, force the door shut if we have issues and after we escape, and hold it there."

"Maybe we should have something heavy to prop against it," I said, "in case it needs to hold."

"You're looking at the strongest men on the ship," said Segni. "We'll be fine."

"The strongest men on *this* side of the ship."

"Horatius, if you question me again, then I'll be sure to include you in our present to the other side. Now, how much longer do we have to wait?"

"Any minute now," answered Nean. "*If* anything happens at all."

"Indeed, *if*," said Segni with a yawn, and sat on the floor with his back against the wall and shutting his eyes. "If it doesn't, deliver the gift basket to my room, refilled, Horatius. I'll be retiring to sleep, as there just so happened to be an interruption last night that cost me several hours, as you know. We'll give it fifteen more minutes, and if nothing happens, then—"

"*Airlock restored,*" said the voice from above, causing everyone in the party to jump, and Segni's eyes to snap open.

With a *crack,* the ice along the seam split, shattering onto the floor and scattering down the hall as the door opened, propelled forward with such force that it slammed against the wall. And peering inside, we saw a long hallway with another door at the end.

A door that had also opened.

And now had three figures peering back.

Chapter 18

The three figures started walking, the two on the sides slightly behind the one in the center. The leftmost swayed with a slight limp, his hand on his belt where a scuffed cooking knife hung on one side and a short black rectangle was clipped to the other. The sleeves of his shirt were too wide for his arms, the red fabric hanging off his bones as if his shoulders were a hanger. He smiled as they approached, two of his bottom teeth missing, and his cheeks forming concave pockets on the sides of his face, and his facial muscles twitching slightly as they held the expression.

The other side figure wore faded blue, the shirt jumping across his skin as his chest spasmed underneath. The contents of his belt were identical to the left figure's and a thin scar ran through his eyebrow to his jaw. He spat on the side of the passageway, his thick phlegm trickling slowly down the wall, the metal similar in most parts to the rest of the ship but interrupted by long arcs of more rough material, globs that were fused to the surface and ran in frozen drops towards the ground.

Then there was the center figure, her clothes entirely grey, the fit far more crisp than the other two, the folds accented with sharp creases. She met my eyes as she led the party, my heart racing as I recognized the familiar pattern of freckles coupled with ginger hair.

Segni and I approached from the other end, him taking up enough of the hallway to push me near against the edge, Tom and Nean following our stride. Segni held a hand against my chest to prevent me from moving past him, his breath coming in puffs as the others reached the halfway point where two double doors were sealed away at a right angle and kept walking. At one-third of the way, we met them, standing five feet apart, and a cluster of heads appeared at the open doorway at the end of the hall to watch and wait.

For a moment, no one spoke—we simply stared, taking in the appearance of those that had been separated for centuries, and viewable only from a distance. Segni's eyes flickered to each in turn, scanning their hands. The men on the left and right of the woman in grey responded by looking him over, their eyes narrowing as they reached his chin, then turning to near slits when they glossed over his stomach. My sight was drawn to the woman in grey, just as they had been drawn there over the years as I had spotted her watching me from her window, and her stare met my own. Then her pupils flicked downward and to her right, where the fingers of her hand danced in a soft flurry of motion, too low to be seen by her counterparts.

Two signs, repeated over and over, one of her thumb overlapping her index and ring fingers, another of her pinky bending in towards her palm. I frowned as I looked towards her face again, and then she spoke, her voice harder and sharper than I was used to.

"I am Airomem," she said, her chin high in the air. "Daughter of Praeter, leader of the Lear tribe. With me are the leaders of the two other tribes, who have granted me safe passage to this meeting between our peoples today."

"Esuri," said the man to her left, scowling at her. "King of the Aquarians."

"Sitient," said the other, his voice raspy and starting before the other had finished speaking. "Chieftain of the Agrarians."

"Segni, chief of the ship," came the answer from our side of the divide. "And on this day of meeting, we bring you a gift."

He extended the basket to Airomem, and she accepted it, while Esuri and Sitient stared at the contents.

"No water?" asked Sitient. "Only food?"

"And not enough to share between the three of us," said Esuri, "with most of these varieties being of the basic species."

"I forgo my share, so that the two of you may enjoy it," said Airomem. "And we graciously accept your gift, Segni."

"Of *course* she would give up *her* share, as if she would even need it," said Sitient, and spat against the wall again.

"*Enough*," said Airomem, her voice sharp just as Esuri opened his mouth to comment as well, and gestured to me. "And you, are you the leader of another tribe from your side of the ship?"

"I am Hor—"

"Him?" Segni laughed, putting a hand in front of me to cut me off. "No, he is the one who prepared the gift for you, a simple farmer."

"Simple farmer?" said Sitient. "Did you come to trade insults as well as gifts?"

"Or to show disdain for us, the leaders, with his inferior presence?" asked Esuri.

"I am sure that he meant nothing of the sort," interjected Airomem. "We must respect that their customs may be different than our own."

"We meant no insult, and I am more than a simple farmer, and act as the hist—"

Segni cut me off with his hand again and spoke, gesturing towards the basket.

"And now that we have provided one to you, where is the gift that you have prepared for us?"

For a moment, all was silent, Airomem's mouth opening slightly as Esuri and Sitient bristled, their hands moving towards their hips as Nean and Tom stirred behind us.

"*Our* gift?" hissed Esuri, and pointed at Segni's stomach, his finger rigid. "*Our* gift, after you send us your scraps? Are you sure that you did not have more to give, fat man, because your offering is a mockery."

"Give it back then, if you don't want it," responded Segni, his face reddening and voice rising. "It's all we could spare with the feast next week."

"A *feast*?" shouted Esuri. "You feast, while the two thousand members of our tribe starve? How many are you wasting this food upon? Perhaps you should set seats for us as well!"

"A thousand," shouted Segni back. "And maybe I would have invited a few of you, if you had been more polite!"

Airomem's face turned white as Esuri and Sitient looked to each other, their heads tilting slightly to the side.

"A thousand," Sitient breathed. "Of course, that would just be your warriors, those invited to partake in the feast?"

"No," lectured Segni as Airomem held up a hand and I tried to interject. "The feast is for everyone."

"One thousand total," muttered Esuri. "Five times less than our tribes combined. With just as much food and water."

"I assure you," I said, speaking quickly, "that our resources are few and stretched thin, much of them destroyed when the Hand of God struck."

"Liar!" shouted Esuri, taking the basket from Airomem and smashing it against the ground, sending vegetables flying down the hallway in both directions. Airomem spun and slapped him, her nails leaving red marks across his face as he reached towards his hip again.

"Harm me, and you know the consequences for you and your tribe!" she shouted at him, then continued to us all, "We came here for peace! We do not know the circumstances of their side of the ship, must assume that they likely have a fifth of the resources we do with their population, and must work with them in the future to assure mutual survival. Together, as four tribes, we will create a future—a better future than our past."

Esuri shook with rage as Segni responded, leaning over to pick up the remainder of the basket, a few vegetables left in the center.

"Four tribes? No, I am chief of the *ship*, just as my father was, and just how I told you earlier. Just how it used to be before the Hand of God struck. And now that we are reunited, I will assume responsibilities of the ship. Not *half* the ship."

And as he straightened up and bit off the end of a green bean in his hand, something toppled out from his shirt pocket. Something red, that bounced on the floor and rolled to Esuri's feet, with a bright green stem and unmistakable among the metal.

It was the result of my labor from reading the *Guide to Gardening*. A plump strawberry, one that Segni had stolen from the basket, the size and color greatly enhanced through my work.

And far more impressive than the other contents of the gift.

Chapter 19

For a moment, the strawberry wobbled, each set of eyes staring down at it as I held my breath. Everyone was still, save for the twitching in Sitient's chest and Esuri's face, causing the shadows to dance on the walls, and for a slight shift in weight of Airomem's posture.

Then Esuri lifted his foot and brought it down on the strawberry, pressing until it was flat against the metal, juice and pulp oozing out from underneath his tattered shoe. And Sitient raised his eyes, his mouth opening to whisper a single word.

"Liar."

Together they lunged, covering the distance between us in an instant as Airomem's arms shot out, sending each careening against opposite walls. And as they bounced away and recovered, I felt a thick hand grip my collar as Segni dragged me in front of his own body. Behind us, Nean shrieked and sprinted away, his footsteps echoing in slow motion in my mind as Esuri and Sitient attacked again.

Esuri's knife was in his hand this time as he leapt forward, slashing downward from above as Segni's grip tightened on my collar, his fingers wrapping around the fabric until it cut off my breathing and I saw black in the corners of my vision. I kicked backwards as the knife came down, Segni twisting me to his left to meet the silver edge that was nicked dozens of times along its length, the short handle stained red where it was clasped in Esuri's fingers. His enraged face was reflected in the blade as it neared my throat, spittle flying from his mouth as he twisted, the blade mere inches away from my skin as it exploded in a shower of sparks.

Reaching around my and Segni's shoulders, Tom's knife met Esuri's, his own arm absorbing the blow as if it he were catching a moderate weight in the heavy room. Then Segni squealed, a high-pitched sound that flooded directly into my ear as his hand loosened and I bucked away, turning to see Sitient at his right, his eyes alight with fury.

And twisting the knife that had just plunged deep into Segni's exposed side as blood spurted onto his hands, and Esuri reared backwards to attack once again.

But then there were two flashes of bright blue light as Airomem stepped forward, an arm extended towards both Esuri and Sitient with one of the peculiar black rectangles in each hand, the blue light buzzing between two sharp metal prongs on the end. With a jabbing motion, she simultaneously jammed one into each of their torsos and they were thrown backwards, screaming as their muscles locked tight and they shook on the ground, their jaws bulging and necks bent.

"Run!" Airomem shouted, pointing towards the door. "They won't be down long! More will surely be coming!"

And as soon as the words left her throat, bodies began pouring through the door at the end of the hall. Dozens of them, screeching as they pushed off each other with too thin arms, and ran on too thin legs, and fought amongst themselves to be first with flashes of blue light and the brandishing of knives.

I turned, slamming into Segni's stomach as he continued to howl, clutching at his side where the knife handle still protruded, his face white and fingers red.

"Segni, run!" I shouted, pushing him, but he barely stumbled backwards. Behind us, the mass of limbs advanced as Esuri and Sitient started to rise, each now holding a knife in one hand and one of the black rectangles that Airomem had used in the other.

"I can't!" Segni shouted. "Your chief is wounded! Stand, stand and defend me, your chief! Avenge me! Teach them who their true leader is!"

The horde was a third of the way now, and picking up speed, their calls more frantic, their movements more fluid.

"Go!" shouted Airomem, strobing the blue light devices. "Go! Now! They will have no mercy!"

"Then we shall have no mercy!" shouted Segni. "Defend me, fight for your chief! In front, get in front of me!"

Behind Segni, Tom stooped down, lowering his shoulder underneath Segni's arm and pulling him into the air as he began to kick. Then Tom started to run with Segni, clearing the way for us to pass as Segni struggled, then eventually reached a hand down to his side and pulled the crimson knife free a quarter of the way to the door.

"Cowards! This ship belongs to *me*! It is *mine*!" Segni shouted and slashed downwards, cutting deep into Tom's shoulder. With a startled yelp, Tom dropped Segni to the ground where he writhed in drops of his own blood as Airomem and I jumped over him, and then he struggled to his feet.

The horde was now half of the way, with Esuri and Sitient leading them by several lengths. Segni turned a full circle, his eyes wide, then his face grew even paler than I thought possible as he saw the advancing horde again as we fled, and then started to hobble after us. Airomem took the rear of the small group, holding the blue lights in front of her, somehow making them buzz louder and glow brighter as Segni struggled to catch up.

"Wait!" pleaded Segni as his breaths came in puffs and he struggled to keep pace, slowing from a jog to a walk with his right hand up. Tom stopped, preparing to turn back, but I took his arm and shouted at him until he budged.

"Tom, no! It's too late!"

And it was.

Segni screamed as the fastest members reached him, their momentum so great that they ran over him as he toppled, but turning back as soon as they saw the blue flash of Airomem. A half dozen knives flashed as he fell to his knees, moving in and out of the skin as he screamed, and then his screams turned to gurgles. And out of his shirt pocket fell another strawberry, coming to a halt ten feet away from him in our direction as we reached the door, just as Sitient reached the center of the mass and buried his open mouth into Segni's throat, cutting off all sound.

We watched as they ripped him apart, a frenzied mass of butchering on all sides. And in front of the spectacle, Esuri stepped forward, a strip of Segni in his hand, and walked ten feet towards us. Then he bent down to the ground and picked up a small object, the strawberry Segni had dropped moments before.

"A feast!" he cried out, his teeth already red before they bit into the fruit, and he threw the stem towards us. "A feast fit for a king!"

And taking the door into both her hands, Airomem slammed it shut, cutting us off from the birthday celebration.

Chapter 20

My breath came in choking gasps as the porters stood with open mouths, shutting my eyes to block out the remains of Segni on the other side of the door, while Airomem started to shout.

"Brace the door! Brace the door; we don't have long!" Her head whipped back and forth over the crew, surveying Nean, who was shaking against the wall, Tom staring dumbfounded at his red hands, and a white-faced and wide-eyed Vaca. "The braces, where are the braces?"

"B-braces?" stuttered one of the porters, as Airomem whirled on him.

"Yes, *braces*, to reinforce the door! They'll be trying to burst through at any minute, first with their body weight, then with a ram! And I give that door about a half hour before it falls in, if that."

"A ram?" I said, my thoughts starting to spin again, fighting the adrenaline that was coursing through my system and still screaming for me to run. "What do you mean by a ram?"

"A battering ram! As in they'll slam into the door with something heavy until it is no longer a door!"

"Why, why would they have something like that?" asked Vaca, still in shock.

"To. Break. Doors," she hissed, clenching her fists, then rounded on me. "When was the last war here? How prepared are you warriors? How quickly can we get a group of guards with weapons, here, to defend this point?"

"W-warriors?" said the same porter that had spoken up a moment before as Airomem bit the side of her cheek, and I answered.

"War? We've never had a war, not in all of our recorded history since the Hand of God struck! I've only heard of them through books. This crew right here, these are the majority of those who would be fit for any sort of defense, minus some gardeners. And Segni's death is the first violent one in at least three hundred years, since the Great Thirst!"

"The what? Wait, no, never mind, that's not important now. Unless we have a way to barricade that door, they're coming through. And if that happens, you'll end up just like your chief! You lot, standing around, I want you pushing against that door as hard as you can! It will buy us time!"

"Don't listen to her!" shouted Nean, raising his face from his hands, his face wet with tears. "She's one of *them*, one of the barbarians that killed Segni! And now she's probably going to kill us too and eat us! Just like they did, just like they did to—"

"Get yourself together!" I shouted back, stepping in front of Airomem. "She did far more to protect Segni than *you* did! She's the reason *any* of us escaped!"

"And I'm not one of them," said Airomem. "Their tribes are separate from my own, with good reason."

"She's still one of the other side," shrieked Nean. "We can't trust her!"

"What if Segni is still alive?" joined in Vaca. "What if he fought them off? What if he's trying to escape now, but we are going to lock him inside? I command you *not* to hold the door!"

The porters hesitated, but before I could speak again, there was the sound of something striking the metal door as it started to swing open on its hinges, and Tom and I both leapt to push our weight against it. There was a screech as the door slammed shut, something behind it scrambling away and scratching at the metal, as I turned to address the other porters who were already jumping forward.

"All of you, against this door, now!"

Their bodies joined ours as several others collided on the other side, but the door held, rattling against the frame.

"We'll need braces," exclaimed Airomem, her voice high. "That won't last long!"

"Hold the door. I have an idea! We'll be right back!" I responded, turning to run down the hallway when Tom's thick fingers gripped around my forearm and he pulled me close. Then he whispered in my ear, so quiet that only I could hear him as Airomem motioned for us to hurry.

"I saw Esuri's knife," he said. "I saw Sitient's knife. I could only stop one. Make sure I made the right decision."

***

"This way!" I shouted to Airomem, streaking down the hallway, sliding on the ice on the floor. Ice that was now melting, I noticed, and air that no longer frosted in front of my face. We turned a corner and my feet nearly went out from under me, but I recovered, pinwheeling my arms as I ran down a small staircase.

"Where are we going?" she shouted, nearly colliding with the wall herself. "There is no way that the two of us will be able to carry back anything big enough to stop them ourselves!"

"We won't need to!" I shouted and continued sprinting, not stopping until I reached the room that Pliny had showed me long ago. The control room.

Together, we burst inside, and I ran to the center table where the book I had studied earlier was still open. And before rushing to the knobs on the far wall, I read the section again that I had found.

The section in the book labeled *Gravitational Controls*. The instructions I would use to defend the ship.

Gravitation for the ship has been preset to account for acceleration and deceleration inertial differentials, read the passage. *Several other applications are toggled, such as the reduction of artificial gravity in hallways to allow for better transportation, or for recreational activities requiring higher values. In the event of special circumstances, full gravitational control is enabled. It should be noted that energy usage grows exponentially with higher gravitational values, and that gravitational changes should be communicated to the inhabitants of the ship to prevent injuries. Furthermore, the ship's intelligence will modulate any set gravitational values accordingly to account for inertial deltas.*

"It exists," came Airomem's voice behind me as she walked over to a wall, reaching out a hand to touch one of the knobs. "It actually exists."

"*Stop!* Don't touch that!" I shouted, and she withdrew her hand sharply.

"Sorry, I was—"

Just then, there was a noise that boomed from above, and rattling thunder that echoed in the control room.

"Damn bastards!" Airomem exclaimed, looking towards the origin of the sound. "They must have had the ram ready, prepared before the meeting, in case they wanted to force their way across the bridge! We should have had more time than this. Quick, we need to act!"

But I was already running towards the section of switches that I had identified earlier, those that corresponded to the other side of the door and to Segni's remains. Without a moment's hesitation, my finger came into contact with a cold metal knob.

And taking a sharp breath, I turned it as far as it would go to the right.

Chapter 21

The sound of a crash slammed into my eardrums again, far louder this time, reverberations reaching us in the control room as the book shook off the table.

"I don't understand, it should have worked!" I said, double-checking the knob and jiggling it to be sure that there was no room left to turn. It was the right one, corresponding with the correct section of the ship, according to the manual.

When I had tested the knob indicated to adjust the control room, it had worked—I'd felt my arms being dragged down to the ground, and my spine crunching under the excess weight, just like I felt in the heavy room.

But this time, I must have been wrong.

"They'll be breaking through now!" shouted Airomem as we heard shouts. "Hurry, we need to get back! We can defend the door for some time at least! With any luck, if we harm enough of them, they'll turn back and we can regroup and maintain the bottleneck. But once they break through that door, there will be no stopping them!"

We ran back the way we had come, thoughts flooding my mind as Airomem removed the black rectangles from her belt and blue light flashed along the walls.

Like she said, if they had broken through, then we would already be defeated. With several more times people on their end of the ship than our own, defending ourselves would be impossible. Even if they did not harm a single person on our end, they would find our crops, and without stores, weakened from the combination of feasting and my actions, then we would starve.

Water had now puddled thick upon the floor from the icy walls, frigid moisture soaking through my shoes with each step. And we were nearly at the corner when the shouts had grown more frantic.

And I wondered what we would do.

We had almost no weapons. In my entire life before that day, I'd never been in a fight whose consequence was anything more than a potential broken bone. And after seeing Segni go down, I knew how this fight would end.

Then we turned, and I saw the scene that was waiting for us.

The porters still stood with their backs against the door, pushing against the metal. Nean and Vaca watched from the hallway, ready to run at a moment's notice.

But nothing had changed except for the screams on the other end of the wall. Which, though faded, now sounded quieter than they should at our proximity.

"What happened?" I said to Tom, my breaths coming in staccato gasps. "We heard the ram; are they preparing for another strike?"

"One hit," he answered. "Then nothing. Only noise."

"It's unlike them," said Airomem. "Typically, when they are blood-lusted, they do not give up that easily, or until they can carry away some of their own dead. Their tribes detest each other, however, and made a peace pact for today only. Maybe it broke down."

"Have you heard anything close in the past few minutes since we left?" I asked, listening, and Tom shook his head.

"Then open the door," I said. "But be prepared to slam it shut again."

"I would advise against that," said Airomem, flashing the blue lights brighter, the porters flinching away.

"We'll be all right," I answered. "I know what happened. Go on, open it."

One by one, the porters stepped away until only Tom was left. With a nod, he grasped the handholds in the center and pulled, slowly cracking the door until it was only an inch open. And stepping forward, I placed my eye against the crack.

"Clear!" I said and pushed the door open as we crowded around the opening.

At the far end of the hallway, several bodies were squirming away on all fours, dragging their limbs along the floor, their hair plastered to the sides of their heads. And directly in front of us was the battering ram where it had fallen under increased gravity, its edge denting the metal floor underneath.

The front of it was the remains of a metal grating, folded over and hammered into a blunt edge. The body was constructed from the tops of desks, dressers, and bed frames bound together, with fabric handholds from ripped apart clothes lining the sides. Inside the hollow frame was gardening dirt, which had given it weight, but now spilled out a crack in the back. Underneath the ram, a shoe stuck out, trapped underneath its weight, and a trail of blood led from it back to the door at the other end of the hallway where the last of the others had disappeared from sight.

I averted my eyes from the red mass past the end of the ram, though little of Segni remained. Instead, it looked as if they had taken him with them to their side of the ship.

"They've fled!" shouted Vaca, "and taken Segni with them!"

Before I could stop him, he crossed over the threshold into the hallway, Nean moving at his side. Or, as Airomem had called the hallway, the bridge.

Confusion crossed their faces as their first step slammed into the ground, pulling the rest of their bodies forward. Vaca's face followed, smashing into the metal, an audible *snap* sounding as his nose arrived first and bent under the weight of his head. Nean caught himself with his hands before collapsing on his chest, his arm muscles bulging as he pushed himself up, his legs which were still across the threshold kicking.

"I'm stuck!" shouted Vaca, his voice nasal. "Help, I'm stuck!"

Tom reached down and took each of their legs in a hand, then pulled them backwards, sliding them out of the bridge.

"The hallway is now a heavy room," I said, pointing as Vaca held his nose. "But much heavier than you are accustomed to. So heavy that making it across is difficult, and we can fend away anyone who gets close. All we have to do is defend this single point, and we defend our entire side of the ship. As long as we post guards, our life will go unchanged."

"Unchanged?" shouted Vaca and sniffled as tears accompanied the blood on his face. "Without Segni, who will lead us? How will we be able to survive?"

"Why, you, of course," said Nean and knelt in front of him, bowing his head. "Just as I protected your brother, I will protect you. And just as he led, you will lead. And I assure you, those that were responsible for his death will pay dearly." With that sentence, he turned to look at me, his eyes narrowed and furious.

"Me, chief?" said Vaca, holding his hands in front of him.

"Not yet," I said quickly. "Without the approval of the council—"

"Then for my first decree," said Vaca, ignoring me and pointing a finger at Airomem. "I want her locked away, for what her people did to my brother!"

Part 2: Airomem

Chapter 22

Airomem would never forget the first time she had seen the power room.

Her father sang under his breath, a song with words long forgotten, then turned towards her as they walked down the hallway. "Oh, Airomem, today is your big day! Are you excited, my little princess? Tell me, what is today? I seem to have forgotten."

Airomem smiled when her father called her a princess, and rightly so. For not only he called her that, but the rest of the Lear tribe.

With one of her front teeth missing and a new one budding in its place, she held up the fingers on two of her hands, and answered.

"I turned six today! Which means I get to start in the power room!" she said, sticking her chin in the air, which she considered very princess-like.

"Oh, I don't know," said her father, wagging a finger and crouching down to meet her eye level, putting his hands on her waist. "Are you sure you are ready? It's a big job, an *enormous* job. The entirety of Dandelion Fourteen depends on you!"

"I'm ready, Daddy," she said, and stuck her chin out even higher, which in her mind could only be more princess-like.

"If you say so!" he said, picking her up and throwing her over his shoulder as she screamed and her fists beat his back in protest. "To the power room we go!"

She giggled as she bounced with each step of her father's until they reached the back of the ship. Or rather, the *very* back of the ship—as a Lear, the back of the ship was all she had ever explored, never leaving the two outposts that were constantly guarded against intruders and led to the front regions. They entered a long room, flashing monitors dotting the walls and displaying flickering information, and headed towards a door in the back, where a word in bold red letters was plastered to the door.

"Nuclear!" Airomem shouted, reading the word, one of the first she had learned as her father taught her to read.

"Yes, nuclear!" he exclaimed and set her on the ground. "This is the entrance of the power room, Airomem. It is time you started learning. One day, it will be your job to be an engineer here, to keep the power running! And if you do that well enough, then one day you might lead the engineers and tribe, like me!" he said and poked her nose.

"Yeah!" she shouted and raised a fist into the air, then quickly lowered it after deciding it was not as princess-like as a raised chin.

"Do you remember the hand signs I taught you? It's loud in the power room, and we have to wear earplugs or else our ears will hurt. Show me *danger*. Good! Now *yes*, good, *no*. Perfect, you're such a great learner, Airomem, one day you'll be among the best."

"Look, Daddy, I made one up too!" she said, and held up her hand, making a new sign.

"And what does that mean?"

"It means I'm tired of waiting!" she said, and her father cracked a smile before continuing to speak.

"Now, Airomem, inside this room, everything is serious. Since the asteroid cracked the ship in half, we have kept the ship entire ship alive. *Both* sides. It's been no easy task—without the main computer systems, many of the things that happened automatically in the past have to be done by hand. And we have to be careful, because only one mistake is all it takes to place us back into peril. That's our job, Airomem, to not make mistakes."

"But what if we do?"

"We can't! We've come so close, and now we are at the final leg of our journey! Remind me, Airomem, what are we getting close to?"

"The new planet!"

"And what is that?"

"It's like a ship, but bigger! I think. It's like where we came from!"

"Exactly. And it is most exciting because one day, you might get to see it, Airomem!" He reached into a pocket and pulled out a piece of paper with seven dots on it shaped in a ring, "When you look out the window, and you see this, it means we are getting close! It could be any year now, Airomem, but most think it will be in your lifetime."

"Will I be princess on the planet?" she asked and stuck out her bottom lip. "Otherwise, I don't want to go."

"Of course," her father said. "And you'll want to go! That's why I'm showing you the power room, dear. We provide energy to the ship until we leave for the planet. Which is good," he said and leaned forward to speak in her ear, "Because we're almost out!"

Then he started singing again under his breath once more, and led her into the power room.

Chapter 23

Airomem's eyes were shut tight as she hid in the dark underneath her bed, gripping the stun gun tight in her right hand and her left flat against the ground, while her toes were coiled like springs against the back wall. In case the locked door of her apartment burst open. In case she had to attack. And in case she had to run.

Her breath came quickly as she saw faint blue flashes through the crack underneath her door, accompanied by far off thuds, and the sound of metal ringing on metal. And she thought back to an hour before, when she and her father had been sharing dinner.

"And how was school today?" he had asked her, holding out her seat as he placed a plate in front of her. "Tell me that Prometh still has enough wits about him to teach the youngsters! He used to be the finest of our engineers."

"Good!" she said, stabbing her fork deep into a carrot and shoving the entire slice in her mouth such that the next few words were muffled. Being a princess came second to being hungry, she had decided. "Today we learned about the photonic crystal! And about what happened to the one on the other end of the ship!"

"Oh, sounds like there was some serious learning indeed," said her father, raising an eyebrow. "Are you sure that you'll be able to keep all that knowledge in that tiny noggin? I hear if you pack too much in, then it'll explode!"

"Dad!" she whined. "I'm not six; you can't play tricks on me like that anymore. I'm eight now! I know better."

"Funny, at thirty-eight, I still think about the same things when I was thirty-six. You can never stop learning, Airomem, and don't let anyone else tell you otherwise."

"Yes, Daddy. You always say that," she huffed, rolling her eyes, and stabbed through another carrot, deep enough that the metal clinked against the plate. And as she brought it to her mouth, her father's head snapped upwards, and she heard *it*.

The wailing of the siren. The sound that made the hairs on her neck stand up and her skin tingle as blood rushed to her face and adrenaline raced along her capillaries.

Her father's hand swept the fork out of her hand as he tucked her under his elbow, then sprinted out of the mess hall. Doors flashed by as they passed the siren wielder, a boy who had just entered his teens, holding one of the stun guns such that its prongs were plugged into a box that screeched as he took off in the other direction, running loops around the Lear territory.

"Starboard!" the boy shouted with every other step, his cracking voice struggling to make it down the corner he had just turned. "Starboard! Starboard! Starboard!"

And then they were at her apartment and her father threw the door open before tossing her inside on the bed.

"Under, down, down! Make no noises, and open your door for no one! Do you understand?" he barked as she nodded.

"Wait, Daddy, what if you don't come back?" she said, trying to grab hold of his hand.

"I always come back," he said, gripping her head between his hands. "Don't you forget that, Airomem. And I'll always be here." He gave her head a squeeze between his hands, then raced away, slamming the door shut behind him. And as soon as he left, she rushed to her dresser and took the stun gun from the top drawer, then waited under her bed, trying to still her breath. Knowing what came next.

The darkness.

And seconds later, it happened, the lights above extinguished themselves, along with every other light in their sector of the ship. Turning the hallways near pitch black, impossible to navigate unless they were already memorized.

Which for the Lear, they were.

She waited, her jaw tight, watching her doorknob as her eyes acclimated, the only light the faint stars outside her window. Her muscles tightened as she heard feet run past, and the siren wailing again, this time the boy shouting "Port! Port! Port!" as his vocal chords strained.

For several minutes, nothing happened as the noises drifted away, their volume decreasing until they were just at the threshold of her hearing where imagination fights reality. Where she imagined all the stories she had heard about the other tribes. How they feasted upon one another after their squabbles, the smell of cooking meat even making its way as far as the Lear's side of the ship. The times that they bothered to cook, that is. Or the screams she heard when she would stray too close to the other side and the battle chants seemed to shake the walls themselves.

And then, in the silence, she heard footsteps. Footsteps that crept down the hallway and paused in front of her door, short ragged breaths coming from the other side.

Her breath held in her throat as she watched the doorknob start to turn, ever so slowly, creaking open in the darkness. And a face appeared around the corner as she leapt out from underneath her bed, the stun gun extended in front of her with both hands, the electricity crackling as she turned it up to full power and bathing her face in blue light.

"Back," she screamed. "Back, or I'll shock you so hard your skin will fry! Back!"

In the light, her father's face stared back, blood trailing along his temple.

"Hush," he said, entering as she burst into tears. "Hush, it's over. What happened to staying under the bed? I told you to stay!"

And though he scolded her, she heard something else in his voice as he looked down on her standing there, the stun gun still buzzing. Something she heard when she brought back top scores on her tests or explained the schematics of the power room to him correctly.

"A princess would fight!" she answered through the tears, her voice shaking, and he couldn't help but smile.

"You're right, she would," he agreed. "Now put that down. And hush."

"Where were we attacked?" she asked as he sat down on the bed next to her.

"On both sides," he answered. "Port and starboard. We defended both and sent them running backwards faster than they came. Now, princess, why is it that we defend those two points?"

"Because those two points are the only way that they can enter our end of the ship," she answered. "They're the only two doorways. But why, Daddy? Why do they attack us?"

Her father frowned and spoke slowly in response.

"Airomem, we live a very different life here than they do. We live an orderly life—but the two other tribes, the Aquarians and Agrarians, are not so fortunate. The Aquarians control the water, having access to the reservoirs, while the Agrarians plow the fields. Unlike us, there are many points of entry for them to attack each other, and they are near constantly at war—what they seem to never understand is that they need each other to survive. They grow greedy, and try to seize the other's resources instead of trading. But what they lust over far more is what we have, Airomem—the electrical power."

With those words, the lights buzzed back to life, and she saw that the blood originated from a long gash.

"Daddy, you're hurt! I didn't think that was your blood!"

"Hush, it's all right; it's shallow," he answered. "Listen, Airomem. We've started this lesson, and now we must finish it. It is something a leader should know as second nature. The Agrarians and Aquarians must *never* gain hold over the ship's power. Can you tell me why?"

"Because, because then we would be dead?"

"More important, Airomem. Even if they let us live, it would be worse. Think, how many years do you need to study before you become an apprentice engineer?"

"Ten," she answered, and her eyes widened. "They would break it! The power room, the reactor, they would break it!"

"Exactly, Airomem. Not only would we die, but so would they, by their own hand. And so would the other side of the ship. So we must protect them from themselves. Now, why do we fight in the dark?"

"Because no Agrarian or Aquarian troop has set foot here in over a hundred years," she answered. "They would become lost and would bump into the walls as they try to attack. It gives us the advantage."

"Precisely. Now, Airomem, the other tribes will not always try to attack us directly. They hate us because we demand tribute from them—we supply them with electricity, and they supply us with water and food. But once, one hundred years ago, they tried to starve us. For two weeks, they stopped delivering food and water, even after we turned out their lights, and we dipped deep into our stores. Tell me, what happened then? How did your great-great-grandfather fight back, back when he served as adviser to the leader?"

Airomem knew the legend by heart, the stroke of ingenuity that had been decreed to have saved the Lear tribe from near extinction.

"They turned the power up, instead of off!" she said. "And the lights burned brighter and hotter than they should have, and it burned the other tribes and their crops. And only then did they pay their tribute, when their skin was so red it broke out in blisters, and they feared the lights!"

"Yes, well done, Airomem. A last resort, but a necessary one. But remember, we can only do that in an extreme emergency— typically, the ship should not let the power rise that high, but after the asteroid struck, the electricity had to be rewired to bypass many of the safety systems. And even worse, the same power that harmed the Agrarians and Aquarians also traveled to the other side of the ship. Surely, they did not know it was us, but we must care for our brothers and sisters, no matter how remote they might be."

Then her father stood and walked to the door.

"I must be going now, Airomem. I personally want to check over the ship, to ensure everything is in order. Go to sleep now, princess, but remember this lesson."

"Daddy, wait!" she shouted as he opened the door. "Don't leave me, I'm scared!"

"We're all scared," he answered. "Some of us are just better at hiding it than others."

"Tell me a story first before you go!" she demanded. "It can be quick. I need to think about something else, or I won't sleep."

He hesitated, then returned to her bed.

"I will, but it has to be quick. Which one do you want to hear?"

"Tell me," she said, thinking, then decided. "Tell me about Necti."

"Ah, your favorite," he said. "Of course."

And he began, his deep voice recounting the tale as she felt her eyelids start to grow heavy. She'd didn't remember her mother, since she had died from a sickness that had taken many of the Lear six years before, but her father's hand on her brow felt just as comforting.

Chapter 24

The asteroid struck Dandelion 14 off center. Of course, it was *very near* the center, which was why the ship split into two parts. The very weakest spot of the ship was hit, the bridge itself, the connector between the two sides and the nose capsule at the front.

As soon as the asteroid made contact, all transport between the halves was halted. No longer was there the air pressure necessary to travel across the bridge, which means anyone who attempted would die. And at the time, Necti was the head engineer of the ship – it was his duty to keep the engines running and the lights on and the systems under control. And when the ship split, Necti was on our side of the ship.

In the confusion of the ship, Necti had two priorities. The first was to the ship itself, and he ran to the power room to keep the reactor from damaging itself as the systems fell off line. Much of the work that is done today was automatic back then, governed by the ship itself, though these were destroyed by the asteroid. So it was up to Necti to preserve the ship, because the ship could no longer care for itself.

But, you see, the asteroid striking the ship was the *second* most important thing that had happened to Necti that day. The first had occurred that very morning—Necti had married his wife, Beatrice, who was said to be even more beautiful than the stars. They had been lovers since childhood, and the ceremony had all but finished—there was but one part left. You see, when the ship used to be whole, the ceremony dictated that married couple would each depart to opposite ends of the ship, then meet in the center, signifying that nothing could ever separate them. That they would overcome all obstacles to be together.

And when the asteroid struck, Beatrice was on the other end of the ship. Which was Necti's other priority.

Because when he looked outside, at the other half, their lights were out. This meant that the power room on their side of the ship had been lost—likely because the asteroid hit their side harder, and caused their reactor to malfunction.

Originally, Necti had saved the reactor on our side because he knew that both he and Beatrice would die without it. But now, he knew that he would not be able to live without his wife, separated far away from him on the other end of the ship. He knew that she would not be able to live without power, and that soon those on the other side would fight for food, and then starve.

He petitioned for the ship to be repaired immediately, but there was a problem. With only one power room, there was not enough fuel to reach the new planet if the ship was fixed. You see, fixing the ship is no small task—the power it requires is *enormous*. And once the ship was restored, one power room would have to support the entire ship as mandatory energy-hungry systems came back online, which was not in the original design. As you will learn in your studies, the more power that the reactor must provide, the more that it wastes. And under that great stress, the energy would run out far before Dandelion 14 reached her destination.

But Necti refused to be defeated. That morning, he had vowed to meet Beatrice at the center of the ship. He had vowed no distance could keep them apart. That no obstacle could stand in their way.

So he devised a plan.

First, he turned off every system still online that was not absolutely crucial, and he turned off those that he could that even once the ship was repaired would draw excess power. And he knew of a room on the other end of the ship, a room where he could tell the ship to repair itself one day by giving it extremely specific instructions when to awaken, and how to fix itself, as he knew we would forget.

You have seen the suits that are kept in the back of the power room, by the engines. In extreme circumstances, these were designed to allow us to move *outside* the ship. With his knowledge of the ship schematics, Necti determined which power cables he would need to connect to the other side of the ship to share our electricity. They wouldn't be enough to completely restore power, but they would be enough for sustenance.

And Necti did something that no one has done since, and likely no one had done before.

He *jumped*.

With the cables streaming behind him, he soared across the gap between the two halves, just barely making it to the other side of the ship. And he restored power to where it was most necessary, plugging our electricity into their systems.

Then Necti reentered the ship through their engines, and their power room, to find his beloved Beatrice. Like us, he knew how to sign with his hands, an emergency precaution used by engineers for situations where communication might be difficult. And as the lights flickered back on from their end, he signed to us what had happened through the windows.

He had found Beatrice still in her bridal gown waiting for him at the bridge, and their marriage became complete. He had found the control room, and set it such that in the generations to come, the ship would awaken, and restore itself just before reaching its destination.

And he signed something else, something as his hands shook and his tears fell upon the window. Something that he kept secret from Beatrice herself.

That when he had entered the other power room, the photonic shielding around the reactor had been cracked open, exposing him with no protection to the radiation. On leaving the room, he welded the door shut, so that no one else would ever enter there again, and warned the other side to never to enter the long room leading to their power room, as that would be contaminated as well but with lesser levels of radiation.

He never told Beatrice – hiding it as long as he could as his hair fell out, and sores formed on his skin. Enjoying his final month with her, with his wife, his love, whom he had let no obstacle short of death part them. And for whom he had saved that entire side of the ship.

We still know the last message he signed to us, one so weak we could barely decipher it, but caused the rest of the engineering team to burst into tears. And which immortalized his name forever among us.

"For her, for you, and for them, I would do it again."

Chapter 25

Airomem fidgeted in her chair as Mr. Prometh entered the room and strutted to the board, taking a marker between his two remaining fingers, and writing in sharp, striking bursts.

"Today," he said to the six engineers-to-be, "today, we learn theory! Today, we forget engineering in the power room in favor of physics—instead of learning which dials do what, and what levers control what, we'll learn *why* they do what they do! We'll be taking this at quite a high level—much of this is not well understood, and I have an inkling that it never was well understood."

"Do we *have* to learn this?" moaned AJ, a student to Airomem's right. "What's the point, if we can keep the reactors running anyways?"

Prometh whipped around and held up his hand, wiggling the three stumps as he spoke.

"I didn't lose three of my fingers while I was under captive by the Agrarians to listen to you snivel, boy! If you don't want to learn, then you can leave! Do you know *why* the Lear spent so many resources on rescuing me, despite my middle age when I was captured? It's because of my knowledge, boy! Because if that reactor goes down, I'm the only one who knows how to fix it, until one of you takes my place."

Then he held his hand to his stomach. "Horrible things the Agrarians did, boy. Would you want to hear more? It wasn't just my fingers they took—oh no, they took whatever they could, bits and pieces of whatever they could peck at. Made themselves a nice Prometh soup while they had me chained down, and interrogated me on how the reactors worked! Ah, such is the price of knowledge."

Then Prometh leaned down to look directly in AJ's eyes from six inches away, his voice steady.

"And the best part was that I didn't even have to keep silent—I told them everything they wanted, because their minds were not trained to receive it! I might as well have babbled nonsense, boy, nonsense about protons and neutrons and gravitational theory. And now you are turning away the knowledge that they would have killed me for! Do you want to hear more of my endurance of their torture? Do you want me to spin your nightmares for the next month? Because I can, boy. The conditions are so terrible there, they are so thirsty and devoid of water that spitting is considered a sign of great wealth. Would you like to know how they treated their prisoners?"

AJ shook his head wildly, leaning back as far away as he could, while Prometh's face brightened.

"Good, then! Now, on to your second worst possible nightmare: physics! Class, much of what we will go over today was developed by a fellow named Einstein. Class, who was this fellow?"

"*We don't know*," chanted the class, as they had been instructed each time the name came up in lecture.

"Correct! While we know the physics, our history going back as far as that name is not nearly as strong. Must have been a bright fellow, or group of fellows. Or maybe we're just not as intellectual as we once were, and he was the average of the lot. Anyways, back to the physics. You see, it's all because of this Einstein fellow that our reactor works."

On the board, he drew a sphere, and shaded in the inner edge of the sphere before filling in a thick dot at the center.

"This sphere, class, is known as the *photonic crystal barrier* – inside the power room, you may have heard it being referred to as *the egg*. We must take the utmost care *not* to break the egg— it would be absolutely impossible to replace with the tools we have, and is quite fragile. And supposedly, in terms of pure material, it is more valuable than the rest of the ship combined. Now, on the inside of this crystal is radioactive matter, which means it spits out energy in the form of super high frequency light faster than AJ spits out stupid questions. The sphere acts like a mirror— all that energy bounces around the inside, none of it can escape, one hundred percent down to the very last photon is conserved. And it meets the target here, in the center, which absorbs it and converts it to electrical energy. Do you follow?"

"Yes, even I knew that," said AJ. "And everything inside the sphere is deadly, like a fire or poison, that can kill us if it escapes."

"Yes, or can be put to great use! You see, that target is able to send the energy *outside* the sphere in the form of a different type of light waves, which pass through the photonic crystal as if it were clear glass! One type of light bounces around the inside, the other type moves freely through—similar to how soup will trickle through the prongs of a fork, but beans cannot fall through the gaps. Now we can use that transmitted energy, or the soup dripping through the cracks, to run the engines, to power the lights, or however else we see fit. Now, does anyone see the problem with this?"

Airomem raised her hand, and Prometh jabbed at her with his two fingers.

"The ship requires different amounts of energy at different times," she said as Prometh beamed. "But the radioactive elements break down at a constant rate."

"Precisely, precisely!" he said. "As I've stated, the crystal is incredibly fragile. This means that there cannot be moving parts on the inside, and it's best that there aren't, as one tiny malfunction would mean our doom. In addition, we have to choose a radioactive material that naturally expels energy slowly, so that if the crystal ever does break, like it did on the other end of the ship, the nuclear reaction cannot spiral out of control. So very tricky, so very tricky, to create something like this! Something that can give enough power to run the ship when needed but will fizzle out otherwise. Now, does anyone know how this can be accomplished?"

Airomem shook her head, and when the rest of the class saw her, they followed her lead.

"Ah, that's quite unfortunate," continued Prometh. "Every year, I hope to have an Einstein in my class, but I have yet to be lucky. You see, this is what he figured out—he found out that under the effects of extreme gravity, you can actually *change* how time flows! So bear with me, and try not to tie your brains in a knot, but by creating an artificial gravity field inside the sphere, we can make the material appear to decompose faster on the outside. Or, in this case, we apply an extremely strong anti-gravity field if we need power, which makes the material inside age *faster than us*, and therefore spit out energy quicker! But creating gravitational fields requires a *tremendous* amount of energy, so the more energy we need, the more we have to burn to maintain that field and consequently speed up the reaction. Understood?"

"No," said AJ as Airomem cocked her head to the side. "It seems like circular math."

"Good," Prometh responded. "That's the best comment you've made so far, AJ. It is indeed—a feedback loop, to be precise. If more energy is needed, then we crank up the gravitational fields. But that requires more energy! So we keep cranking them up, until we can sustain the ship's power. Anyways, I didn't expect you to understand it all. Hell, even I don't—but now we can say you've had an equal opportunity to the Agrarians who I taught this to! Though I hope you learned more than they did."

"I'm not sure about that," said AJ, scratching his head.

"Even with you, AJ, we can always hope," said Prometh. "But that's it for today. If any of you want to know more, feel free to stay after."

As the rest of the class departed, Airomem waited behind. And she listened to Prometh for several hours, absorbing all she could, whether or not it made sense. For Necti had once understood it, and if she ever wanted to live up to her favorite story character, she would need to too.

Chapter 26

Airomem shadowed the engineer as he walked around the circumference of the egg, watching as he checked off sections of a notepad, taking temperature readings and anti-gravitational values as he adjusted his hearing protection. She frowned as she followed him, running through the effects of every one of his actions in her mind, tracking the physics as he adjusted each knob, or imagining the consequences should one of the parameters rise too high or fall too low.

And imagining was important, since there was nearly no physical response to each of his actions. Numbers would change, and the pitch of the sound might slightly modulate, but for the most part, there was no tangible effect—unless a visitor owned the eye and ear of a trained engineer, they would have no recognition of an alteration in the engine room.

But Airomem; Airomem always knew.

She knew that the shrill tone that accompanied the roaring of the engines meant that the resonance of one of the induction coils was out of tune, and that excess energy was being shed as a result. And she knew that fixing it would increase the engine efficiency by several percent—not only reducing the induction losses, but also reducing the antigravity field to be generated. A bead of sweat travelled down the side of her face as she kept an eye on the temperature reading, knowing that she would keep a tighter monitoring of it than the current engineer, who had let it rise two degrees above what her calculations determined optimal.

She drew a sharp breath as the engineer nearly ignored a slight spike in energy output, releasing it just as he noticed, then looked about the room to check each of the systems working to keep the reactor online. And every time she tracked them, her mouth opened slightly in wonder at the design of it. At the perfect way it all fit together, at how even with the engineer's occasional blunders it could survive, at how it provided power while nearly the entire ship did not have the slightest idea where it came from. And as she stared, she saw her father enter and wave her over outside the room.

"Four weeks in!" he whispered excitedly as she exited, the door closing behind her and sealing the power room away. "Four weeks of shadowing instead of just learning. How do you like it?"

"It's great, it really is!" she said. "But, Father, I've been wondering something. How, how did all this happen? Where did all this come from?"

"The power room?" he asked. "Why, it was constructed when Dandelion 14 was, at the very beginning."

"The entire ship, then! How, exactly, did it come to be? I know that it was built, but why? And by who?"

"Are the intricacies of the power room not enough to satiate your curiosity?" He laughed and touched her nose.

"Come on, Father, I'm not twelve anymore! I'm almost an engineer! How did all this start?"

"Dandelion 14?"

"Dandelion 14."

"Let's take a walk, Airomem. A lap around Lear territory. This will take a moment to explain."

"Sure," she answered and followed him as he started at a meandering pace.

"Airomem, Dandelion is not only the name of the ship. Back before we lived on the ship, it was the name of a plant."

"From the gardens?"

"Well, yes and no. You see, the plants back then were not always grown by us. In fact, they existed before we did—and dandelions were a type that bore no fruit. Instead, they only bore seeds. Seeds that were clustered in such a way that at the lightest of breaths would scatter them across the earth, where they could have a chance to grow."

"Why does this matter, if they weren't brought on the ship?"

"It's more of the principle of the matter," said her father, and he took a breath. "The point is, that this plant was considered undesirable. But it was so proficient at reproduction that it refused extinction and instead spread its seeds in the face of adversity." And closing his eyes, her father began to recite:

"A farmer went out to plant some seeds. As he scattered them across his field, some seeds fell on a footpath, and they were eaten. Other seeds fell on shallow soil with underlying rock. The seeds sprouted quickly because the soil was shallow. But the plants soon wilted, and since they didn't have deep roots, they died. Other seeds fell among thorns that grew up and choked out the tender plants. Still other seeds fell on fertile soil, and they produced a crop that was thirty, sixty, and even a hundred times as much as had been planted! Listen, Airomem. Where we came from, where Dandelion 14 was built, we left there because it was headed for destruction. But we weren't the only ones, Airomem, who left. Supposedly, there were others. Dandelion seeds scattered among the stars, each seeking new life."

"So there are others then, for sure?" she asked excitedly.

"Airomem, wait, before you take too much hope," her father said. "Remember, of the seeds that were cast out by the farmer, only a few survived. Only some made it only to fertile ground where they could live."

"So you're saying that once we find our new home, the others might not survive? And they might not find us?"

"No, Airomem," he answered, his face solemn. "I'm saying that our ancestors spread seeds like a dandelion because only a few would find fertile soil. For all we know, we might be among those that land on rock and cannot take root. Even after all this effort to survive, even if we find the new planet home, we may still die."

Chapter 27

"Line up!" shouted Prometh, standing in front of his class of six. "And pay attention! I may be old now, and my hair may be gray, but I could still knock the life clean out of any one of you in a fight! The Aquarians and Agrarians will move much quicker than I, I assure you! And not just that, they'll have all their fingers! Plus three of mine, which each put up enough of a fight to bring one of them down with them!"

Airomem was squared off against AJ, with another student on her left and right side, and two others on his. An open door frame had been constructed between them, just wide enough that each of them could reach across to the other side without fully entering the frame, and a wall jutting out for a few feet on each side.

"Now, there are two entry points to our territory. The Starboard, where Agrarians can attack, and the Port, where the Aquarians can attack. As warriors, you have *one* priority—defend these two doors with your lives! So long as they are not breached, we hold the advantage as they cannot overcome us with their numbers. So use the bottleneck to your advantage! Of course, these two doors can be locked and braced, but that's no guard against stubborn perseverance—only you can guard against that."

"But what if they get through?" asked Airomem, "Won't we have to fight them then?"

"You better pray they don't!" exclaimed Prometh. "But we are prepared in the case that they do. Each the port and starboard sides have three bottlenecks—the others must fight through all three doors to enter into the soft underbelly of our territory. Each bottleneck empties into a larger room, so if they try to ram their way through, you can hit them with stun guns from the sides as they come through the door. And due to their frequent wars with each other, it is almost never necessary to retake a room if we have lost it—instead, when one tribe senses that the other is weakened, they attack. And the Agrarians or Aquarians will pull their forces back in defense, especially since they know that we won't pursue them past the initial bottleneck."

"And why not?" asked AJ. "Why don't we storm through and kill them when they are busy defending themselves? Why don't we take their land and defend that as an offensive front?"

"*This* is why," said Prometh, pointing to the wall where a hand drawn map was plastered. "These are the schematics of the ship—found in an engineering book in our territory. Written, mind you, which is good because I have yet to hear of an Agrarian or Aquarian that can discern a vowel from a consonant. Now, as you can see, once you break past our bottlenecks into their territory, there are many more points of attack. Instead of defending two doorways, if we advanced, we would have to defend six, then eight, then ten as the corridors fan out! That's why the Agrarians and Aquarians are always at war—there are dozens of entry points between them, so they have no strategic buffers."

"But we could take them slowly, and we fight better than them!" claimed AJ. "Even you say that. Though our numbers are far fewer, we have far more stun guns and better strategy, so our firepower is much greater!"

"True, true, I agree with you there. In terms of weapons, we do have more stun guns, but they have plenty of knives—and while a knife will lose to a stun gun, a knife exists to kill, while a stun gun will only incapacitate. But have you ever farmed, AJ? It's truly backbreaking work. It would cost hundreds of lives and several years to make that territory advance, all so that we can just be farmers. Instead, so long as we defend our entry points, we lose a life or two every year—most of them from guards being inattentive. And even if we did take the land, we do not have the numbers to farm and support ourselves."

"Rather, it's far easier to demand tribute for the power that we provide," said Airomem, and Prometh nodded, then he continued.

"But now, enough on strategy! Stun guns set to low! If you are struck, you are out and must clear out of the doorway. Airomem and AJ, you are the keystones. Akil and Helen, you are left flank. Priam, Aga, you are right flank. In this mock battle, AJ's team will be trying to advance through the doorway. Airomem, your team will be defending it like the bottleneck on Port or Starboard. On my call, you start, and remember your techniques!"

Airomem squared her feet as AJ crouched on the other side of the door, his eyes flicking left and right as he searched for a weakness, his freshly formed facial hair sticking out in odd directions from just underneath his chin. She held two stun guns, one in each hand, the blue light just barely visible under the low setting, the buzzing just at the edge of her hearing, and the vibrations traveling up her arms. On each of her sides, her flanks turned their stun guns on as well, just as AJ's flickered to life.

Then Prometh blew a whistle hanging around his neck, and the mock battle began.

Airomem took a sharp step backwards as AJ jabbed forward, the edge of his weapon whiffing just under her chin. On her right, Aga swept in, trying to catch AJ off guard as he recoiled just in time, the blow catching air where he had been just an instant before. And in her mind, Airomem recited her strategy learned from Prometh while she watched for AJ's next move.

The keystone holds the formation together. It is the keystone's responsibility to plug the hole, to stand strong and open opportunities for corner attacks from the flanks.

And she took another step backwards, opening up space between her and the doorframe as her flanks moved forward to the walls in front of the doorframe, using them as a shield to hide their bodies. Together, they formed a triangular pocket. A pocket where anyone who entered would be attacked on three sides—from keystone, who was to stop momentum, and from the flanks, who dealt the finishing blows.

Without warning, Priam darted through the door from the other side, barreling low so that Aga's taser struck too high. Then Helen arced down from the left, jamming the taser into Priam's shoulder blade as he tumbled past Airomem, who allowed him past her without interference. Stunned and disqualified, he now posed no threat.

But as she pivoted back to the keystone position, her eyes widened, watching as Akil bent down with his hand on his knees just beyond the door, and AJ took a running start from several feet behind him.

"Aga, Helen, strike low!" she shouted as AJ launched himself upwards, arms flailing through the air. Aga and Helen struck Akil at the same time as he passed under AJ, but now AJ's trajectory was headed directly towards Airomem, his stun guns pinwheeling in blue streaks.

She grit her teeth as she staggered her stance, her bangs falling over one of her eyes as AJ descended without grace, holding both her tasers directly in front of her in a single outstretched point. They struck AJ directly in his chest as he crashed through them, his far larger body bowling into hers as they collapsed together, loose stun guns shocking them repeatedly on the way down. She slid against the metal floor in a tangle of limbs, AJ's body jerking with each electrical impulse, stars forming in her vision as the breath was knocked out of her chest.

And as she sat up, she heard Prometh start clapping to the best of his ability, a smile on his face.

"Well done. Well *done,* Airomem. Had your tasers been on full power, this would have ended quite differently. And AJ, though somewhat unorthodox, that move would be similar to something the other side would try. And you cleared a hole. I would declare a tie, but considering Airomem has no casualties on her team, she holds a slight victory – careful, Airomem, it appears that AJ gets sharper with each passing day! Now, pick yourselves up; it's time to go again. This time, Airomem, you will attack."

Chapter 28

Airomem spent much of her time now in the power room. She would watch as each of her engineers ran through the necessary checks, smiling if one of the new recruits caught a temperature that was trending out of range, and remembering the years when she herself had been fresh on the floor. But that had been long ago—back when she was just out of school, in the years when Prometh still taught her combat tactics.

She'd risen among the ranks quickly—in part, because of her father's influence, but also due to the extra time she spent listening to Prometh's recounts of every possible piece of information about the reactor. When she was on shift, the reactor ran without hiccups. And those in the Lear leadership were quick to pick up on that correlation.

But in addition, Airomem volunteered at the Port and Starboard entry points, disregarding her father's best wishes.

Engineers were considered high-class contributors to the Lear on their own – as a result, they were not expected to contribute to guard duty, similar to other skilled workers such as the doctors and the teachers.

"What you are doing is an unnecessary risk!" her father said when he found out the first day she had volunteered. "You belong in the power room. And more importantly, you're my daughter, and as leader, there is a chance you might take command upon my passing!"

"Then why was I trained for combat?" Airomem demanded. "Everyone else is required to defend the ship. I'm no better than them."

"You were trained in order to understand how to make proper decisions," her father replied. "But this is impractical."

"Unless I experience it, my judgment is hollow. Besides, I know you did the same at my age. You were said to be the best, and I will uphold your name. And the chances that I will be on guard during an actual attack are minimal."

Begrudgingly, and with his arms folded across his chest, her father relented. But she noticed that those days when she served, there were more guards than typical, and they were the largest. And always, she served on the flank, out of the way from direct strikes.

After her second month of volunteering, she arrived at her shift early and rooted herself firmly in the center.

"Today, I am the keystone," she said when the other guards arrived.

"But, Airomem, on direct orders from your father—"

"I don't care. Today, I am the keystone, unless you want to fight me for it. And if you do, I'm sure he'll love to hear about how you jeopardized the wellbeing of his daughter," she said as the stun guns in her fingers came to life, her arms hanging loose near her waist.

The guard bit his lip, then moved aside.

"Fine," he said, "but this doesn't come back to me. If your father asks, Earnest let you."

"Earnest has been dead for a year," she said.

"Exactly. And I'll be dead tomorrow if he finds out it was me," he answered.

"Earnest it is," Airomem replied and took up the center. She stared down the hallway, doors ajar down its length, dark stains covering the floor in increasing frequency the nearer they were to her. Occasionally, she would catch sight of a gaunt face, of cheeks tucked too far in to be healthy, and eyes sunk too far in to know hope.

And on her third month of guard, she saw an Agrarian emerge from around the corner and walk their way, his mouth ajar, his posture swaying with each step. Behind him appeared ten other faces, each watching as he approached the doorframe, edging closer from a distance with a knife tucked loosely in his belt.

"Lone straggler," she said as the other guards jerked to attention. "Carrying no tribute, armed. Approaching at thirty paces. I've got this."

"No," said the guard accompanying her and pushing her to the side. "I'm afraid I cannot allow that."

"Have the Lear grown so complacent that they send tiny girls to defend their borders?" shouted the straggler, now only ten paces away as he cackled, "Come back out, little girl. I wonder how you taste? Not so gamey as my usual meals, but everyone knows that Lear taste the best!"

He licked his lips as Airomem pushed herself to the front again, switching on the tasers, adapting a staggered stance.

"Not a step more!" she shouted, "or we will be forced to take action!"

"Not a step, not a step," chanted the man, his arm muscles twitching as he danced forward. "Step. Step. Step."

He leered as he slinked closer, the breath out of his mouth putrid even from a distance as Airomem's arms stiffened. "I've been exiled, little girl, exiled by my own people! I have nothing to lose. Figure I might as well get a last meal in!"

Then he darted forward, pulling his knife from his belt and slashing as he crossed the doorframe. And Airomem jammed both of her stun guns directly under his ribcage, turning the power to maximum.

He shot off the ground, his own legs propelling him as his clothing smoked, crashing against the ceiling before toppling down again, the faces at the end of the hall recoiling as he landed. Airomem stepped over his body out into the hallway, her stun guns still burning bright, and her voice shouting.

"Let it be known!" she said, the faces flinching as each word lashed across them, "that these doorways mark not only the entrance into Lear territory, but into death! Let it be known that I am next in line for the crown, and I will tolerate no uprisings! That I will bring darkness upon your lands, and burning light, until no plant grows and no child goes unhungry! Let it be known that our tolerance for you has come to an end, and if you do not make peace, you will face far greater consequences!"

"Are you trying to start a war, princess?" hissed the guard as she crossed over the border again, and they dragged the body away.

"It's for their sake, as much as ours," she responded. "And we do not have much time left."

Chapter 29

"What you did was downright stupid!" shouted Airomem's father back at her apartment, where he had come as soon as he heard news of the incident. "It could have gotten you killed, and worse, it could have started a full-on attack! Airomem, this is not behavior conducive to Lear survival. Nor your own!"

He paced her short floor, biting his lip as she sat on her bed.

"The other tribes need to know we're a power to be reckoned with," responded Airomem. "They need to know not to attack us."

"They *do* know that, Airomem! If anything, it's best that they forget it, and forget us entirely! The Agrarians and Aquarians know one way to deal with fear, an instinct that has been bred into their cultures – to attack and to destroy. You must understand, Airomem, that they are not like us. They have little order, they thrive in chaos. Their attacks against us are rarely planned, and nearly always are a faction broken off from the whole. To send a message like that only gives them cause to unify against us. No, it is better that they forget our existence than to remember and act."

"But you said it yourself, Father!" Retorted Airomem, gesturing out of the window to where the stars lay beyond. "You said that we are coming to the end of the journey! And when we do, we won't have the doors and bottlenecks anymore to protect us!"

She stared at her father, waiting for his response, her chin high and her eyes blazing. But instead, he stared past her to the window, his mouth slightly open, the starlight mingling with the grey in his hair.

"What's wrong?" Airomem asked, as his eyes widened as she turned her head to trace his gaze. But she only saw darkness accented by the lights on the other side of the ship, in addition to the flickers of movement from within its windows. Then her father reached a hand into his pocket, uncrinkling an old piece of paper and flattening it against the window.

"Look," he whispered, the color drained from his cheeks, his other hand taking her chin and pointing her face into space, past the paper, past the seven points shaped like a ring that were inscribed on the paper. "Look."

And towards a cluster of seven stars in a ring the size of her thumbnail, glowing from the depths of the beyond.

"Airomem," he whispered, crumpling the paper within his fist. "Airomem, we're here."

***

Airomem watched the ring deep into the night, unsure whether she could tell it was getting larger or if it was her own imagination.

If what her father said was true, then they would soon be leaving the ship behind. They would soon be emerging into a new world. And they soon might be sharing it with those who threatened to end their existence with every chance they were given.

She swallowed and let her eyes wander, straying to a window at the other end of the ship. Usually, a farmer filled that window, working the fields nearly every day, his own gaze occasionally meeting hers, his actions just barely visible through the visible portions of the windows. In the past, she had tried to sign to him, but he had only stared back before returning to the soil. Perhaps he was too far away to understand, or they did not know hand signs there, or the light made her own figure too difficult to see. And only occasionally would she get a good glimpse of him, only when he crossed the windows just right, his silhouette fleeting.

He didn't look like the Agrarians—from what she could tell, his cheeks were not puckered, and his face was not gaunt. And he moved slowly, methodically, with purpose, unlike the Agrarians and Aquarians that twitched and jerked when they walked. Surely the farmers on that end of the ship would be different, like the Lear themselves. Like distant cousins, that had survived apart, but were really the same.

At least, she hoped.

The Lear would need allies.

Chapter 30

"In my absence," said Airomem's father to the room, fifteen of the Lear's most experienced members within, "each of you shall command over your areas of expertise. Airomem, you shall take charge the power room. Prometh, I give you council over the young of the ship, and over education. To matters of war, to the military committee. Each of you shall act independently until I return, and should I not return, make plans for the appointment of a new leader."

"But who shall accompany you?" asked Prometh, seated in a chair in the front, his few fingers stroking a silvered beard. "And more importantly, what is the goal of this expedition?"

"I suspect I will have to go alone," her father answered. "The Agrarians and Aquarians will be suspicious enough, and should I try to bring additional people, their suspicion will only increase. As to why this mission is necessary, it is because we will need those on the other end of the ship in order to survive. They'll help us fight our way out."

Her father pulled a large roll of paper out from underneath his chair, then unfurled it on the table, pinning down the corners with dinner plates until it was as long as a man lying down.

"This paper," he said, gesturing, "was left to us by Necti himself from those before him, and details what will happen as we reach our destination. First, and most importantly, it mentions the awakening of this ship. For those of you in the power room, that means we'll have to crank up the reactor to levels higher than ever intended by the original designers. Efficiency will be low, but we should only have to maintain it for a limited amount of time – which is fortunate, for our dwindling fuel stock will be exhausted quickly."

"This is preposterous!" said a voice from the back, belonging to AJ's father, named Tela, one of the older members of the war committee. "If Necti is wrong, and our power is exhausted, we will have no bargaining chips against the Agrarians and Aquarians. If the lights go out, we will be starved, starved then overrun!"

"Then you better hope he isn't wrong!" snapped back Prometh, popping the edge of his chair back against the edge of a nearby table.

"By my estimates, the ship has twenty-five years of fuel left until the reactor fizzles out through normal consumption. And that's a best-case scenario! So either we take the risk, or your children face certain darkness."

"Is this, is this true? Why were we not informed?" demanded Tela.

"The arrival of Dandelion 14 at its destination is beyond our control," answered Airomem's father. "For this reason, the fuel stock was kept secret to prevent general panic. We had plans within the next two years to start rationing energy more strictly, however, we are now close to arrival. And that is why we must act. This concern lies close to you as well, Tela, for we may be in dire need of your military strategy. Come here, where you can see the paper."

Those within the room crowded forward, standing around the table, squinting down at the minuscule handwriting and stenciled diagrams on its surface.

"Where did you get this?" asked Tela, his voice suspicious.

"It has been passed down from chief to chief since Necti left us," said Airomem's father. "Aside from me, Prometh is the only other person to know of its existence. Now, the paper itself is simple enough to read – it moves from top to bottom, detailing each stage the ship will enter."

He pointed at the top and they leaned in, following his fingertip as he spoke.

"Necti programmed the ship such that the halves would come together when the destination planet became close. That is what will happen first—the ship will repair itself, and systems come online. This has two implications—one, as I mentioned, is the power requirement change. And two, due to our position at the back of the ship, the Agrarians and Aquarians will be the first to meet with the other side, which could be disastrous."

"You said we may need the other side to survive," said Tela. "Why is this?"

"We do not know what awaits us on the new planet," Airomem's father responded. "The more of us to face conflict, the better. But that is not the only reason—whoever remains on this ship will die. Those on the other end are our brothers and sisters—we cannot condemn them to that fate."

"For all we know, they could be as bad as the Agrarians and Aquarians!" responded Tela.

"And for all we know," said Airomem, "they could be an enormous benefit. We'll have to give them the benefit of the doubt. We'll have to meet them before we pass judgment."

"Precisely," said Prometh. "And we may need their help sooner than we think."

"Yes, we may," said Airomem's father, "for the ship itself will never land on the destination planet. No, as I mentioned, Dandelion 14 will continue sailing past it. Only a small piece of the ship will detach itself and carry those within to safety, which is the true reason we will need the others. Since that piece of the ship is currently unattainable to us, beyond our reach."

"It's the third broken segment, which will be repaired along with the rest of the ship," said Prometh, his eyes glinting, "And with the new allies, we'll have to fight our way past the Agrarians and Aquarians to the only entrance. To the bridge."

Chapter 31

"We should kill you here and now," stated Airomem. "You've intruded upon Lear territory, and we have no use for prisoners. Maybe you came here to steal our secrets as a spy."

"I could only wish," said the man strapped down to the bed, his chest muscles twitching as he spoke. "I am not so lucky, not lucky at all! I'm exiled! Go on, kill me now! I'd rather die here— I'm a dead man anyways!"

A frown creased Airomem's face as she stared down at him, the wretch of a man, scorch marks still on his skin from where she had stunned him as she guarded the bottleneck. He grinned back up at her, his eyes darting from side to side in a way that made the hair on her neck stand up, and his breath coming in quick gasps.

"And what, exactly, did you do to deserve such a fate?" she asked, raising an eyebrow.

"Stealing!" he screeched. "I stole, and I stole well! For years upon years. Stealing, you see, is in our blood and in our bones. You can even taste it in the best thieves when they die. But I stole from the chief, dozens of times, many times. I only had to be caught once, and should I return, he'll steal my very heart."

"Almost sounds romantic," said Airomem. "Stealing your heart."

"Not if it's pulled out of your chest still beating!" he shouted back, the veins in his neck throbbing, and spittle flying from his mouth. "Not so romantic then!"

"Indeed not," replied Airomem, "But consider, consider if you had a way to make your chief forgive you."

"Impossible," he spat. "I'd have to kill twenty Aquarians alone to seek his forgiveness."

"But what if instead of killing them, I gave you the *means* to kill them," she said, and reached into a bag at her side, pulling forth two black rectangles and setting them at a table beside the man as his eyes widened. "I know these are near priceless among your kind. By our counts, only four of them that still work exist outside the grasp of the Lear. But you, you can give them to your leader in exchange for your life. And maybe as a clever thief, you can even keep one for yourself."

"And why," said the man, "why would the Lear, the cunning Lear, the slave-master Lear, give me such a gift? It is a trick, and I know it!"

"It is no trick," Airomem answered, "but rather, a trade."

"A trade for what? I have nothing to offer."

"Oh, but you do," said Airomem with a smile as the man's attention focused upon her. "All you have to do is deliver a message."

***

Airomem and her father watched as the lone straggler departed, dancing down the corridor away from the entry point bottleneck, an occasional blue flash accompanying his cackling.

"You gave him two?" protested Tela from behind them. "Two stun guns? This is a dangerous game, arming the Agrarians. I won't have my men die without cause, should they attack us."

"It would be for a great cause," Praeter answered. "The greatest cause, our survival."

"Besides," added Airomem, "the stun guns we gave him have nearly no power left, and haven't been charged in the power room for over three years. They may look flashy, but they won't last long, and he won't know the difference until it is too late."

"True, but his chief might," said Tela.

"But the bait is too great for them to resist," said Airomem's father. "Ten stun guns, all for ensuring my safety to and from the bridge."

"You're giving them more?" shouted Tela, his face red. "We won't be able to hold them back!"

"You won't have to," responded Airomem, staring as the blue flashes disappeared around the corner. "We plan on supplying both the Agrarians and Aquarians with new weapons. The new tension will pit them against each other, hopefully starting a wave of battles strong enough to cripple both sides. And even if they should turn on us, we only have to hold out for a short time, until we arrive at the bridge. After that, nothing else matters."

"Again, assuming you're right," said Tela.

"We're praying that we're right," said Airomem's father, walking back towards the back of the ship. "And you, Tela, should pray too."

Chapter 32

It took three days for the Agrarians to respond.

The chants echoed far into Lear territory to clash with the shouts of the siren boy as the Lear military scrambled to the bottleneck, lining up in ranks behind each of the doors, stun guns turned to high and braced for attack. And when Airomem arrived with her father, nearly three-quarters of their military faced off against the Agrarians, while the remaining quarter had fallen back to wait at the opposite end of the ship in case of a planned Aquarian attack.

Airomem's breath caught in her throat when she saw the entire force—never before had she witnessed a full attack, but she had heard the stories of their numbers.

The Agrarian ranks stopped just thirty feet from the entry point doorway, the four front men lined with ropy scars across their faces and arms, their eyes hard and their skin tight. Behind them was another row of nearly identical men, and behind that another, dozens of rows that extending back as far as she could see—more warriors in that corridor, it seemed, than the entire population of the Lear.

And together they chanted, their voices forming sounds rather than words. Guttural noises that lashed against the ranks of the Lear in unison, funneled down the hallway to strike like a battering ram.

"Show no fear!" commanded Praeter as he walked forward through the ranks of his men, Airomem at his right side and Tela at his left. "It's all intimidation. They know that their casualties attacking the entry point would be too costly to merit an initiative. Stand tall, chests outwards, faces stoic. Be proud, for you are the Lear, and as each strong as ten of their men!"

And as he passed, their heads rose, and their expressions steeled, and their stances widened. Then he took his place at the front of the group, their spearhead, his own life first among them.

The voices of the Agrarians grew louder, and they stamped their feet until the walls began to shake, their faces turning red as something approached from far behind them. It passed over their heads, supported by a sea of hands as it moved forward, a dark shadow that nearly brushed against the ceiling of the hallway. And as it reached the front of the crowd, Airomem made out its shape.

It was a couch, or rather, couches, lashed together by liberated electrical wires to form a platform. The legs and lower half of the couch were dyed red, the tied shirt fabric coming away in sheared and dangling strips. Bones jostled from the sides, clacking together as the platform swayed and then was passed down to the front of the Agrarians directly in front of Airomem's father.

Silence washed over the horde as a figure stood up from the couches, brandishing two stun guns and letting electricity crackle between their prongs, illuminating a long scar that ran down his face and yellowed teeth.

"I am Sitient of the Agrarians, and I hear you have a deal for us, Lear!" he shouted. "A deal for us that may put our troubles with the Aquarians to an end!"

"Indeed," responded Airomem's father, stepping forward. "We come offering you a trade of ten stun guns, for safe passage."

"And why do you seek this deal, Learman? What have you to gain?"

"The reasons are twofold. First, we seek to explore the ship and update our records."

"Lies, Lear lies. But go on."

"And second, we have been stiffed by the Aquarians for far too long in their dealings. Their water arrives to us tainted and off color, smelling of rot. Should you take their lands, we ask for fair tribute, as they have cheated us in our trades. Furthermore, we find it easier to trade with one unified tribe rather than two, and if that means wiping out the Aquarians through enhanced weaponry, then so be it."

Sitient smiled and opened his hands.

"Then so be it! We too know the Aquarians for their treachery. But how should I know that you will make good on the deal? You are old, perhaps only a decade away from death. Perhaps your plan is to die among us, and for the bargain never to be completed? Perhaps this is a Lear trick, a Lear lie?"

His voice rose, and the chanting behind him surged to meet it, rattling the walls for a full two minutes before it subsided and her father was able to respond.

"I assure you, we have no ill intentions. We simply seek guidance and guardianship. In return, you'll have your weapons."

Sitient's eyes narrowed, and the skin over his cheekbone twitched, his scar dancing.

"Do not take me for a fool! I smell lies better than I smell flesh. No, should this deal be completed, it shall be on my terms." He cast his gaze around the Lear, the pupils coming to rest on Airomem.

"No, I shall not take you, the aged leader. Instead, I'll take her, to ensure you make good on the deal!" he said and pointed, his index finger aimed at Airomem as chills raced down her spine. "Besides, she took one of our own just a few days ago—is it not fitting we take her in return? A fair trade."

Chapter 33

"Absolutely not!" shouted Airomem's father after the Agrarians had left, and they had returned to her apartment. "Absolutely not! They'll use you as a bargaining chip, as a way to get even more out of the deal. You had no authority to accept his demands!"

"It's too late now," said Airomem, her arms crossed over her chest, her heart still beating rapidly from when she had stepped forward to counter Sitient with words of her own. As the ranks of Lear exploded into applause, she had lit her own stun gun to form a challenging beacon, watching Sitient wince backwards as her mouth formed words.

"Take me, then! But do not suppose I will be an easier burden!"

Back at her apartment, Prometh spoke up from the door, from where he had followed them.

"Strategically, she's right," he said. "You forget your position as not only a father, but also as a leader. The Lear need you now more than ever as the ship joins together. Should you leave and not return in time, there is a chance that none of us will survive."

"But if she should leave and not return—" started Praeter as Prometh cut him off.

"The Agrarians may not possess the most acute intelligence, but even they can sense the wrath a father will feel for his daughter. They know that if the Lear attack, then they will have their flank exposed to the Aquarians, and they shall not risk it. And they know that with ten stun guns, they will have a strong upper hand against the Aquarians, an edge they have been seeking for centuries. No, they will return Airomem; the motives are too great for them to consider otherwise."

Her father's face contorted, and Airomem turned away, looking outside the window to avoid his eyes.

"Leader or no leader, I cannot allow it," he said. "We will take the time to plan out a different alternative, as I cannot—"

But then his voice was cut off, and the ground underneath Airomem lurched, nearly knocking her off her feet. Above them, a voice spoke as she regained her balance.

"Systems rebooting," said the voice. "Ship damage assessed. Reuniting the two halves of the ship and restoring airlock, approximately twenty-four hours until complete."

When Airomem turned to face them again, her father's lips were pursed shut, and Prometh's eyes were lit by an inner fire.

"I'm leaving," she said once more, her fists clenched, "and I'll come back. I always come back."

***

"Come with me," her father said, three hours after he had stormed from her apartment, his face one of tired resolution. "Before you leave, I wish to show you something. To give you my council."

She followed him, wordless, as he strode away, her footsteps in the shadow of his and her thoughts upon what he might have to say. They continued walking to the back of the ship, to the power room, and then to a small side alcove. One she had been to before, but that had not been used in hundreds of years.

The room that held the suits.

Dust fought to hide the gleaming of helmets as her father strode in front of them, waiting for her to take a seat at a chair towards the back of the room. He glanced backwards to where they were fastened to the wall, eleven in all, bright white with oxygen tanks bulging from the back, and small utility belts clipped to the sides. Towering over him, their silence majestic, their presence reminiscent of a time long past. And one missing, the one Necti had taken long ago to the other end of the ship, which had never returned.

Then her father began to speak.

"These suits once allowed us to travel *outside* the ship," he said and she nodded, knowing the lore well behind the equipment. "I want you to consider their purpose, Airomem. They are like small ships in themselves—they keep the wearer safe. But the smallest of cracks in the glass, or the tiniest malfunctions, and the user enters extreme peril. Just as we have entered extreme peril."

"Of course," she said, trying to understand his point. "Outside the ship, the vacuum forces would mean near instant death should they be given the chance."

"Exactly, Airomem. The suit serves as a layer insulating against danger. But there are other dangers besides the exterior of the ship, other environments that cause peril. Environments such as the Agrarians, which you will soon enter."

He took a breath, and she saw resentment cross his face, before he continued.

"I have brought you here because when you walk among them, you must walk in a suit of your own. Not *these* suits, but the suit of royalty. The suit of the Lear. If you show but the slightest sign of weakness, they will rip you apart faster than the exterior forces of the ship. So, daughter, hold your chin high. Remember your heritage, and give them no chance to strike."

"Of course, Father," she said. "Just as you do, when they approach for battle."

"Precisely. There is another reason I brought you here, though, Airomem. One far more grave." And from his pocket, he produced a key ring and walked to the side of the room where a small cabinet was recessed into the wall.

Three locks were on the outside of the cabinet, and he inserted different keys into each, unlocking them one at a time. Then he pulled the door open, the metal over an inch thick, and reached inside to pull out a device the size of a drinking cup. He held it a half arm's reach away, his hand gripped tight around its handle, and his eyes slightly widened.

"What is it?" Airomem asked, leaning forward, inspecting the bright yellow handle and dark red prongs that extended from the top, as well as a trigger that her father's index finger avoided with care.

"This," her father said, "is the most dangerous item on the ship—more dangerous than knives, or stun guns, or potentially even the reactor. Only two exist—this one, and its counterpart in the power room on the other side. For this is an Omni-Cutter, a device capable of shearing through nearly *any* material on the ship. One accidental slice from this, and the ship itself could be breached. Back when it was used by those who wore the suits, only the most senior among them could remove it from its cabinet, and only for the greatest of emergencies and most dire of repairs."

"But why are you telling me this? Do you want me to take it with me?"

"*Absolutely not*," he said and walked back to the cabinet, fastening the device inside once more. "It's another lesson for you to consider. Despite its size, that device can be the end of us all. As you travel, Airomem, realize that even the smallest of your actions can bring death to the entire ship. Realize that *you* are an Omni-Cutter, that one mishap may very well be the Lear's last."

"But even if the hull was breached by the Omni-Cutter," objected Airomem, "the ship automatically shuts off the areas where pressure has dropped until it is restored, correct? So even if you *were* to cut into the hull, would the ship not protect us?"

"It would, yes. But I fear you may not be so lucky, with the Agrarians. Our time is short, and even one potential pathway that is closed off could eliminate our odds of survival."

Then he walked forward and placed his hands on his daughter's shoulders.

"I say this not to put a burden upon you, Airomem, nor to dissuade you. But rather, so you may know potential outcomes of your actions. That you may *think* like a Lear before acting. And that you may act as a chief would, as the chief you will one day become when my time is no more. So go, and go with my blessing. But go with the utmost caution."

Together, they left the room, her father casting one last look upon the suits. And he muttered under his breath, his words just audible to Airomem before following her.

"For though I walk through the valley of the shadow of death, I will fear no evil."

Chapter 34

The Lear military followed Airomem to the bottlenecked entry point, then stopped as she crossed the border, saluting her back as she entered Agrarian lands. Four Agrarians waited for her at the end of the hallway, four that had stood there waiting since the deal had been made. Now they folded around her as an escort, encapsulating her in a bubble of foreign silence interrupted only by the shuffling of their bare feet on the metal floor.

"Touch me," she barked before they enveloped her, her voice hard and her hands on the two stun guns at her belt, "and I will ensure you feel the pain of the Lear. That I will go down fighting, and the lights above will burn you as they burned your ancestors."

But the guards' faces formed scowls instead of answers as they led her deeper into the ship. Deeper than anyone she had known, besides Prometh, had ever traveled. And as she walked, she remembered his parting words with her before he left her at the entry point, his eyes turning dark as he recalled his experience as a prisoner among them.

"Show no fear and give up no ground. They will do their best to unsettle you and to pull you down to their level—resist both of these and remember that you are Lear. Lear *royalty*, untouchable to them, a goddess among men. Let the idea that you are the same as them never enter their feeble thoughts."

Then he took Airomem by the shoulders and whispered.

"Stay safe, student. We can't afford to lose a mind like yours."

And remembering Prometh, she swallowed, keeping her chin high and her shoulders straight as the hallways began to reek with the stench of rotted flesh. Gouges dug into the walls and floor, scratches of knives and unrepaired dents of bodies thrown against metal in their final moments. The occasional red splattering marked the ceiling overhead, the dots elliptical in shape as they dried, their mark frozen forever in time. Bones collected in forgotten corners, piling up in tribute to the people they had once lived within.

The guards led her three to four lengths of the Lear's entire territory, crossing through fields filled with both stooped plants and people, dozens of sets of eyes following her and hands gripping shovels as she passed. Tongues flicked across lips as jeers sounded from those far enough away that their words could not be deciphered, their harsh tone making her imagination race.

But then they turned, and the fields fell away, and they led Airomem into a large room with the same lashed-together couch that she had seen carried by the crowd during the negotiations. Seated upon it was Sitient, his eyes upon her as she approached. And he raised a hand to his mouth—not his own hand, but one that had been removed from an arm, and took a bite out of one of the fingers with a crunch.

They will do their best to unsettle you, echoed Prometh's voice in her mind, followed by her father's. *If you show but the slightest sign of weakness, they will rip you apart faster than the exterior forces of the ship.* So she met his eyes as he took a second bite, her irises like steel, and spoke.

"Let's move."

***

Like the Lear, the Agrarians had heard the voice in the ship, and they had seen the other half of the ship coming closer through the windows. Sitient's eyes had narrowed when Airomem explained her destination was the bridge, and demanded to accompany her for two reasons—first, of curiosity. And second, that to reach the bridge, they would have to traverse a small strip Aquarian territory.

Sitient was able to negotiate safe passage through two promises, that the Aquarian leader Esuri would be permitted to accompany them, and that Sitient would provide an exorbitant amount of food to the Aquarians in the near future. Likely, he would turn on the deal once he had his hands on the stun guns, but it did not matter to Airomem. All that mattered was that she reached the bridge, and she initiated contact.

Sandwiched between Sitient and Esuri, Airomem had waited for the air locked door to open. She had prayed that whoever was on the other side would prove to be a powerful ally.

And that perhaps, with each other's help, they might survive.

Part 3: Departure

Chapter 35

"I want her locked away for what her people did to my brother!"

Vaca's words hung in the air as the porters failed to move, and Nean bared his teeth. From my side, Airomem spoke three words in a challenge, punctuating each with a flash of blue light as defiance crossed her face.

"Then take me."

Vaca's mouth fell open, and Nean turned to face the still porters.

"Do you hear her? She speaks openly against your new chief! She defies him to his face! Are you going to just stand there or are you going to act?"

Their blank faces met his, and Tom spoke for them, his words slow and deep as they shuffled, their heads nodding in agreement.

"She fought, and she closed the door. You ran."

"Fine!" shouted Nean, "Cowards, all of you. I'll do what you are afraid to do!"

Pulling out his knife, he approached Airomem, several inches taller than her and twice as wide. Her chin rose with each of his steps and he faltered, pausing a mere two feet away, his figure entirely eclipsing her in stature.

"Surrender," he said, "or –"

"No, that is not what I came here to do," she interrupted.

"Or I'll –" he continued, attempting to ignore her.

"I must warn you, this will not be pleasant," she added.

Nean's speech became flustered as she refused to budge, and he extended the knife in the vague direction of her neck, his arm clumsy and hesitant as he spoke again.

"Then I must take you prisoner by force, in the name of –"

The jab was fast, almost too fast to be seen, a blur of blue that crackled through the air as Airomem's stun gun connected with the underside of Nean's arm. With a jolt, he pivoted, blown backwards as his muscles contracted and he uttered a sharp scream of surprise, slamming against the metal wall and sliding to the floor.

"You killed him!" shouted Vaca as Nean started to drool. "You —"

"I stunned him," said Airomem. "And he deserved it. He will be back to normal in only a moment, but perhaps he will think twice next time he threatens me."

"That he should," I said, speaking over Vaca, who had opened his mouth once more. "As I said previously, the council will decide our next actions and appoint a new chief. I'm sure they will want to hear what she has to say regarding the other side of the ship, as well as how to defend against them. She saved our lives today, and likely the lives of our entire community. We should be grateful to her, not trying to imprison her. And the council will be even more grateful for her guidance."

"Which I will be only too happy to give," spoke Airomem, "for that is why I traveled here, risking my own life to make contact. Our time is short, and we must make all haste."

"Our time until what?" asked Vaca, and the porters leaned in as I held up a hand before Airomem could speak. Whatever secrets she carried, it would be best that they were not exposed to the ship's community by Nean and Vaca first.

"That is for the council to discuss. Now, the first action of the council is to meet, and to meet at once. Tom, free any members of the council that Segni held confined, and ensure they have been given a proper meal and a chance to wash. In one hour, we meet outside of the chief's old quarters."

Tom nodded and started to lumber down the hallway away from the bridge with the other porters as Airomem's sharp voice rang out.

"No, not all of you! Half of you must stand guard – under no circumstances must you leave, no matter what anyone says."

"Listen to her," I said, pointing back to the doorway. "I will ensure that your meals are delivered here. Take Nean's knife as well, and pray you don't have to use it. No one should be able to cross that hallway in anything but a crawl, but be prepared in case they attempt it."

Then I turned to Vaca as I led Airomem away and Nean began to stir.

"One hour until the council meets. Show up this time."

Chapter 36

"Before anything else, take me to a window," said Airomem. "Towards the back of the ship."

"Alright," I said, shaking the water from my shoes as ice continued to melt from the walls with the rising temperature. "But first, how much trouble are we in? How big is this threat?"

"So long as the hallway is blocked, you have nothing to worry about," responded Airomem. "At least for now."

"And are you the reason that the ship came back together? Did you do this?" I asked as we walked.

"Us? No, the ship came together on its own, just like it was supposed to after it was reprogrammed when the asteroid struck."

"What do you mean, reprogrammed?"

"How – no, what exactly do you know about the ship?" she asked, stopping. "How much history do you actually have recorded?"

I smiled and pushed my chest out.

"I'm the most knowledgeable of anyone on the ship's history," I said. "What do you want to know?"

"You are the most knowledgeable?" She coughed, giving me a sideways look as we started walking again. "What's your plan for departure to the new planet?"

"What exactly do you mean?"

Airomem sighed just as we rounded a corner and a window came into view. "This is going to be difficult. Much of what you know is about to change, Horatius. Radically."

Then she walked over to the glass and pressed her face against it, searching. She pulled one of the black rectangles from her belt and gave off three quick blue flashes. Squinting past her, I saw three quick blue flashes respond from the other end of the ship as a face peered back at her, the features difficult to make out in the distance.

Taking her hands, she formed several slow signs, exaggerating her movements and squinting at the person across the void, who was forming signs of their own.

"What – what are you doing?" I asked as her fingernails clicked against the glass.

"Letting the other side know what happened," she answered, her face in concentration.

"With your hands? You're speaking with your hands?"

"Well, yes, and no. I can't fully mimic human speech – there aren't enough signs for that, and we only use them in emergencies. But I can get the general message across. Words like *safe*, *past-danger*, and *attack*, but nothing too complicated."

Then we started walking again as I took care to bring her along more deserted hallways on the way to the chief's room at the very back of the ship, and I spoke up after a moment's thought.

"Why wouldn't you just speak normally instead of with your hands?"

"Because sometimes, in the power room, it's too loud to talk."

"The power room?"

"Yes, where – ah, never mind. We'll cover all that soon. All you need to know now is that I need to speak with your council, and that it is crucial that they listen to me. What is the current status of your side of the ship?"

"We're limping but making it. As Segni said, he was our leader – and recent events have hit us hard."

"Events like what?"

"The ship coming together was the worst – we weren't prepared for the lurch, and it claimed many of our lives as well as causing a number of injuries. We would have been able to handle them, but we're low on supplies, which complicated matters further."

"The lurch must have hit you harder than us, or at least at a worse angle. And supplies? As in food?"

"Yes – we're low on food, and more importantly right now, medicine. The food should be back up soon – after learning how to alter the lights in the control room where we just were, I've been able to enhance our growing conditions to be much stronger than the past," I said, eager to prove to her that there were parts of the ship that our side knew more about than her own. "That action, combined with more frugal stewardship and rationing, should place us into a much more sustainable position. Speaking of food, what, ah, exactly do you eat?"

"We're not like them," said Airomem, gesturing backwards and guessing my thoughts. "Our food comes from the earth, from plants. These paths that we walk, they feel familiar. They're mirrors of our own, on our end of the ship. We just entered what would be my tribe's territory on the other end. The rest belongs to the Agrarians and Aquarians."

After a few more minutes walking, we reached the chief's room, where Elliott was already waiting outside, and the door was open for entry. And Airomem stopped in her tracks, her eyes wide in realization and her hand clutched around my forearm, pulling me away.

"I'm not going in there," she hissed and started backing away. "And neither should you, if you value your life."

Chapter 37

"Elliott, this is Airomem," I said, casting a confused look at her as she took another step back, "Where is the rest of the council?"

"Inside and waiting. A pleasure to meet you, Airomem," he said. "Don't be scared. I'm not going to hurt you."

"They're *inside* there?" Airomem cried, her voice alarmed, "Get them out, now! Quickly!"

"Look, I heard about what happened on the bridge," he said. "But we're not like that here. There is nothing to be afraid of – no one here will hurt you. There is no danger. Now, we are all very eager to hear your story, and I assure you that you will be safe when telling it."

"No, I won't," she said, planting her feet. "Not in there."

"Airomem, I saw you take on two grown men at once," I said as Hannah waved from within the chief's quarters. "Trust me, should you want to fight us, we would lose quickly. We know nothing about fighting."

"No, I don't know how to explain this," she said, her foot tapping against the floor anxiously. "Open the door a bit wider so I can see in. Oh God, what have you done? Where are the warning signs? The monitors? You must have removed them ages ago. You see, on my end of the ship we have a hallway just like this, and a room just like yours on the end. See, look inside – do you see that red C plastered to the door at the end?"

"Yes," said Elliott, starting to grow impatient. "C for chief, since this is his quarters. And we've tried to open that door but had little success. It's stuck shut."

"You tried to *open* it!?" Airomem shouted. "That's insanity! That C doesn't stand for chief – it was once part of a larger sign, one that has been scraped away. That door once said nuclear – as a warning to what lies within. You don't understand; it's poison, poison of the worst type. That door blocks most of it, but some still leaks through to where you stand now."

"This is ridiculous," said Elliott. "Every chief we have had has lived here contentedly, for as long as I can remember. If it's poisonous, then why is the heating so convenient, making a comfortable gradient from the back to the front? That's one of the reasons it's so habitable; obviously, that was planned for maximum comfort."

"The heating is part of the problem!" she exclaimed. "The heating *comes from* the poison, from radiation! Look, have your chiefs ever exhibited any abnormalities? Any growths or discolorations on their skin?"

"Why, of course," said Disci, the head doctor, appearing behind Elliott. "Such is God's mark upon a successful leader."

"No! That's wrong, so wrong. Did they die soon after? Each time they were *blessed*, did it last long?"

"Well, no," said Disci, his face scrunching together. "The Lord only blesses those near the end of their life on the ship."

"You have it backwards," she said. "Those growths are why they died. They're signs of the poison, signs of death coming. Regardless, I refuse to come any closer. I'm something of an expert on this poison, and I know what it can do to people. We need to find another spot for our meeting, and you should board this door shut – it should have enough shielding to contain the poison. I can explain everything to you – the poison, the other side of the ship, everything – but not here. Those are my terms."

Elliott paused, his face flickering between disbelief and uncertainty, and I spoke.

"Elliott, do you really believe that a chief marked by God would have allowed Segni to become our leader?"

And as he mulled over the question, his face turned closer to uncertainty, and Disci took a quick step away from the room.

"To our normal meeting room, then," he said, rubbing his wrist, "despite the memories of what last happened there."

Chapter 38

Airomem finished speaking as she completed a hand drawing on the board on the wall behind her, depicting the ship before and after the Hand of God. The other members of the room squinted at it, trying to absorb all the information that had come their way, except for Vaca, who was staring into the speckled stars outside the window.

Hannah, Elliott, Disci, and I sat on the same side of the table as him, accompanied by Ruth, who had refused to leave her parents' side since their imprisonment. But despite her young age, even she had been far more attentive than Vaca, her eyes following Airomem with each description and her forehead wrinkling at some of the more difficult parts of the story.

We'd decided to keep Vaca on the council, not for his opinion, but to prevent him from stirring up trouble in other areas of the ship. There were those who would follow him, those that still believed that he was the rightful chief. And though they were no longer the vast majority, keeping him in leadership kept them satisfied and acted as a safeguard against mutiny.

"So let me get this straight," said Elliott, gesturing at the drawings, "Prior to the Hand of God, the ship was one piece. We knew that, and we can agree upon that. Then, the Hand of God struck, and the ship broke apart, and we lost much of what the ship used to be able to do. We also knew that.

"But what you're stating is that we originally lost much more – that we were in total darkness, that we lost all the heat, and that there were no heavy rooms but instead extremely light rooms. All because there is a room full of poison that gave us these things, which was damaged in the Hand of God, and now can kill us instead. How can something kill us and give us life at the same time?"

"Think of it this way," said Airomem. "When you plant seeds, you do not eat the dirt and compost that you plant them in – that's poisonous to you. However, your food comes from that soil. The power room, the poison room, is like that."

"That follows," I said, remembering how I had learned about plants drawing pieces of soil into themselves to grow. "But what about how your side keeps us alive now?"

"After the asteroid," she said, tapping her foot, "we were able to give you back some of the capabilities of the ship through wires. Without them, you would have died long ago. And we've taken special care to keep these wires alive, to keep you alive."

"I'm sorry, but this all sounds a bit ridiculous," said Elliott, spreading his hands and taking a step back from the table. "We've just met you, and now you claim that you've been caring for us our entire life, in addition to our ancestors. After what happened to Segni, I can't help but be suspicious, even if you story does hold some merit."

"I thought you might say that," said Airomem, pulling out the black rectangle from her belt and flicking it on as Elliott flinched back. "See this? This is called a stun gun. This blue light here, this spark, is what keeps you and the ship alive inside the wires. It's complicated, but you're going to have to believe me."

"Can you open up some of the wires and show us then?" asked Disci as we leaned forward.

"No, it's very dangerous. More dangerous than the stun gun itself without the proper tools," she said, then saw Elliott's suspicion returning. "But wait, I can do something!"

Then she walked over to the window and gave three blue flashes, and her hands started weaving signals again as Elliott cocked his head.

"She can talk with her hands," I explained to the group. "The other side of the ship is concerned for her safety, so they are constantly watching for her to appear in the windows and receive messages from her. From what I understand, at this distance, they can only convey simple messages and at a slower rate than typical."

"Wow!" said Ruth from the table. "Can you teach me that? I want to learn to talk to them too!"

"Of course, if we have time, though only a few on the other end of the ship know how to converse," said Airomem. "Now is everyone ready?"

"Ready for what?" I asked at the same time as Elliott.

"For proof that we've kept you alive."

"I just don't think you have any way to adequately prove it," said Elliott, waving a dismissive hand. "There's no way –"

But then, Airomem flicked her wrist to give one final signal, and Elliott's mouth closed with an audible clicking of teeth.

Above, the lights shut off, pitching the room into instant darkness. Vaca shrieked as the legs of his chair left the floor and he started floating upwards, along with the rest of us, each pinwheeling our arms to keep from turning upside down. To my right, the vent that had been spewing warm air suddenly ceased to work, cutting its breeze as suddenly as the lights had been extinguished.

Then, a two-second period after it began, it was over. The lights snapped back on as we clattered to the ground, the chairs nearly rocking over and air flowing through the vent again. Disci's face had turned a pale white, Vaca's eyes were wide with accusation, and Ruth's expression was filled with wonder. Elliott's hands shook as he smoothed his shirt, and Airomem cleared her throat as she waited for him to speak.

"Yes, erm, well, that will do Airomem," he said, his voice slightly higher than usual, "You've made your point. Go on."

Chapter 39

Rations were lower than ever the next week, the sound of forks scraping on plates becoming common during meal times to account for every last crumb. And though we worked in the fields with the best possible techniques, our backs bent over the soil for long hours of the day, plants take longer to grow than stomachs take to shrink.

Each night after meeting with the council, Airomem spent time in her own personal apartment that the council set aside for her, often accompanied by Ruth, who she was teaching how to speak with her hands, plus me as I told her the lore from our side of the ship. And each day, Airomem taught us about the other side of the ship – everything from their government structure, to what we now knew as the power room, to the methods of bottleneck defense, which we immediately taught to the porters guarding the bridge. Each day, she communicated with those on the other side of the ship, asking how many more days left until arrival, and getting little in the way of answers.

"The problem is, they don't know," she told the council after one week on our side. "We should be approaching the planet soon, and we should be landing soon, but it could be a month away or six months away. We don't know how much time Necti left us to be prepared, and we can only assume that he erred on the side of caution and gave us more time than we needed. But what does matter is that, once we are close, we are able to evacuate the ship."

"That won't go over well," I said. "It's easy to speak with us about leaving, now that we know what you know. But the rest won't want to listen."

"If they don't, they'll die – in day or weeks, but they will still die. We have to make sure that when the time comes, they are ready to move, and move quickly. We need to tell them now."

Elliott raised a hand in caution, and spoke, the wrinkles that had started to form on the edges of his eyes over the last few weeks becoming more pronounced.

"Remember, the majority of them do not understand what is going to happen. But they do understand that their chief was killed, and he was killed by people closely interlinked with you, Airomem. And they do understand being hungry. We'll have to break this news softly, and in increments. Over time, they will accept it."

"But it could happen at any time!" protested Airomem. "And if they are not ready to evacuate, we might as well have put a knife through their hearts!"

"Airomem, we are not like the Lear," I said, frowning, "despite how much I wish we were. There is much that your kind understands that ours does not. Trust me, teaching them the simplest of changes took years and gratuitous reinforcement. If the day comes too soon, then we can handle it to the best of our ability – if the ship truly is a danger to anyone who remains on it, then we are justified in giving them a little push if necessary."

"What, what exactly do you mean by that?" asked Elliott, and he cast a searching eye over me as I fidgeted. He still did not know about the power room, nor my antics in pushing the people into adopting my agriculture methods. But Elliott was too sharp to stay in the dark for long, and I would need to inform him soon. Perhaps when everyone was not so hungry.

"Like Airomem could shut off the power again," I said quickly. "And if they think that the ship is too dangerous, then they'll have to follow us out of fear."

"Don't you think that they should get to decide if they stay or leave?" said Hannah, raising an eyebrow.

"If they decide wrong, then they die," I responded. "Should we allow that to happen instead?"

"But what if we decide wrong?" she objected. "What if we evacuate, and it kills us? As much as I would like to place my faith in this plan, you must admit that it is an unprecedented risk."

"Even if we do give them the choice," I said, "there are many who would follow us, many whose eyes have been opened over the last few months. There are likely just as many who would remain entrenched in their ways, but we could at least save half."

"Regardless, this conversation stays between us for now, the members of the council," said Elliott. "We should make plans for each possible scenario so we are prepared."

We nodded in return as he walked to the board and started to draw out possible plans.

And even Vaca nodded as he continued to stare out the window.

Chapter 40

I'd been accompanying Airomem most nights after her meetings with the council, bringing additional questions and jotting notes down as she ate her sparse dinner. Each day, she seemed to bring a new surprise, a new alien trait that made my eyebrows shoot up and my thoughts spin.

I was so interested because I was a historian, I told myself. It was my duty to learn not only about my side of the ship and our past, but theirs as well. These were stories that I had never been able to access, ones that had been sealed away for hundreds of years by the void of space, pages unread for generations. Ones that to them were old, but to me were brand new.

But there were other reasons too – how Airomem walked so confidently, how she demanded attention from everyone in the room simply by being present. How her face had been the first I had recognized on the other side of the ship, and now was speaking to me, something that just weeks before I would have declared impossible. And how I yearned for a way to impress her as well, since her side of the ship seemed far more extraordinary than my own.

"You said you knew about the control room before I took you there?" I asked as she finished her rations, a disappointed look on her face as she set the plate on the floor. "How exactly?"

"It was mentioned in our stories," she said. "We remembered a time when the ship would do much of the work for us, and the engineering in the power room was such that many of our tasks could be accomplished from a distance. Since we always had the ability to change the power on other areas of the ship, it took little imagination to understand that perhaps we used to be able to change much more than that, or to change it more precisely."

"And the power on your side of the ship, did you ever try to enhance farming with it?"

"Considering that the Agrarians did the farming, it was not in our interest," she said. "If we helped them too much, then they would grow too strong and become a threat. Conversely, if we starved them off, then we would starve our own food supply. And even if we were allies with them, we wouldn't know where to begin in terms of the science."

"Wait, you're saying that you've never actually farmed?" I asked, eager to teach her something new, something in which I was an expert. "Would you be interested in learning?"

"Of course!" she said. "Trying on our end of the ship would be suicide due to the Agrarians' grasp on the land. But learning how to do it can only prove useful – whether in fighting our enemies, or upon arrival on the new planet, where I suspect we will have to do it ourselves anyways."

"I can show you, then!" I exclaimed, beaming. "Tomorrow, just after our meetings, I'll take you to the fields. It's simple, really, especially since you already seem to understand the conceptual parts."

"Deal," she said as Ruth came to the door and paused in the frame. Then she put her hands in front of her, her tongue tucked around the corner of her mouth, and started forming symbols as Airomem laughed.

"Yes, you can come in," Airomem said and made another sign, after which Ruth looked to me and laughed.

"What did she say?" I asked as I stood up to leave.

"Oh, it's a secret, Horatius," said Ruth, wagging a tiny finger and laughing. "You'll have to learn sign language to find out!"

The next day, Airomem joined me in the fields, and I taught her the basics of how to plant seeds, of the varieties, their preferred soils, and light optimizations. Her presence on our end of the ship was well known by now, through an announcement by Elliott, who had temporarily taken control as chief by vote of the council, at least until the ship was no longer in crisis. He'd also made the announcement of Segni's death, assuring the crowd that he would, in fact, be remembered.

"But what about her!" Skip had shouted from the back of the crowd as others murmured. "Segni was killed by her people, and you're going to let her walk among us? As if she were one of our own?"

"Airomem's people are enemies of those who killed Segni," Elliott had responded, keeping his voice level. "And they have been giving us crucial information about how to keep them from harming anyone else. In addition, she explained how the ship created an extremely heavy room on the bridge for our protection as its systems came online. She is an incredible resource and will do far more good than harm."

I coughed as Elliott had mentioned the ship creating the heavy room, turning away slightly to avoid the eyes of the crowd. I'd instructed Airomem to tell that lie, informing her that the control room was a long-kept secret, one that it was best if the remainder of the population did not know about. All it would take was one twist of the wrong knob and there could be another Great Thirst. This close to our arrival, another catastrophe might prove to be the last event we would experience.

I sighed in relief that the crowd's perception of Segni had been so negative at the time of his death – they still felt the hunger attributed to his feasts, many fought infections from lack of medicine, and others had family members that had perished or were close to perishing from the ship coming together. Segni's death was a distant tragedy compared to their own, washed away in a river of sorrow that hoped for new beginnings and redemption. There were some who cried at his funeral, and others who paid their respects, but the general shock smoothed over any sense of retaliation.

The death of a chief had happened before and was eclipsed by the shock of the other recent events.

In times of crisis, our people had always learned to listen to tradition and to orders. Now Elliott, as the new temporary chief, was able to provide both of those. The majority of people were willing to overlook the events that had led up to Segni's death, and to focus upon the future.

The majority, but not all.

We planned an assembly in the next week as Elliott met with each of the local leaders to discuss his plan, instructing them to keep the details extremely confidential. He spoke with Tom, who would move the porters to action. He reached out to the eldest cooks and doctors, relaying on to them that he would need their support to ensure survival. And he asked me to start convincing the gardeners, to bring Airomem out there under the pretext of teaching her our ways, but to win over as many people as possible into trusting her. To acclimate them to her presence, to convince them that there was no danger.

Only then would we cascade the evacuation plan, speaking through localized leaders to win over the whole. By Elliott's estimations, that would gather support from over three-quarters of the ship. And the last quarter, while we could prod and goad them to follow, we could not force.

That last quarter, if could we not convince them to follow us, if we could not convince them to *change*, then we also could not convince to live.

Chapter 41

I'd been teaching Airomem in the gardens for a week when it had happened.

She'd been among my quickest learners, due to her mind being a blank slate to gardening and her focus upon science, but even for her, the techniques were not instant. And in that week, Airomem had become acquainted with the other gardeners – there were children who crept in close to watch her or to ask her questions about the other side of the ship. And there were the early adopters of my gardening endeavors who ventured forward to offer a handshake and exchange names, or to offer their assistance in accommodating her.

A group of people gathered around her each morning before work began, a group to which she told stories. She spoke of Necti, and how he was among their ancestors. She mentioned how our and her people had once been the same, and perhaps they could be the same one day again. And together, stomachs would be full, thirst would be quenched, and the children would prosper. Heads nodded at her words, at the idea of a unified ship, of returning to the former glory of what *we* once were – though Airomem neglected to mention that we would be doing so *off* the ship itself.

They watched her as she taught Ruth sign language, even sending some of their own children to learn as well. They nodded in approval when, during mealtimes, she would wait until last to be served. And they marveled at her uncanny ability to remember their names, as well as where they worked in the gardens – but what they didn't know about were the long hours at night she and I spent going over them together, rehearsing so she could regurgitate them the next morning.

"What do you think is going to happen once we arrive?" I said once as we sat back in her apartment after learning a new set of names. "What do you think it will be like?"

"Well, if I was in charge of building the ship," she said, "I would try to make it as similar as possible, so that when we arrived, the shock would be minimized."

"That makes sense," I said, thinking back to some of the oldest stories I knew. "But I think some things will be different. Like sheep; I wonder if there will be sheep."

"Sheep?" Airomem asked, an eyebrow raised. "What are those?"

"I, well, I don't really know. Something from the stories, but they showed up quite a bit," I responded, drumming my fingers on the table.

"How are you going to know when you find them then?"

"I didn't think that far," I said. "I'm not sure if I *would* recognize them even if they are there. Then again, we didn't know who *your* people were either, besides the stories, and I think I understand them pretty well now."

"I think I'm still working on yours," she said letting her gaze rest on me. "But for now, let's continue learning names. If we're ever going to win their support, they'll have to like me first."

Those who agreed with Airomem largely consisted of the people who had trusted me in the past. Then were others who slinked to the other end of the garden when she passed, or who cast dark looks in our direction. And there was Skip, who never permitted himself to be within fifty yards of her.

Until Airomem and I worked through lunch, our hunger forgotten in the lesson, and those who were amicable to us already had departed for the midday break. When I looked up from planting a row of new seeds, I saw Skip facing me with a quarter of the gardeners at his back. Behind them there were others, others who I had seen scowling in the hallways, or huddled around Nean's table at dinner.

"We've had enough!" shouted Skip from the spearhead of the group, now only fifteen feet away and still approaching. "We want her out, *now*. It's an insult to Segni and to us, and she comes trying to change our ways far more than you ever did, Horatius."

"There is no reason to overreact!" I replied as Skip stopped only inches from me, his face livid. From beside me, Airomem's hand instinctively went to her belt as Skip pushed forward.

"Overreact?!" shouted Skip. "While you've been leading this intruder around our ship, and while you've been meeting with the council, what have we been doing? We've been here gardening, praying that there will be enough food to support us! And what's more, what's more is what I heard what *the council* are planning for us! The treason!"

"Skip," I said, "calm down. Whatever your issue is, feel free to take it up before the council and it will be addressed. As far as food goes, we should have a surplus. It's just going to take time. You know as well as I do that growing vegetables is not instant. And Airomem has done nothing but help us."

"The council? The council? I *would* take it up with the council, if they weren't brainwashed by *her*! Did you hear what they are saying now, what their plans are?"

He was shouting to the mob behind him now, their attention acute as he spat the next few words.

"Their plans are to rip you away from your homes! To move us all somewhere else, somewhere we might die just as Segni did. And how do I know this? Because Vaca himself told me; Vaca, the true chief!"

Chapter 42

"Hold on –" I said, putting up a hand, but Skip was shouting again, enough spittle flying from his mouth to water the garden. Beside him, another gardener picked up a shovel, sinking the blade deep into the earth and leaning forward against the handle.

"Ever since you've been born, Horatius, ever since that first day you joined my class, it's been nothing but disaster after disaster! Now we're in a worse position than ever, with you planning to make things even worse!"

"Make things worse? I *saved* you! I showed you how to plant more efficiently, and I got us through Segni's feasts!"

"You would slander him before his body has even gotten cold, you would attempt to place the blame upon him! I've half a notion that you somehow brought the ship together to do him in too! That *you* are responsible for *her*." He raised a finger like a knife, its quivering tip aimed at Airomem, as the glares of those behind him matched its violence.

"Impossible!" countered Airomem, waving a dismissive hand as the crowd flinched back. "That was controlled by the ship's systems, which are inaccessible to us. It's not like altering the lights in here to enhance growth."

For a moment, all was silent as the muscles in my back tightened and blood flushed to my ears. Skip's eyes widened as his breath came out in a hiss, and Airomem's hands flew back to her belt as her face flooded with realization.

"Altered the lights to enhance growth," whispered Skip, turning a slow circle to where dead stocks still piled around from where they had been burnt. "Ever since you arrived, Horatius, you've changed our ways, luring us in with false promises. And each time, our crops died. To think now that you intended to kill them entirely, to kill *us* entirely."

He shook, his face as red as Segni's strawberries, his gaze turning upwards to where the steady glow of the lights shone overhead, then falling back towards me like a hammer.

"Treason!" he shouted. "Treason! We hunger not from our own mistakes, but because of *you,* Horatius! I knew it, all this time, I knew it!" He brandished a shovel in his hand, his clenched knuckles white as shock crossed the other faces.

"Back away!" commanded Airomem as the crowd began to push forward, spurred forward by their stomachs, their voices joining Skip in shouting.

"Away!" repeated Airomem, and she flashed the blue lights as the crowd winced. But they continued to move forward, their faces reddened with anger and their footsteps instigated by Skip.

"She *dares* pull a weapon on us! She *dares* threaten us!" screeched Skip.

"Skip!" I shouted as Airomem and I retreated, quickly backpedaling through the soil, "Skip, you are making a huge mistake! A bigger one than this ship has ever seen, one the council will surely punish."

"No, you *already* made a huge mistake!" he retorted, kicking a clod of dirt so it exploded on my chest. "I don't give a damn about the council. It's time for the true chief to take charge! For Vaca!"

Behind him, the mob cheered, raising their gardening tools into the air.

"Horatius," hissed Airomem, "we need to get out of here. *Now.*"

"No!" I countered, planting my feet and squaring my shoulders as Skip's chest pressed close to mine, pieces of earth still imprinted in my shirt. "No! I'm done with hearing this! Vaca and Segni only caused trouble! It's their fault that we are in this situation, and I did what was necessary to save the ship."

"Because killing our crops and killing our chief and killing our hope was the solution? Why can't you just do things the right way?" A deranged smile crossing Skips lips, his words now catalyzed by an incredulous laughter.

"Because that's the *idiotic* way, not the right way!" I shouted as Skip popped his palm on my right shoulder to push me back, and Airomem's stun guns buzzed louder. Blood rushed to my face and I raised my own fists, stepping forward to return the blow, oblivious to the crowd that pressed forward and Airomem pulling against my elbow.

And even more oblivious to Nean, who had snuck behind me in the heat of the argument from the hallways beyond the garden. And who cracked the handle of a spare shovel across the top of my head so hard that white light flashed and my knees buckled.

White was followed by blue as I tumbled, landing face up in the dirt while Airomem's twin stun guns dashed in ellipses above me, mingling with the stunned stars that filled my vision. I saw Nean reach back to strike again and he instead received a prompt jab to the neck, his eyelids shooting upwards while his body crumpled downwards. Skip followed shortly, a stun gun catching him under the chin as Airomem spun and the tips of her hair whipped against his shocked face.

The edges of my vision closed in as I saw a shovel blade thrown from within the crowd connect with her forearm, causing one of the stun guns to go flying, accompanied with an angry cry. Then, as darkness took me, the single blue streak danced with renewed vigor, and I heard more thumps hitting the ground until sounds too dissolved into nothingness.

Chapter 43

I slept in darkness, and I awoke in darkness.

My head slammed against something hard as I sat up, doubling the already throbbing headache as I fell to the floor with a grunt, my palm clasped against my clammy temple. My heart raced to keep pace with my rapid breaths as I felt around me, searching for clues about my surroundings.

"Hit the shelf," came a quiet voice from beside me as I jumped to my feet, stumbling to a thin strip of light on the ground that would be the bottom of the door. I found the handle and pushed, the door emitting a dull rattle as it bounced against the frame but refused to budge.

"Locked," came the same voice through a sniffle, and I froze, realizing that I recognized it. "Barricaded from the outside; they've piled things up so we can't escape."

"H-Hannah?" I said, sinking to the ground with my back against the wall. "What's going on? Where is everyone?"

"Nean," she sniffled. "He had me seized out of my apartment and taken here, where I found you passed out. There – There's a crowd of gardeners in the hallway outside, all calling for justice, and Nean is keeping us prisoners here until Elliott relinquishes his position as chief to Vaca. W-We thought Vaca was not listening in the meetings, but there was one topic he *did* listen to – Airomem's lectures on bottleneck defense. They have this entire corridor blocked off, Horatius, and defended. They've taken the knives, along with Airomem's stun guns, and are guarding both ends."

"I – I'm sorry, Hannah. It's only a matter of time until they run out of food and water, though, and then they'll have to give in. They'll have to – they can't last long, and we'll bring them to justice."

Hannah's sobs doubled for a moment in the darkness, then she found the strength to speak.

"Before they blocked off the corridor, they raided the food and water stores. It's *all* here, stored away in the apartments nearby, and they're not rationing it. They were able to take it by stationing their own guards at the stores, and since there wasn't much left, there wasn't much to carry. You've been knocked out for a day – last night, they had a feast in Segni's honor. Tonight, they're having another. Since they're only a quarter of the ship, they don't have to ration."

"Oh God," I said in realization, realizing the true reason that Hannah was crying. "Everyone else, all those outside the corridor –"

"Have nothing to eat," she cried. "Ruth, Elliott; they'll starve!"

"They won't," I said, thinking. "There's enough food growing in the gardens to keep them sustained for two weeks at least, and enough water in the reclaiming units to stave their thirst. It'll be tight, and they'll be eating crops before they have a chance to mature, so they're borrowing crops from the future. But after that..." My voice trailed off, and I bit my lip, not wanting to think about what would happen after that. We were silent for a moment, then I spoke up, fighting to keep my own voice from cracking. "I – I'm sorry, Hannah. I only did what Pliny would have –"

"What's done is done," said Hannah, managing to make her voice hard as she pushed away the sobs. "And while I can't say I disagreed with your actions, doing them as a team would have been far more effective. Elliott and I had a suspicion of what you were doing in the gardens and we turned a blind eye, so we are just as guilty. Ruth kept a watch over you for us, and her reports were positive, so we stopped short of questioning you. And Nean confirmed my suspicions – he's kept it no secret what you have been up to."

"And Airomem? Is she locked away too?" I asked.

"No, she's gone. Back to her end of the ship. He gloated about that as well, said he took the trash back where it belonged."

I paused, my swallow audible among the voices outside the door. Over the next two days, I racked my brain, my ear pressed close to the door to where I could hear Elliott negotiating down the hallway, while Nean and Skip refused to budge on their terms. That Elliott turn himself over to them, serve six week's confinement for his act of treason alongside us, and declare Vaca the true heir.

At times, I stared outside the window to where I could see the other end of the ship, and I wondered what Airomem was planning, or even *if* she was planning. If she had convinced the Lear that we were worth saving, or if they might try to block us out from the new planet after the way we as a people had treated her.

Hannah and I spoke of possible escape, trying to think of ways to get past the barricaded door. But beyond would be the mob that we would have to fight through to escape – we were weaponless, and though none of the gardeners were well trained in fighting, neither were we. Eventually, I resigned myself to looking at the rightward wall of the apartment, knowing only a few walls separated me from farmland.

On the third day, as I racked my brain for possibilities and I heard Elliott pleading at the end of the hallway, a voice came down from above. The voice that had changed all our lives just a few weeks ago, and now prepared to do so again.

A voice that chilled me more to the bone now than the first time I had heard it.

"Twenty-four hours until arrival," it proclaimed from above, accompanied by a siren and repeating itself three times. "All members of the ship, report to the departure vessel. Immediately."

I swallowed, meeting Hannah's eyes in the darkness. Knowing that if nothing changed, we would be left behind. And knowing if God were to exist, he was not with us.

Chapter 44

Airomem was tossed into the air and came down to the ground far harder than ever before in her life. Her arms strained against the metal floor, pushing downwards as muscles bulged, barely able to lift her head upwards. Even her hair seemed to drag her down, yanking against the roots as she turned back down the corridor.

"Fools!" she shouted as she watched them slam the door of the bridge shut. "Incompetent idiots! Bringing upon your own deaths!"

The she turned back to the long corridor of the bridge before her, its gravity still magnified, and began to crawl. With each struggling motion, she thought back upon the previous few hours, and grit her teeth.

Twenty-four. *Twenty-four* farmers she had stunned before they had managed to strip her of her weapon, and now that she was thinking about it, twenty-four new reasons for them to hate the Lear.

Until they'd figured out what to do with her, they had locked her away inside an abandoned apartment for three hours. Three hours that she had searched for any means to escape but had found nothing outside of breaking the window into space beyond, something that even if she had wanted to do, she would not have had the strength or tools. And something she knew would be suicide.

But then, a dozen of the farmers had come back for her, armed with knives and her own stun guns, and had ushered her back to the bridge. A few porters looked on as they threw her back in, but Tom was not among them, and they parted with little resistance before the mob.

Now she was crawling back to the Agrarians, her posture low and her pride lower. With failure pushing down upon her shoulders as hard as gravity, and the knowledge that the Lear's potential allies would not only be a burden if it came to war, but would also be unreliable to call upon for aid. But even with that knowledge, there were those who she could save among them, those like Ruth, whose neighbors would sentence her to death out of ignorance.

People that she had an obligation to save, because they could not save themselves. People who the Lear could adopt as their own and who held valuable information about the methods of farming that could prove crucial on the new planet.

So she forced herself forward, knowing that each second that passed was an enlarging portion of their time left on the ship. That the marathon to the end of the corridor was already taking far too long, and that the information she held was of utmost importance.

When she made it to the end, she collapsed, her lungs heaving in the suddenly lighter environment. She allowed herself thirty seconds of rest before climbing to her feet, her hand against the wall to steady herself, and peering down the deserted walkway. This was Aquarian territory, but it was deserted – they had no reason to come this close to the edge and were likely clustered near key points of defense for the water reclaimers. So, keeping her head down, and with quick but silent feet, she began to trot towards the end of the ship where the Lear resided. But first, that meant crossing through Agrarian territory.

And unlike the Aquarians, the Agrarians were waiting.

The same four guards that had escorted her on the way to the bridge were nestled behind a corner and she nearly ran into them, except she was never given the chance. Instead, they enveloped her once more, this time with the hint of smiles upon their faces. And they deposited her in front of Sitient as he reclined on his couch, his leg tapping against the bones dangling from the fabric, his eyes hard as they looked over her.

"I demand safe passage," she said, forcing her own eyes to match his, "as determined by the negotiations between you and the Lear."

"Your father has promised me ten stun guns for your release," replied Sitient, his voice hard, "but you have injured me, *princess*. For that reason, I am raising the price to fifteen. Until then, you will remain under our guard – for your father demanded your safe passage, but he did not specify what condition you would be in when you returned."

"You can be sure," she barked, "that if you lay a finger upon me, there will be no end to the wrath of the Lear!"

"That's the beauty of it, that *I* don't have to," responded Sitient, the corner of his mouth turning upwards. "But I only have so much control over my people, princess. With the tribute that the Lear demands, they grow so hungry – hungry enough that they might want a Lear snack of their own. So I suggest you only travel where my guards take you, or the only thing I will provide safe passage to your father are your bones."

She paused, suddenly aware of the eyes that stared out from the shadows, of the distance she would have to travel to make it home, and the sheer *number* of the Agrarians she would have to pass through to get there.

"Then make your demands," she said, "but do not be so foolish to think that he shall bend beneath your thumb."

"We shall see, princess," he said. "Until then, you shall wait until I fetch you. Your guards are departing – for your own safety, I would suggest you hurry to depart with them."

Pursing her lips, she followed, leaving Sitient laughing behind her. For five minutes, they walked towards the center of Agrarian territory, crossing through fields still filled with hollow-cheeked workers and yellowed plants. Then they led her into a side hallway filled with several apartments, opened the door to one, and barricaded the door once she was inside.

During the first day, she heard nothing – no food or water was delivered, and no guards checked upon her status. The second day was the same, and she tried pounding against the door or searching for weaknesses in the barricade, but found none. She bit her lip, the dry skin cracking if she wondered if they would leave her there to rot, if she would die of thirst before Sitient was satisfied with the deal.

And as she waited, one word brought her comfort, a single name scratched into the wall long before by someone else who had once shared her torment.

Prometh.

Chapter 45

"Your father has conceded," sneered Sitient as he thrust open the door to her cell. "Time for the princess to return home. And with the weapons he's providing, it might be soon that we meet again."

He smiled, and she retched as his breath struck her, watching the open door quiver under the grasp of his shaking hand.

"When I'm back with the Lear," she rasped, her throat dry from lack of water, "the next time we meet will surely be the last."

"What's that?" he asked, cocking an ear towards her. "I couldn't quite make out the words. Are you thirsty? Don't worry; we've prepared quite the drink for you. With the weapons, I don't think water is going to be much of problem for us anymore. We have *plenty* to spare."

She stumbled after him as he departed, her legs weak from the heavy rationing on the other end of the ship plus the lack of food over the last few days. Ahead, she could hear voices, a commotion of activity that grew louder with each step, until she broke into the lighting of the farm fields.

Hundreds of the Agrarians extended before her, stretched in two long and waving lines from one side of the fields to the exit at the far end. Between the two lines there was just enough room to form a narrow path through the dirt, but it was no longer only dirt – buckets lined the sides, buckets full of manure and water that had been cast into the earth, creating a foul mud concoction that Airomem could smell from the entrance. Her pangs of hunger dissipated under the stench as the guards prompted her closer, then stopped at the front of the two lines.

Behind her, the guards hoisted Sitient into the air on a chair and he began to speak, the crowd quieting as his voice bellowed over their own and his spittle mixed in with the mud.

"On this day, we welcome Airomem, princess of the Lear – for she has fetched us the price of fifteen stun guns, more than our tribe has ever known!" He raised his arms and the crowd erupted into screeches and stomped, spraying flecks of mud into the air. He waited until they quieted, and he continued, "On this day, we are no longer one of the three tribes. On this day, we become part of the one tribe! We take the Aquarians and their water, and then we take the Lear! In thanks for their gift, we have spent our remaining water until our conquest of the Aquarians in Airomem's honor! Be sure, I repeat, *be sure* not a single drop of it goes to waste!"

Airomem felt a foot thrust forward into the small of her back and propel her forward, sending her sprawling into the mud. Jeers erupted ahead of her as she rose to her knees, muck clinging to the front of her clothes and tips of her hair, and before she had a chance to stand, a ball of the manure slammed into her right cheek, exploding over the entire side of her face and up one nostril. She shook it off just as another smacked against her side, launched by a woman with no teeth twenty paces up the line as others scooped up the material to make their own projectiles.

Airomem clenched her jaw, then raised her chin upwards.

And she began to walk, her feet sinking ankle deep into the earth.

By the twentieth mudball, she hardly felt the new ones, and by third time she had been tripped or shoved, there was no part of her body left uncoated, no patch of skin or hair that stood naked. Their voices laughed and their eyes flashed as she moved past them, the lines constricting in places to make it near impossible to cross while thickening in other areas to allow for more projectiles. For ten minutes, she endured it, making no sound, meeting none of their eyes. Staring directly ahead, plowing onward until at last the lines split and she reached a corridor, the one that she had initially taken when she had departed the Lear.

Refuse rolled away from her with each step down the deserted hallway, her feet leaving dark tracks on the metal, the commotion still loud behind her. And after two hundred paces she came upon a group of twenty waiting Lear soldiers circled around a pile of stun guns.

"Halt!" commanded the first as the others recoiled. "No entry is allowed by any Agrarian past this point until Princess Airomem has been returned to the Lear!"

"I *am* Airomem," she hissed, throwing her matted hair over one shoulder. "Daughter of Praeter. And I have seen the other side of the ship."

The soldiers gasped as they recognized her and parted, allowing her to pass and escorting her to the first bottleneck a mere minute away. Upon arrival, she turned to the soldiers and spoke.

"I seek my father's council, at once. This matter cannot wait for cleaning or rest – bring him here, now! We have but only minutes to act!"

And standing in the doorway, she shook the mud from her feet and shouted into Agrarian territory, her voice harsh and her eyes cold.

"The wrath of the Lear will not be felt with weapons or words! No, it will be felt with our absence, for our departure is the departure of your lifeblood. There will be weeping and gnashing of teeth, and the wicked will have no peace!"

Chapter 46

"What in the name of –" Airomem's father started, his face turning red as he saw her scraping mud from her arms with rags provided by the soldiers.

"It can wait," she said, cutting him off, her voice refreshed by water from a soldier. "I'll include it in my full report. But first, we must act. The Agrarians have nearly exhausted their water supply and plan on using their newfound weapons to attack the Aquarians, then us. We must cut them off by providing five stun guns to the Aquarians, in exchange for all the water that they have, plus three more stun guns every six hours they provide us with more water. When the Agrarians find out water is not being delivered to them, they'll initiate attacks, only to discover that the Aquarians have them matched in weaponry."

"You're sure of this?" he asked, pausing. "What if the Agrarians turn on us instead?"

"Absolutely sure. The Agrarians know that without water, they only have a few days, so they'll attack the Aquarians first. And if they do attack us first, the Aquarians will respond by attacking their exposed flank with their new stun guns. Either way, the Agrarians and Aquarians are in gridlock and will hopefully weaken each other to the point where we can stroll through their territory when it is time to depart. The Agrarians have greater fire power, but no water, which will keep the battles raging."

"I'll bring it to the war council at once," he answered. "It's a dangerous hand, but one that needs to be played. And you; you will be appearing when?"

"After an hour. I need to clean up," she responded, then turned to the soldiers beside her. "Food and water; I'll need them both at my apartment. And, Father, it will be difficult, but we *must* convince the others that we have to save the other side of the ship. Otherwise, we have provided them with power for the last hundreds of years for nothing, and that energy has gone to waste. They're like us, the Lear, but there are those similar to the Aquarians and Agrarians among them. And we must save the Lear."

***

Nearly half an hour passed before Airomem was satisfied with cleaning herself, certain that she had missed a patch of excrement *somewhere* as she tossed down the fifth soiled cloth. Her teeth gritted with each stroke as she remembered walking down the aisle, and her forearms tensed as she remembered Sitient's smile. The only comfort she felt was that soon the Lear would be leaving their problems behind, literally.

She took a bite out of the meal that had been provided for her, savoring the taste as her stomach cried out in excitement with each passing morsel. Already, she was nearly full to bursting with water – usually, she would feel guilty for wasting so much of it upon washing and quenching her thirst, but by that night, the Lear should have more water than they'd had in a century.

She took a last bite and dressed herself, knowing that her father and the other leaders were awaiting her report. Casting a glance outside the window, she frowned as she looked over the other end of the ship, wondering how she could tie their futures together. Wondering if they would *let* her.

And just before she turned away, a flash of white light caught her eye, a flash that repeated two more times. She squinted, trying to make out the distant object through the narrow ship's window, nearly turning away before she saw the flashing repeat again in a staccato burst. Her hand fell to her dresser, and she pulled out a spare stun gun that she kept in case of emergencies, the same one that she had pulled on her father long ago.

Holding her breath, she raised it to the window, and responded with three blue pulses.

Three white flashes immediately responded, three flashes she now saw was simply a window near an overhead light being covered and uncovered, and her eyes widened as she saw a face fill the window, the forehead pressed against the glass. A child's face, one she had seen only three days before.

Ruth's face.

Then the face was replaced with hands that raced through a flurry of signals, signals too fast and far away for Airomem to understand. She pulsed her stun gun to capture Ruth's attention, and signed two words, her fingers taking long and deliberate pauses between each.

Slow down.

Ruth's hands flashed back, and then the words began once more. In the time that Airomem had spent with her, she had only been able to teach her a portion of the words, and they came across rough and disjointed. It felt as if she was reading a paragraph with holes in it, that someone had written with their left hand, handicapped with darkness.

Help; that part was clear. *Stuck. Two stuck. Stuck like you.*

Stuck? she signed back.

Danger. Man and woman stuck. Help.

Airomem frowned, and then Ruth continued to sign.

Radioactive people stuck man and woman. Need help.

Radioactive? thought Airomem. *What did she mean?*

And then she remembered the word she had used for radioactive among them. Poison. And Ruth's message began to make sense.

Poisonous people have stuck a man and a woman. Need help.

The poisonous people could only be those who had exiled her: Vaca, Nean, and Skip. They had Horatius; that was what stuck had to mean, that he was captured. But woman; who was the woman?

What woman? she signed back.

My woman, came the answer. *My woman.*

Her mother, Airomem realized. Both Horatius and her mother were captured. She had seen Horatius being taken, but not Hannah as well. And then Ruth signed again.

No leave man and woman. Help. Stuck.

Where?

Six, came the sign, followed by a gesture, and Airomem counted over six windows until she saw one that was dark. It was in a portion of the ship that she had passed through on her way back from the bridge, as it was mirrored on the Agrarian side. And a lump swelled in her throat as she realized it was a lone corridor, with easily defended entry and exit points. And she realized how it might be defended.

How are they stuck?

You. You teach. Your power.

Her bottleneck defense lessons. Her stun guns. She was the reason Horatius and Hannah were captured.

And she realized that when the bridge opened, and she had crossed, it had not only allowed *her* to pass through. Rather, she had brought other pieces of her side of the ship with her, sections of their culture, ideas that had long been dormant in Horatius' people's minds simply because of the naivety of their side of the ship. Because they hadn't experienced them in centuries, until the opening of the bridge had awakened the concepts once again.

Violence. Warfare.

Murder.

Chapter 47

The voice came from above as she walked to the meeting room, causing her to redouble her pace, nearly reaching a run.

"Twenty-four hours until arrival. All members of the ship, report to the departure vessel. Immediately."

She broke into the meeting room just as her father stood atop a chair, calling for order among the arguing members.

"You heard it! Twenty-four hours until arrival! I want every member of the Lear notified to pack no more than a knapsack of belongings and to be ready to leave at a moment's notice! Everyone but the most senior members here will be supervising. In one day, this ship becomes a wasteland – anyone who stays will not be under my protection, and even if they were, they wouldn't survive longer than a few days. Dandelion 14 is about to become a husk, devoid of food or water, and with no power. To stay is to embrace death. Go! Now! Except for you, Airomem. We need your report."

Before she could speak, Tela cut her off, his voice sharp with desperation. "Their military, how large is it? How well can they help us fend off the Agrarians and Aquarians as we flee? Are they potential allies?"

She raised a hand, signaling him to pause, and took a breath. Then she began.

"The," she paused, realizing they had no name for themselves, and restarted, "The *Nectians* have a population of approximately one thousand, separated into their leaders, their chefs and doctors, and their laborers. They have no warrior class, nor do they have weapons among them – I suspect there may be racks of stun guns locked away in their power room, where we recharge ours, but it is too dangerous to enter there."

"So it was fruitless," muttered Tela, his eyes narrowing as his fingers gripped the tabletop. "Our weapons traded away for an empty expedition."

"Not quite," she answered, holding a finger in the air. "Actually, quite the contrary. The Nectians may be unable to lend a hand in leaving Dandelion 14, but they could prove crucial once we land on the new planet. The majority of them are farmers – assuming that's how we will find food. They will be indispensable when we disembark."

Tela frowned, and her father spoke.

"And their disposition? Will they cooperate with the Lear? As farmers, are they like, well, are they like the Agrarians?"

"I would estimate that seventy percent are compatible," she answered, "but the other thirty percent will balk at the notion of leaving the ship, and will be left behind of their own accord."

"This other thirty percent," growled Tela, "are they the reason for your return? We received no message from you that you were coming back, and had the guards on the border stationed there in case you arrived, not because you were expected."

"Yes, the thirty percent mutinied," responded Airomem, "which is another reason we must help them. They took prisoners, two of the leaders of the Nectians. Without them, many of the Nectians will not be convinced to leave. We'll have to rescue those two, or risk losing them all."

"So you're saying that thirty percent were able to overcome the vast majority," countered Tela. "Meaning the majority we are to bring with us is far weaker. In addition to that, they can offer no assistance against the Agrarians and Aquarians, but rather *require our assistance* to leave the ship. Airomem, do I need to remind you that we now have twenty-four, no, twenty-three and a half hours left to disembark? To force our way through to the bridge, and to protect our own kind first? We cannot afford to take them under our wing."

"But there is something they can do to help fight!" she exclaimed, her face brightening. "On their side of the ship, they have discovered a control room, and they can wreak havoc upon the Agrarians and Aquarians from there! They could incapacitate them from a distance, a tactic that could prove invaluable. One that already *has* been invaluable."

But across the table, Prometh shook his head, large bags recently formed under his eyes.

"I'm afraid that will not be possible," he said. "I'm familiar with this room from old drawings of the power room schematics, and Airomem is correct. It does hold a great strategic advantage."

"And?" pressed Tela as Prometh paused.

"And it also requires power to operate." He sighed. "For the past twelve hours, our engineers have detected the electrical draw of the ship to have tripled and to be steadily rising. We checked everything – from wiring faults to misreads, and until I heard the announcement, I assumed that we were simply missing something. But now, I realize what has been happening – the ship is drawing power to the bridge, preparing the vessel that will take us to the planet."

"And why is this a problem?" said Airomem.

"Because at the rate that the power is increasing, due to the exponential burn rate," said Prometh, "I would estimate that, at best, we have about twelve hours of power left."

For a moment, the table was silent. Then Tela's chair flew backwards as he stood, his face red as he shouted.

"So not only do we have to fight our way through our enemies, but we have to do so *in the dark?*"

"Well, yes," answered Prometh, his voice tired. "But I suspect that will be the least of our worries."

Airomem's eyebrows shot upwards as Tela prepared for another outburst, but her words cut his off.

"Gravity!" she exclaimed. "Without power, we'll be weightless! Weightless *and* in the dark."

"Precisely," said Prometh.

"With this information," stuttered Tela, "it is absolute madness for us to attempt a rescue mission. Those of the Nectians who come of their own accord will be admitted. But the rest – the rest have decided their fate."

Airomem bit her lip as Praeter spoke up, his voice slow and deliberate.

"The Lear come first," he said, his head down. "Our duty is to serve them before all others. I'm sorry, Airomem, but under the extreme circumstances, we have no choice. The Nectians will have to make their own choice, as you made them aware of the situation in your envoy."

"Except for the prisoners!" Airomem exclaimed, rising to her feet. "They don't get to make a choice, and they're the ones who saved their people! Now they are dying for it!"

"They chose to be heroes, Airomem. And being a hero means you put yourself at risk for the sake of others."

Her eyes flashed as she whipped around to storm out of the room, her voice coming out in a hiss.

"You're right, Father. That's *precisely* what being a hero means. And once, I would have believed we fit that description."

"Prometh," she heard her father say as she left, "see to it that the power room lasts as long as possible. And my daughter has always listened to you; talk some sense into her as well. This is a difficult decision, but I can't afford to put our people into more danger. Compromises, difficult compromises, must be made."

"Of course," said Prometh, following Airomem from the room. "Talking sense is what I do best. She will be ready to depart promptly."

Chapter 48

"Airomem, hold up!" Prometh called, his breath coming in gasps as he rushed down the hallway. The accumulation of his age and the sleepless night had taken its toll, and he grimaced with the knowledge that rest was still far away.

"I heard what you said," she hissed, whipping around to face him and still walking backwards, "and you won't *talk sense* into me."

"Not if you kill me first with this pace," he responded, and then pointed at her with one of his remaining fingers. "But at bare minimum, you owe me a discussion, Airomem, a discussion of the other side, and of the survival of this ship as a whole! Time is short and we cannot afford for it to be wasted by your temper!"

She stopped, blood rushing to her face. Prometh was right, just as he had been countless times through the years. Her storming away solved nothing, and she had no plans developed for what to do when her anger subsided. She paused, then spoke as he caught up to her.

"What do you want to know?"

"These people you found; you said they were like the Lear?"

"Yes."

"And that they may prove critical to our own survival?" he inquired.

"Absolutely."

"And, when they turned upon you," he held a hand up as she started to protest, "was it violence and greed that drove them? Or was it fear and ignorance?"

"Ignorance," she answered, and Prometh smiled. "Ignorance of what was for their own good."

"That's fortunate," he answered, his voice soft, "for that can be fixed. Oh, yes it can – knowledge can be given, and the stupid can be led, but character is far harder to change. Now we must discuss the Lear departure of the ship. Stop trying to speak over me. We'll come back to the issue of the Nectians in just a moment."

From his pocket, he pulled out a folded paper and began to open it, gently prying the creases apart and setting it on the ground.

Airomem recognized it as the schematics of the ship that had hung in the classroom during her studies, as Prometh had taught her the methods of bottleneck defense.

"It is critical that you remember, Airomem, the path to the bridge," he said, smoothing the map with his palm. "This map is old. In the years since it was created, there could be blocked corridors or there could be malfunctions in the ship that block our progress. Do you remember any of these?"

"No," she answered with a frown as Prometh handed her a pen. And she traced the route she had taken on the paper, her face wrinkled in concentration as she fought to remember if it was correct.

Prometh shook his head as she traced a particularly long line through the farming fields.

"No, that won't do," he whispered, shaking his head. "It's too much distance."

"Why does that matter?" she asked. "If anything, it's the quickest way as a straight line and it points nearly directly at the bridge."

"You forget, Airomem, that we will be weightless," he answered. "We will not have the privilege of running along the ground. Our speed will come from kicking off the walls, and in a stretch as long as this, the air itself will slow us down! And should we get stuck near the center, we are as good as dead. Easy targets from the sides."

He took the pen from her and traced around the inner edge of the fields, squinting as the tip raced through the narrow lines, and speaking once he finished the alternate path.

"This is better, with more right-angled turns that can be used to keep speed. More dangerous, though. More dangerous for sure. But the procession of the entirety of the Lear would be greatly accelerated."

"It's nearly at the center of Agrarian territory," she answered. "It doesn't seem dangerous; it seems suicidal. You would be surrounded instantly."

"Not quite," he answered. "With the sudden influx of weapons, all it will take is but the tiniest of sparks to drive the tribes to full war. I'm certain the Lear can find a way to initiate it. Just a few of the right words when giving stun guns to the Aquarians should be enough. That means that the majority of the Agrarian forces will be at or past their own boundary, and those few who may be lingering will be incapacitated at the front of the procession by our own soldiers. We'll have surprise on our side as well, since we will cut power to the ship mere seconds before we depart, and the darkness will help shield us from prying eyes. With no notion that weightlessness is coming, or even the idea that it exists, the Agrarians' ability to react will be severely diminished."

"So cut the power," she reiterated. "Then flush our people through the hall in a single line as fast as possible to the bridge. From there, we defend the entrance like a bottleneck until it is time to depart."

"Exactly," said Prometh. "And there are only two who can lead the Lear to the bridge, two that have walked the paths before. I and you, Airomem. But since I'm a frail old man, I fear there are journeys I can no longer attempt alone."

She grimaced, turning to the window where she could see the other side of the ship with the Nectians, and bit her tongue. She hadn't considered that the fate of the *Lear* rested just as heavily upon her shoulders as the fate of them.

"When the Lear arrive at the bridge," continued Prometh, "it will be too late to save the Nectians. Without gravity and in the dark, they'll have panicked. Even if they *do* decide to depart for the bridge, the loss of power several hours before they leave means that many of them will be left behind. I anticipate that only a few stragglers will make it, if any at all."

"I," started Airomem, her voice thin, "I'll cross the Agrarian lands on my own then, now, before the power is out, and lead the Nectians to the bridge. Then I can come back for the Lear."

"A suicide mission that will help neither," said Prometh. "You'll be killed long before you reach the Nectians if you travel by foot. I'm afraid that way is barred to you, Airomem."

Her throat tightened, and Prometh turned to embrace her in the hallway, his arms around her as she felt hope fleeting, watching as a few members of the Lear hurried away from them, carrying the message of the soon-to-come departure. At any other time, his gesture would have seemed inappropriate – but she found herself welcoming the comfort of her old mentor. And she felt his fingers entwine around her own, her eyes widening in surprise as something hard and jagged bit into her palm, held firmly in place by the pressure of Prometh's hand. He angled his head, and he spoke into her ear, his words coming slow and heavy.

"As I said, Airomem, there are journeys I can no longer attempt alone. But leading the Lear through Agrarian territory is something that I *can* do. Your presence shall be missed."

He took a step backwards and gave her a slow wink.

"I hope I have talked some sense into you, Airomem. As your father commanded, be ready to depart *at once*."

Then he turned away as she glanced at her palm, her mouth opening as she recognized the objects she held.

"I'll see you at the bridge," he said over his shoulder and waved a hand in departure.

"You as well, Prometh. Thank you. This may be the most important lesson you have ever given me."

And she raised her own hand in a fist, mimicking his motion, but not daring to open her fingers and expose the three keys and folded note that she clutched within.

Chapter 49

Airomem had no need to read the note to know her next destination. Instead, she felt her legs carrying her forward against the current of the frightened crowd, attracting stares as her shoulders rubbed against those preparing to flee. Whispers chased her down the hallway, whispers that threatened to distract her from her task.

Snippets like "I bet she knows more about what's going on" or "Why isn't she preparing to leave?" or "Hard at work, even on the brink of disaster," accompanied by a knowing glance or worried frown, though none of the speakers followed her. And when she arrived in the power room, it was emptier than she had ever seen – posts were abandoned in favor of preparation, knowing that reactor failure was soon imminent and that there was little the extra hands could do to help.

Despite knowing what was occurring, chills still ran up her spine at the distress alarms and flashing lights that called out to her to fix them, and her eyes widened as they saw the energy expenditure levels high above anything she had ever observed, yet still rising.

Prometh was right, she realized. The time to act before power was completely lost was rapidly dwindling. And turning away from the machinery she had dedicated so much of her life towards, she opened the note Prometh had written her and started to read, keeping an eye upwards at the few workers who had stayed behind.

She recognized one of them, Abraham, an engineer in training that she had personally helped instruct as he neared the title of full engineer. He was brighter than most his age, yet still had to grow into his gangly body, his arms and legs possessing an uncanny knack for bumping into tables and chairs. She raised a hand and beckoned him over, leading him outside the power room to where they could hear each other speak.

"I think I know what's wrong with the reactor," Airomem said, avoiding his eyes, "and I'm going to need your help to fix it."

"But everyone says it's already destroyed," he said, brushing a bead of sweat away that raced down a strand of his dark curly hair. "Even Prometh said that."

"Well, I think he's wrong," she countered. "And if it is already destroyed, there is little harm we can do. Don't forget that you're still an apprentice, Abraham – there's much you still don't know about the reactor, information that I *do* know. And if you work with me, we might just save the entire ship."

"But how?" he asked, his eyebrows scrunching together.

"Not many people know this, Abraham, but there is a way that we can cause the reactor to reboot," she said. "Do you know the panel on the side wall, the one with the number keypad on it?"

"Yes," he said. "But I've never seen anyone interact with it. And I do know that if I touch it, that I'm no longer allowed to become a full engineer."

"Abraham, if you *don't* touch it, then there will be no full engineer position," stated Airomem. "But besides, you have my full permission. More than that, you have my command. Here's what I need you to do – I'm going to access some of the wiring on the other end of the wall, in the side room. When I give you the signal, I'll need you to enter in the code I give you and hold down the green button. Okay?"

"Sure, but are you sure you know what it will do? And what is the signal?"

"Abraham, I know *exactly* what it will do. Remember that afterwards," she said, and avoided his eyes again. "The signal will be when I flash my stun gun. You'll be able to see the glow through the window on the door to the room, but I'll be too busy to come into full sight. Understood, Abraham? From this point forward, you are under my strict orders to complete this action. No matter what anyone says, now the fate of the ship rests upon your shoulders."

"Understood," he said, straightening upwards. "And the code?"

"One four four zero," she said and asked him to repeat it. Then he reentered the power room and she walked over to the side room, looking at the small circular window set into the metal that Abraham would see the glow of her stun gun through.

Taking a breath, she cast a look back at the struggling engineers and the limping reactor. She looked at the door that led back into Lear territory, where her father would be waiting for her, where the Lear were preparing to depart, and where all she had ever known was locked inside.

Then she nodded to Abraham and placed a hand upon the cold metal, entering the room as the door clicked shut behind her. Her own breathing was the only sound as she was cut off from the power room, and she struggled to keep it under control, raising her chin to look outside the window at the stars beyond.

Completely alone, except for the eleven suits at her back.

Chapter 50

Airomem, you know where these keys belong. And you know the one other way to the other side of the ship, the way least traveled. Over the years, I've kept the suits on their place on the wall in case of an emergency such as this. And I inherited the books on how to operate them. Consider them my gift to you. Once you are ready to depart, enter the code on the back of this paper simultaneously into the two control panels, one the main in the power room, the other inside the room of suits. And beware, Airomem – should you lose physical contact with the ship once you depart, you do so forever. Heed the safety section with utmost care. I cannot stress this enough.

Airomem swallowed as she reread the note and turned back to face the suits. On the ground, in front of the first one, a book lay open – a book with three slips of paper marking pages. *Read me first* was scrawled upon the first in Prometh's handwriting, centered on the already open page. Turning the book over, she mouthed the title of the cover, *Ship Maintenance and Exo-repair Manual*, then returned to the parted page.

Mandatory Safety Precautions

Section 1: Any and all excursions outside the hull of the ship shall occur in teams with a bare minimum of three participants.

Airomem grimaced as she paused. She'd only read one rule, and already she was breaking it.

Section 2: Excursions must be approved by the ship council prior to departure, and must be supported by the mission team in the control room.

Rule two, broken.

Section 3: Proper gowning and tethering procedures listed below. Prior to departure, each item must be checked and approved by a minimum of two other authorized members of the excursion team.

A list appeared beneath the section, detailing the proper way to ensure the suit was airtight, check over the tool belt, and connect the user to the ship via a double coil of wire spooled around the left hip. From what she could read, at all times, the user was to be tethered to two different points in the ship and was to scuttle along the outside edge of the ship while reconnecting to different points as the spools of wire ran short.

There would be no one to check her list, but she could ensure that she at least followed half of rule three, which was better than none.

Then she turned the pages to the second bookmark, a section titled *Emergency Boarding Procedures*, her eyes widening and a nervous laugh growing in her throat with each passing line. After committing the section to memory, she flipped to the last bookmark, *Departure Procedures*.

Closing her eyes, she reviewed the steps line by line, making sure she missed no part of what she had to do. That every step was as clear as it could be, that she could identify no discrepancies, knowing that even a small deviation meant death.

Then she turned to the wall of suits, running her hand along them until she came to the empty space at the end, and selected the one adjacent. The suit itself was intuitive – the boots were built into the pants, internal straps tightening the fabric to her heels automatically as her toes found the inner edge, the soft compression cupping her arch. Then the sensation travelled up to her ankle, the fabric compressing inward, small wrinkles forming upon the surface from where the outermost layer was designed for thicker calves. Her hamstrings were next, then her hips and stomach, the suit forming more of a skin than an article of clothing up to her shoulders, then moving down each of her arms until even individual fingers were intimate with the material.

As the fabric tightened, she noticed the weight of the tools at her belt and the air tank on her back become alleviated, the suit itself taking on some of the downward force from each. Moving an experimental step forward, she felt the suit not only conform to her movements, but *contribute* to them – stretching in regions to accommodate the strain of her muscles, while constricting in others to remove weight.

Then she reached forward and took the helmet in her hands, a curved trapezoid constructed of glass and metal that fit atop her shoulders and interlocked into her back, and slid it over her head. With a *hiss,* the fabric latched onto the harder helmet, constricting around the rim of the helmet like a bottle cap over a glass bottle, until no path remained for air to escape. She took a breath and felt the suit respond, a slight breeze smelling of plastic wafting upwards from her collarbone.

Reaching towards her belt, she zipped open the container, checking that all the tools that she would need were present. Then she picked up the three keys she had left on the book before gowning and strode over to the cabinet her father had opened for her just before she had left the Lear. Taking each of the keys, she unlocked a separate lock, surprised at the dexterity of her fingers as she turned the keys, an uneasy feeling growing inside her at just how easy it had been to open the most secure vault on the ship as she recalled her father's words.

Back when it was used by those who wore the suits, only the most senior among them could remove it from its cabinet, and only for the greatest of emergencies.

As the last tumbler settled, the door creaked open and Airomem reached a careful hand inside, pulling the Omni-cutter from the box with a steady hand. It was heavier than it appeared, and she gripped it tight, afraid that it might somehow leap from her fingers. Holding it an arm's length away, she flipped upwards the red guard, and put her index finger over the trigger.

She would need to test it, of course. It should be simple – just to see if the machine reacted to her at all, but she hesitated. Dropping it at the wrong angle would tear a hole in the floor, while an accident could send it into the wall, ripping a hole that would suck her into space. But she pushed the thoughts away and slowly commanded her finger to move, her muscles tensing with each millimeter that the trigger twitched, its internal mechanism resisting her.

Then there was a click and her index shot backwards as the trigger gave way. Bright white light exploded into the room as she gripped the Omni-cutter, accompanied by a buzzing far louder than even the full power setting of her stun gun. She cursed and released the trigger, seeing stars, and realizing that Abraham would have seen the light as well. That he would think it was the signal, and if she didn't move now, he might come to investigate.

Her hand fell to her belt and she pulled the cord out of its winder, snapping the connector at its end to a railing intended for anchoring according to the procedure book. Then she rushed to the panel, the cord trailing behind her, and entered the numbers on the keypad with flying fingertips.

One.

Four.

Four.

Zero.

Go.

As she held the *go* button down, she flashed her stun gun repeatedly in case Abraham had missed the first light. She'd already been in the room for twenty minutes, and she prayed that another engineer had not distracted him from his post or noticed him touching the keypad.

She held her breath as seconds counted by, keeping one eye on the door's window and her other eye towards the stars. Then she saw a face appear in the window, Abraham's, his eyes wide as he saw her. She saw him shout and watched as his face turned down to look at the handle, then his hand pounded against the glass.

Then she heard the sound, a soft humming that filled the room, and felt her suit adjusting its grip upon her as the pressure dropped. More faces appeared at the window, red-faced engineers that pushed Abraham aside, their expressions confused. She raised a hand to them, and she signed two words.

My task.

Their looks turned to panic as she looked back out towards the stars and saw that the wall had begun to slide downwards moving until its lip was flush with the floor. She walked to the edge of the ship, the abyss surrounding her on every side, the cord spooled behind her, and the other end of the ship waiting.

And she gasped.

There, far to her right, there was an object among the stars, but far larger than any of them. What appeared to be a disk the size of her fist, a swirl of blues and greens, of color among the darkness.

The planet.

Their planet.
Home.

Chapter 51

For a full minute, she stared, her mouth slightly open, her toes just over the edge of the ship. And for the first time in her life, she felt *small*. The Lear had always stood above the other tribes, and she had stood above most of the Lear. She even felt more significant than the stars, tiny pinpricks of light that she sailed between, that she commanded to fall past her as she fed power to the engines.

But this, this was something completely alien to Airomem. Something that would soon change her life forever. Had *already* changed her life forever.

She drew a sharp breath as the lights above her flickered, and she peered over the edge into nothingness, extending her leg outwards and feeling the force of artificial gravity fall away with each passing inch. She'd have to crawl along the side of the ship, moving in a "U" shape over Agrarian territory, crossing atop the bridge, then moving over the Nectians, a process that would be extremely slow going. And she frowned when her eyes turned towards the bridge, and bright white light illuminated her mask.

There, she could see just the uppermost tip of the third part of the ship – a metallic dome that rose behind rectangular metal of the bridge. On the other side, the white light emanated in bursts and spasms, illuminating the edges of the bridge and casting long shadows on the rest of the ship. Sparks accompanied the glow – long, trailing arcs of light that showered the top of the bridge, danced on its roof, and dripped off its surface as remnants of artificial gravity took hold of them.

Her shoulders sank as she looked upon that, raising her hand to look at the fabric separating her from space, wondering if it was made to withstand sparks like that. She could be impaled before coming anywhere close to the Nectians, or the temperature could rise higher than she could stand. Effectively, the bridge was no longer a passageway but rather an obstacle.

Her muscles tightened as the precious seconds dragged by and she fought to come up with another solution. Perhaps crawling under the bridge would help, but she did not know the extent of construction in that region. She could try to leap through the sparks, but as Prometh had said, losing contact with the ship likely meant she would float away, then suffer a death of eventual suffocation or thirst. But if there was a guide wire, maybe, *maybe* she could make it.

And her heart fluttered as it came to a realization.

All she needed was a guide wire. And long ago, when the ship had lost power, Necti had connected the halves to bring back power. There, nearly as thick as her arm, and spanning the gap directly between the two halves, was the cord he had once laid. A cord coursing with enough electricity to char her to the bone, that waved loose in the void. And that might be her only way across.

She swallowed and looked left again, considering chancing her way among the sparks just as a thicker ball of molten metal sailed from the repair site and skidded along the bridge, slag spraying away as it made contact and rolling to a red hot stop just on the edge. Airomem watched as it cooled, imagining that it had struck her in the back and had melted the material of her suit away in fizzling hunks as it sought her skin. Her mouth dried and she turned back to the cable, her thoughts fighting adrenaline for control over her body.

It would be impossible to crawl across, she realized, since her tether was metallic. That meant that if the insulator covering was not sufficient, current could flow through her body back to the metal of the ship, short-circuiting the electronics. Shutting off all the lights and killing her in the process as she lit up like the filament of a light bulb.

She tapped her foot, eye spanning the gap, and wondering if she could make the jump with the tether behind her as a safety in case she missed the other side. But if she misjudged, even just slightly, she would come back into contact with the wire. And this time, the momentum could carry her around the wire, tangling her with the cause of her death, and leaving her crucified between the two parts of the ship for eternity.

Considering her options, she frowned. To the left, she would likely die from exposure and heat. To her right, the cable would fry her from the amperage through her tether. Either way, the risk was too high.

But there was one way, she realized, one way just short of death. One way that meant she followed *none* of the safety precautions provided to her by Prometh or the procedures. A way insane, yet the least so of her options.

The only way.

So she reached behind her, and unclipped the tether, watching it recoil back into the spindle on her belt.

She took two steps forward in a running start.

And Airomem jumped.

***

In the meeting room, Prometh spread the map he had showed Airomem against the tabletop, speaking with Praeter and Tela as they peered down at the track he had marked.

"When we give the command," he said, "the power room will cut all power to the ship, and our window will be opened. *All* the Lear must glide single file down the hallways, as fast as possible, before the Agrarians have a chance to react. The head of the group should be soldiers, ready to stun anything that moves, then soldiers should be peppered throughout the line to prevent disruptions and provide general aid. Then, the end of the line should be capped by soldiers, to ensure no one is left behind and that we are not attacked from the rear."

"And you expect our citizens to naturally know how to glide?" criticized Tela. "This is a pile-up waiting to happen. We'll be lucky if they make it down the first corridor without broken bones."

"He has a point, Prometh," added Praeter, clasping his hands together over the map. "We have difficulties enough mobilizing them now, and we still have gravity and light. This could easily lead to disaster."

"We've considered that," said Prometh, "and I currently have engineers cutting through the electrical lines of the main corridor. Within the hour, conditions within will replicate those during the final stages of evacuation, and nearly everyone will become accustomed to weightless travel. On your mark, Praeter, they will finish the conversion to weightlessness."

"We'll need to communicate the message first, then –" started Tela, but he stopped mid-sentence, his mouth still ajar.

"What is it?" pressed Praeter as Prometh's gaze followed Tela's, his voice filled with awe.

"We're here," he gasped, eyes glistening. "All my years, I have waited, and we have truly made it."

There, in the corner of the window, they could just see the shape of an orb among the black of space. Beyond it, they could see a star far larger than any of the others they had ever encountered, a mammoth among pinpricks, their new power room.

In unison, their chairs screeched backwards as they rushed to the window, similar to like when they were children and a classmate spotted an interesting constellation or star cluster.

"It's *enormous*," breathed Tela.

"It's beautiful," whispered Prometh, his gaze upon the star. "Absolutely stunning."

But Praeter's fingers were clenched on the edge of the window, and when he spoke, his voice came hard.

"What," he barked, "in the name of Dandelion 14, is *that*?"

Though he raised a finger, there was no need for him to indicate as a dark form passed in front of the star, the silhouette inching slowly along until it moved over the planet. It was a slim figure, bearing the shape of the suits from the power room, with its legs clasped around a cable that ran between the two sides of the ship.

"A hero," choked Prometh. "A hero, for the stories to remember."

Chapter 52

Airomem panted as she inched across the power line, every one of her movements creating reverberations that whipped down the line and back, threatening to unbalance her and cast her into space. She inched her hands forward, careful to maintain contact with the cord, and gripped tight each time a particularly violent vibration raced towards her. Then she shimmied her legs upwards, all too aware of the electrical hum trapped underneath her as her shins glided against the insulation. Then she repeated the process, her eyes glued to the other end of the ship to prevent her pupils from being lost in the blackness below, and curses streaming from her clenched jaw.

Just moments before, she had made the leap, crossing from the solid metal of the ship to the power cable, suspended in space for what felt like years. Her hands had been extended outwards until her fingertips grazed the cable and she latched on, gripping fast as her legs streamed behind. Then they arced forwards as the wire became taut under her momentum, her center of gravity swinging as she fought for control. The full load of her momentum snapped against her shoulders as they bore the tension of her swinging body until she pulled herself tight along the wire. For a moment she had paused, trembling, knowing that without the tether, one wrong move could mean death.

And now, she was slowly approaching the other end of the ship, each movement taking her closer to the midpoint. Images flashed through her mind of space debris, smaller versions of *The Hand of God* that would punch holes in her faster than she would be able to react. Thoughts that perhaps the wire was not secured tightly on the other side, and that she might yank it free. Or that the old oxygen tank on her back might have become defective through years without use, and that it might run out prematurely.

But with each pull against the cable, she pushed these thoughts away, forcing herself to concentrate on the next foot forward, then the next steps of her plan. And praying that she had not forgotten any of the steps in the procedures.

After ten minutes, she was halfway and she paused from her suspended position to look beyond the ship. There, reflected in the glass of her helmet was the new planet, with the burning star just beyond, its light illuminating her red hair. After hundreds of years, this was their final destination. And she couldn't help but wonder what they had left behind, and if this new world would prove any better.

By twenty minutes, she was three-quarters of the way there. And by twenty-five, the other end of the ship was ten feet away, and waiting. She would have to jump, clearing the last remaining gap to avoid the same short circuit problem that she had encountered earlier. But now, instead of her feet firm on the ground, she had only a swaying cable, and the closest handhold was thirty feet away, a tethering point just visible to the left of one of the windows.

The ship shuddered as she hesitated, and she cast a nervous glance to beyond the bridge, where the white light intensified temporarily. The longer that she waited, the more of a chance there was for something to go wrong, something she had absolutely no power to predict.

Gritting her teeth, she extended her arms forward as she arched her back. She hung there for an instant, like a string pulled tight and ready to snap, quivering under the tension. And then she launched herself forward, opening her arms wide as she drifted through space, her expression turning to horror as she streaked off target.

Halfway across the tethering point was now several feet beneath her, with the lip of the ship falling at the same pace. By the time she reached it, it would be too far to grip with her hands, and her toes would just barely graze the metal plating. She drew in a sharp breath as she saw the result of her trajectory, a beeline between two stars countless miles away, and felt adrenaline rushing just under the surface of her skin as the realization that not only would she be doomed if she missed, but so too would the Nectians.

In desperation, her hand flew to her belt where it found the coiled tether, and she whipped it towards its contact point. It sailed past the target, slamming into the side of the ship instead and skittering away, then retracting back to her side as the spindle drew it back in. She aimed a second throw, but it was too late, as the angle of opportunity for the opened hook to catch had closed, and she was now directly over the ship, the smooth top surface too flawless for her hook to catch. Eddies of the ship's artificial gravity below caught hold of her and she started to fall face first, her emotions flaring as she crashed against the metal and bounced back upwards, her fingers scrabbling along the surface but finding no purchase.

She slammed downwards again once more, skidding across the slick metal, turning a full circle as she started to slow. Ahead, the edge approached, but she was still moving too fast, the fabric of her gloves doing little to reduce her speed, now just above a jogging pace. Then the metal fell away once more, and the ship began to depart, leaving her behind in the void.

But there, on the flank of the ship and just at her eye level, was the mirror of the tether point she had tried to connect moments before. And as she drifted away, the gap between her and the ship growing larger with each second, she cocked her arm backwards for one more throw and let the hook fly, watching as it struck metal and danced around the contact.

Chapter 53

There's no sound in space – meaning that the tether was silent as it soared. The click Airomem waited for was purely imagined, and she had no way of knowing whether the connection was successful. But she could see the hook lodged into place, and at her belt, the wire started to spool away from her, the umbilical cord back to the ship and her sole chance of survival.

Further and further, she travelled, too scared to move and dislodge the hook, her form rigid as it waited for the wire to run out, her hip bone registering a slight vibration with each full revolution of the spindle. And in that moment, her rotation carried her around to face the planet, now slightly larger than the last time she had looked at it. The planet where she would lead her people – the Lear *and* the Nectians. The planet that was the culmination of Dandelion 14, that she and countless others had spent their entire lives tending to the power room to reach.

At that moment, she knew that if the tether connection broke away, she would become a slave to the planet's gravity, pulled in until she crashed down long after her death. Inferior to its will.

So she squared her shoulders, glaring down her nose at the new world. The new world that belonged to her. And she raised her chin, just as the tether caught and whipped her into a spin, the breath nearly knocked out of her by the jerking motion. Then, at her belt, she felt the vibration again as the tether started to retract.

Click, one revolution of the spindle, drawing her closer to the ship.

Click came the second rotation, followed by a third, then a fourth, the frequency increasing with each vibration as she accelerated. She stretched out her hands, releasing a small sigh of relief just as they made contact with the metal, her fingers clutching around a handhold, the tether at her belt still pulling with a slight tension. Breathing hard as she realized she had made it to the other side, and step one was complete.

She blinked, looking left and right down the row of windows, her toes extending just over the glass of one below her. And, consulting her memory, she tried to determine where the nearest collection of apartments would be. Most likely left, she realized, though there would be some on the right as well, though about twice as far away.

Leaving her tether in place, she crawled downwards until the window was eye level, and looked inside.

Directly in front of her were farms, farms that were disturbingly empty. A few figures walked in the distance, but there on the left, just as she had predicted, was a hallway that led a row of apartments branching away from the end of the farms. Taking care to ensure at least one of her hands always firmly grasped part of the ship, she started scuttling over the outer edge, watching as the hallway approached with each passing window. Then she breached the internal wall, and there was a stretch twice as long before the next window began.

In moments, she was in front of it, one hand against the glass, squinting to look through, a triumphant smile flashing across her face as she recognized the structure of some of the ship's smaller style of apartments characterized by the wall-mounted bed, receded shelving, and sliding door closet.

And in this one, there was even an occupant – a child whose eyes bugged out as he stared at her, held frozen in place, strands of his dark hair sticking up in the back as if they too were astonished. She raised her hand in a wave, and slack-jawed, he slowly raised his own, opening and closing his fingers as if he couldn't remember how they worked. Then she moved to the next window, peering inside to see the door closed and the room vacant.

Thinking back to a short time before, she recalled what the procedures book had said, in the *Emergency Boarding Procedures* section.

Upon designing the ship, special precaution was taken to limit the points at which people and objects could enter and exit. These points form a natural weakness in the hull, as well as a general

*opportunity for problems to arrive, and as such were limited to two –
one on each end of the ship.*

*However, this design possesses faults: it does not consider
emergencies that may occur to maintenance workers on distant areas
of the ship, the potential for the exits to become inoperable, and other
unforeseeable circumstances. As such, the following section is
provided as a guide in absolute emergencies, and should be used only
as the very last resort in the most dire of situations. For this method to
even be considered, no fewer than three hundred lives should be at
risk, and the full council must make a unanimous emergency vote.*

This certainly qualified as the most dire of situations, Airomem
decided, and she began checking the room inside for the aspects
denoted by the next section of the procedures.

*First, the target room should be small and must have a closed
door. Clutter within should be kept to a minimum, and there should be
no occupants present. The window must not be damaged, and there
should be no objects of high value in the room, including any sort of
ship controls. Water vessels should not be present if possible, nor any
sealed containers.*

Continuing to scan the contents, Airomem nodded and moved
on to the next section.

*When designing windows for the ship, layers of ultra-strong
plastic were interlaid between the transparent ceramic compounds,
allowing for a barrier to retain the pressure of the ship even if the
window should shatter. As you prepare to make your incision, be sure
to puncture these internal layers, and prepare for the event of
shattered glass. Make the incision short, keep tight hold of your cutting
tool, and ensure your body is clear of potential fractures and
pressurized gas. Utmost caution is to be used, and remember – this
method is not simply a last resort due to the damage to the ship, but at
the high potential for injury or death of the technician.*

Swallowing, Airomem's hand fell to her tool belt where she
had stored the Omni-cutter, and she held it as far as possible away
from her, inching along the side of the ship until only its tip brushed
the corner of the window. Pulling the trigger, she watched as the white
spark danced at the edges of the prongs, and her finger hovered over a

second button on the side of the tool. The button, as she had read in the procedures, would force the arc outwards in a short parabola, stripping away anything in its path.

She paused, her grip growing tighter on both the tool and her handhold, her teeth clenched, her second tether secured moments before to a point just a few yards away. And with a sharp breath, her finger danced forward, pushing the button inward as the arc leapt away from the prongs and rushed into the waiting glass.

Chapter 54

It was the planet that drove me back into action.

Until this point, talk of departure from the ship had simply been talk. In a way, it was like the stories – I knew them to be true, but they still existed just beyond my own experience. I walked the same halls as they had occurred, yet they were removed. Facts lacking physical sustenance, like a smell without a taste.

But seeing the planet made me realize that we *were* actually leaving, that it was an event and not only a story, as the realization shifting from the informational part of my brain to the tangible part with a *clunk*.

"It's incredible," Hannah had breathed when she had seen it through the window, the light reflected off of it playing across her face.

"It's a countdown," I'd responded, my knees wobbling as I stood, the slim portions of food and water sapping away at my strength.

Each day, the light under our door grew dark, and Nean's voice had floated through the clamoring of those outside.

"Rations!" he shouted to those outside. "Rations they fed us while we were hungry, instead of actual meals! Instead of the feasts that you have now! And now, we shall feed them rations, so that they can experience what they put us through!"

Then scraps of food would be forced through the crack under the door, mixed with water to form a sludge of the unwanted bits of vegetables, the hard stems and rotting parts that others had cast away.

At first, I'd recoiled in disgust against the far wall, my nose pinched as the smell wafted from the pile into the room. But then the thirst had begun, and I'd soaked a shirt I had found in the closet in the mound, then squeezed the sour liquid into my mouth. And eventually, I started picking through the bits of sustenance, my standards decreasing with each passing hour and the intensifying growls of my stomach, minimizing my energy to preserve my strength.

But now, with the planet still shining in Hannah's eyes, energy started flushing back to my body and mind. And casting my eyes around the room, I stopped searching for a way to escape.

Instead, I remembered the way Airomem had fended off the horde of gardeners as I had fallen down, helpless from Nean's strike from behind. How Tom had blocked me from the blow of the Esuri's knife, and how I had felt when I had brought the gravity crashing down upon the Agrarians and Aquarians.

So I searched for a way to fight.

In general, the ship was engineered in ways to make it difficult to detach furniture and objects – but remembering Airomem's story of Sitient sitting upon his couch throne, as well as bits and pieces of junk that had accrued over the centuries, I knew it was possible. I rummaged through the closet, finding only smooth wall, bundles of clothes, and a few shoes. Then I tried the bed, but it extended as a single shelf, its interface seamless with the wall with no parts that could be removed. The paneling around the window also refused to budge, though I applied far less effort in trying to remove it, fearful of opening a hole into the outside.

But finally, I found something – something that, while not perfect, would suffice.

The vent set into the wall above us.

Standing on the bed, I stared at it, examining the vertical bars which split the flow of air as it traveled outwards. Placing my hand against them, I pushed, feeling them barely flex inwards under my strength. Beneath me, Hannah stared upwards, watching as I rocked the vent back and forth in place, gaining little ground in actually removing it.

"Try this," she said after a few minutes, handing me up a sock. "Wrap it around one of the bars, and try to pull it free."

So I wove the fabric between the metal and yanked, pulling one of the bars outwards such that it bent in the middle. Pushing it back in, I repeated the action, the center of the grate heating up with each flex until it snapped, the sock flying loose so suddenly, I nearly toppled off the bed. The two halves of the thin bar now stretched away from the vent, their ends jagged, and with several more cycles, they broke at the base to come free.

Two sharp points of metal, each about as long as my middle finger, and about a tenth as thick. After a few more minutes, I had broken away another bar to make four, and jumped off the bed, handing two of them to Hannah.

"Our only chance," I said, holding one of the miniature spears up, "is to catch them by surprise if they open the door, and to make a rush for the exit before they recover."

"You do realize," she responded, her face skeptical though she clutched the rods, "that fighting kitchen knives with these is suicide."

"No, Hannah," I answered, pointing to the floor, "this, *staying on this ship*, is suicide."

Chapter 55

The current of air from the freshly cut hole was less than Airomem had expected.

Instead of an explosion it was like a tiny faucet – a thin, spindling tube of air visible by dust jetting out through the hole into space, emptying the apartment in front of her.

Like all doors on the ship, the one in front of her had sealed itself as the pressure fell – a precaution that prevented a single hole from taking down vast swaths of the ship. From her position, she could see that the crack underneath had turned solid, the frame itself swelling to form a barrier, and though she could not yet touch it to test, that lock would be held fast. Until pressure was restored, the room would remain that way – sealed away and preventing any more of the precious air from escaping.

She clung to the side of the ship as she waited, watching the flow slow and thin, until only a trickle exited that she could just barely sense through her glove. And taking the Omni-cutter once more, she placed it up against the hole and let the spark fly out to meet the glass.

The plasma curve traced through glass quicker than she expected as the arc eroded the material, her hand gliding along the outer edge with a speed that attested to the sheer power of the Omni-cutter. In seconds, she had cut away nearly three-quarters of a hole the size of her shoulders, and she slowed down at the last portion, careful to make sure the connecting cut was clean and that there would be no rough edges, or a jagged snap that might cause cracks to spider web across the surface.

Ever so gently, she completed the circle, the white light flashing as it cut through the final finger length, then inch, then sliver. Catching the outside eddies of the ship's gravity field, the circle cutout of the window fell the quarter of an inch of a gap the Omni-cutter had left behind in slow motion, then began to tip inwards.

Airomem's hand shot out and caught it just before it fell, the sharp edge biting through her gloves. And she breathed a sigh of relief as she felt the ship's gravity take hold of her fingers through the hole and she experienced the sensation of becoming grounded once more.

And slowly, without releasing the glass or her tethers, she placed her right foot through the hole, then her left, so that she sat scrunched half inside and half outside the ship, the gravity gradient making her insides feel imbalanced. Then she slid the remainder of the way, her feet connecting with the floor in a silence that should have left a *thud* had air been present, and turned to glance back into space. Space that had nearly claimed her, but she, Airomem, princess of the Lear, had conquered.

It took another few minutes to place the window back over the hole, and to pull the temporary repair kit from her utility belt. Two strips of tape held the window in place as she applied a sealant around the edge, one designed to stop any microcracks from propagating as well as reduce airflow through microscopic channels, the thick yellow putty conforming to the shape of the gap. Then the remainder of the job was a layer of tape over the gap, an amount that seemed to Airomem like far too little but would at least temporarily hold, according to the procedures. She could feel wire mesh in between the polymer layers, the adhesive itself so strong that she gave up on removing a piece that had attached itself to her gloves and now dangled from her index finger, and the black finish obscuring the yellow underneath.

She tested it, placing a palm against the window and pushing outwards, feeling the circle bulge slightly into space but hold tight. Then she turned back to the door, locked under the pressure differential, and considered her next steps.

It would be easiest to simply slice through it with the Omni-cutter, making a hole just as she had with the window. Her fingers twitched, greedy to use the instrument again to save time, her fear forgotten after her first use. But she paused, looking behind her at the patch. Cutting through the door might be a shortcut, but if the patch gave way due to a quick pressure change, then she could potentially lock down an entire portion of the ship. And the rapid decrease in pressure for anyone not wearing a suit in the nearby hallways would mean near instant death.

So instead, she placed the Omni-cutter back into her tool pouch and reached around to her back where her air tanks connected to the rest of the suit. There, just under the last of the vertebrae in her neck, she felt the valve that was used to quickly replace air tanks in the event of a longer than usual maintenance project. And remembering the instructions in the procedure book, she gently turned the knob until she could just barely hear a *hiss*. Too much, and the safety would kick in and close the air pathway to the suit. Too little, and she would be waiting for hours for the room to fill with air.

As the hissing continued, she paced, her eyes flicking back towards the patch every thirty seconds. And she thought about her next moves – first to find Elliott and Ruth, then to rescue Horatius, then to lead the charge back to the bridge. Saving all who would follow, and leaving those who would embrace death to their fate.

As her pacing quickened, the hissing slowed until it became just barely audible, then stopped entirely. Raising both hands in front of her, she clapped, a smile breaking across her face as she heard the sound and knew that pressure had been restored. Her heart quickened as she placed two hands against the door, prepared to sling it open, ready to enter as the first person who had traveled from end to end on the ship since Necti, both through internal and external means. Her chin raised of its own accord, and her stance widened, prepared to make a strong reemergence.

She shoved, putting all her weight behind her palms.

In front of her, the door rattled, the latch caught. The pressure in the room was not quite high enough to completely release the safety mechanism, though her air supply was depleted.

And cursing, she reached back to her belt, pulling back out the Omni-cutter, the white arc illuminating her face as she began to slice through the metal, cursing again as pressure was restored and she realized the lock had jammed.

Chapter 56

The hallway was nearly empty when she kicked through the door, an oval portion of it just a few inches shorter than her falling forward with a ringing *clang* as it struck the floor, skidding forward under its own momentum until it rammed against the opposite wall. Only one set of eyes watched her as she stepped outwards, the Omni-cutter still emitting its white arc, her suit still covering every inch of her body. Behind her, there was a *click* and the door swung open, the lock releasing as reverberations from the falling metal shook it loose. And though the window bulged out slightly more than usual, the tape, mesh, and putty combination held. Hopefully, for at least a few more hours – that was all she needed.

Across the hall, the lone figure stared as she reached a hand around to release the clasp that held her helmet in place, shaking her hair out as she set it on the floor. His eyes widened as he recognized her, then widened further as they looked past her to the hole in the window, then to the other end of the ship, and coming to rest on the Omni-cutter just as she shut it off.

"Hello, Tom," she said, standing atop the fallen door to be only a head shorter than him. "Ready to save Horatius again?"

"Of course," his lumbering voice responded, a slow smile uplifting the words. "But what is that? Stun gun?"

He pointed towards the Omni-cutter, and Airomem raised it upwards for him to get a closer look.

"Just as you are the strongest man on this side of the ship, this is now the sharpest knife. There is little, if anything, it cannot cut."

Tom reached a hand forward, his eyes sparkling, but Airomem retracted her arm, speaking, "And because it is the sharpest, it's also the most dangerous. It should only be used when absolutely necessary, and I fear now is one of those times. Do you know where Ruth is, Tom? Can you take me to her?"

"Her, yes. Horatius, no."

"Then let's start moving," said Airomem, following Tom as he began to walk towards the exit of the corridor. "I fear our time already runs short. And if we are to depart, we must make haste."

"Depart?" asked Tom, and Airomem gestured back to towards the window.

"To our new home, Tom. To the planet that you see out there, the purpose of our long journey."

"But this Tom's home," he answered, confusion crossing his face. "Here, the ship."

"Your *old* home, Tom. This one is falling apart, but the one that we are going to, that one is full of life and promise."

Then they broke out of the corridor and into the farmland beyond, the overhead lights significantly dimmer than just a few days before, the soil harder under her feet from lack of maintenance. At the far edge, a crowd milled, clustered around the entrance to another corridor, their voices melding together into a buzz by the time they reached her ears. And from the tip of the crowd, just beneath the doorframe, she could see the glint of knives behind a barricade of furniture.

Halfway across the fields, she heard a scream that differentiated itself from the crowd, one that emanated from a small figure that rushed across the earth towards her, her haste so great that flecks of soil flew into the air behind her.

"Airomem!" shouted Ruth, barreling into her. "I knew you'd come! I *knew* it! There, in that corridor, they have my mother and Horatius! We have to save them!"

Behind Ruth, the crowd began to turn around, the words stopping in their throats as their eyes traveled from her face to her suit. Awe took hold of them in a wave, young and old, big and small, literate and illiterate. Ruth let go of Airomem and moved to her right, while Tom stood at her left, their heights forming a downward slant.

And when the silence was so thick that it felt impossible to breach, Airomem bent down and gathered a handful of soil from the ground at her feet and held it high in the air, allowing a trickle of it to pass through her fingers like water.

"One thousand years ago!" she shouted as the dirt fell. "One thousand years ago, our ancestors departed upon a journey for new life! A journey that took them far from what they called home in search for another. And today, we embark on a similar journey."

She took a step forward towards the crowd and gathered another handful of soil.

"Today, we complete our voyage among the stars! We remember that this is but a step along our path, that the ship itself is not a destination but a bridge into the future of us all. To the planet you see outside the windows, a place where the lights shall never dim, where the plants shall grow, and the water plentiful. Where all shall be fed, and none greater than their neighbor. And we shall bring the dirt our ancestors left us, our only true piece of their home that we have left, and mix it with the soil we find ahead. As a remembrance of the past, the seeds that shall grow the future."

Then she let the handful of dirt fall in front of her, the clump thudding against the edge of a shovel and spreading out in all directions.

"I will not force you to follow me. I give you the option to choose, but I warn you, just as a plant with no water withers and dies, so too will this ship. Already you have seen the signs that all is *not* as it once was, that you no longer can do what you have always done and survive. So I charge you this: wait here for death or spring forward for life! And I, Airomem, your chief and your equal, shall lead you there!"

The clapping started in the back, closest to the barricaded entrance, Elliott's hands coming together in short powerful strokes where he stood. Dozens of others joined in, a small peppering interspersed in the masses, but with heart.

But then the jeers started from those who had been listening behind the barricade, and the crowd erupted in response, their faces red as they shouted and hands moving in a flurry of motion, the thunderous applause drowning out all other sound.

Airomem brushed the earth from her hands as she walked towards them, glimpsing the planet through a window in the corner of her eye as she did so, and whispering in a voice that stood no chance against the roar.

"To dust we shall return."

Chapter 57

Ruth, Tom, and Elliott were gathered around Airomem as she drew in the dirt with the toe of her shoe, recreating the corridor where Horatius and Hannah were trapped.

"It bends a little there," said Ruth, bending over and adding an arc to a previously straight line. "And here there is a closet."

"Other than that, it's correct," said Elliott, and Tom nodded. "There are only two entrances, as you've drawn, both barricaded and defended by knives. Even if we could get past the barricade, we'd be cut to pieces. If they have the spine."

"From what you have told me, they have the food rations holed up in there as well," said Airomem, and she thought back to the wars between the Agrarians and the Aquarians. "Men are capable of much more evil than you would anticipate when they are defending their stomachs, and much more good when defending their hearts."

"Good or evil, it's still a barrier," said Elliott. "Negotiations are failing – I believe they are holding on to Horatius and Hannah to exchange for food in the future, as well as to ensure their own safety. But even more so, I fear it is an attempt at petty revenge for Segni's death, in which case, I fear for the life of my wife."

"These are the same people who assaulted me," said Airomem through clenched teeth, then pointed to the rooms she had drawn in the dirt. "We are past the point of negotiation. Now, where are they keeping them? And where are they keeping the food?"

Elliott turned and waved to a woman who had been waiting twenty feet away, her gaze turned towards the crowd still milling at the entrance of the corridor. With a start, she walked over, long bags under her eyes and scratches on her shins.

"Airomem, this is Angie; you may recognize her from your time in the gardens," said Elliott. "Angie was asleep in her bed in the corridor when the rest of the gardeners moved the food and hostages inside, and woke up to the current barricade situation. She escaped by crawling through the barricade – if you can call it an escape. Nean was all too happy to have one less mouth to feed. They practically drove Angie out."

"I see," said Airomem as Angie stood opposite her, her lip trembling, her face flushed red as a quick flash of recognition spread across Airomem's own expression. As she remembered that face from when she had fought off the gardeners with her dual stun guns, not participating in the mob but not helping Airomem and Horatius either. But standing to the side, watching and following. And certainly not asleep during the ordeal.

Airomem met her eyes and spoke slowly, her voice portraying no emotion.

"Quite unfortunate for you, Angie, though it is good you escaped. But now that you are here, that is all behind us. All that matters is what lies ahead. Can you point out on our map everything you know about inside the corridor?"

"Here," said Angie, her own voice with a slight warble and gesturing at the second room on the outer edge of the corridor, one that faced the stars, "is where they are keeping Horatius. And here," she pointed opposite, to a room that receded inside the ship so that it shared a wall with the edge of the gardens, "is where they are keeping the majority of food supplies. They keep that door shut tight, and distribute food from there twice a day."

"And the times that they open the doors?"

"Morning and night for food, and they don't really open the other ones. Nean wants to ensure there is no chance for escape."

"Thank you, Angie," Airomem said as the other woman looked down. "Your actions will help determine the fate of the ship."

"I know," she whispered, eyes watering.

"When we arrive," said Airomem, "you'll be remembered for this crucial information, as the reason why Horatius and Hannah were freed. If you remember anything else, Angie, do not hesitate to tell us. For now, that's all we needed, but we may have more questions later."

"Thank you, Airomem," she said, departing. "Thank you."

"Now," said Airomem, ignoring Elliott's questioning look, "we have two objectives. One, to rescue the hostages. And second, because everyone here looks so famished, is to recover much of your food. I'd rather everyone had energy for the next few hours. Here is what we are going to do."

Crouching down, she illustrated the plan in the dirt, drawing two lines to show the proposed movement. Elliott shook his head when she finished, speaking.

"The things you have shown us that are possible, things I never would have dreamed of, have changed everything."

"Let's hope," she said. "In one hour, we will act. That should give us enough time to prepare. During that time, Elliott, I need you to make it clear to your people to prepare to evacuate. Pair them up, ensure that your elderly and young have a strong counterpart. They should only bring the most *essential* of items. In addition, have your porters bring as much water as possible. Warn them that at any moment, the power may cut, and should that happen, they should reconvene *just outside* the entrance to the bridge. Make it clear that they should not enter that hallway without us, as it could mean death. And make it clear that anyone who waits here will be left behind. Be back here quickly, so we can start negations."

"Of course, we will start immediately. I thought you said we were finished with negotiations?"

"We are. I just need you to hold Nean's attention. Work some insults into them, get him and his people flustered. Tom?"

"Yes?" responded Tom, who had otherwise been silent, his eyes slightly narrowed as he tried to make sense of the diagram in the earth.

"Are you feeling strong today?"

"Tom always feels strong," he said, stretching his arms in front of him and looking down them.

"Good," said Airomem, holding her own arm next to his, the suit contrasting skin. "We're going to need it."

Chapter 58

"I've come again to negotiate!" shouted Elliott through the barrier, a crowd milling behind him. They were those who had finished packing first and were ready to evacuate, only ten percent of those who had been present earlier, but clustered directly around the corridor entrance. In their cone-like formation, and with each of them generating a nonstop high volume chatter as Elliott had instructed, it would appear to Nean as if their ranks had not diminished.

"Look who's come crying back to my doorstep," came a sneer through the barrier as Nean's face appeared between two stacked chairs. "Are you ready to recognize your true chief? Turn yourself over, Elliott, and only then will we free you and your wife – after six weeks!"

"Can't do that, Nean," responded Elliott. "But what I *can* do is offer you and Vaca positions as vice coordinators of the council – each of your votes would count as half of my own. And to do this, you would only need to serve one week in our captivity for your crimes."

"What?" hissed Nean through the gap. "I have the food, Elliott! And unless you kneel before your rightful chief, you'll die of hunger!"

Elliott shrugged, laughing, and responded, "Did you really think that the council didn't squirrel away our own food, Nean? Why do you think we had such shortages – we saved it for an event like this!" He pulled a strawberry from his pocket, the *last* strawberry that had been found in a forgotten corner of the storerooms, and took a bite. "I bet Segni would have loved this one. We always did keep the best for ourselves, of course."

Spittle flew from Nean's mouth as he shouted, flecks nearly making their way through the barrier, "I still have your wife, Elliott! I still have her, and I could kill her before your eyes!" Then he turned to where his own crowd was amassed and shouted, "Do you hear that? Just as I have always said, they kept you hungry! *They* are the traitors!"

His hands gripped a chair in front of him, and he shook the barrier, others from behind him rushing to join in generating the *clack*ing sound that reverberated around the garden. From Elliott's prior instruction, his own crowd surged to take hold of the barrier, shaking the furniture just as hard, their screams slamming through the holes where they met the mutineers ten feet beyond.

Then they started propelling handfuls of mud along with their voices, and the inside retaliated with half rotten food. Elliott stepped back to watch, remembering the words he had said to the crowd who now only half faked their anger.

Make noise, engage them, cover them in mud. But make no attempts to take apart the barrier or enter.

And under his breath, as he watched the conflict escalate, Elliott muttered, "Make all haste, Airomem. Your window is open."

***

Five porters trotted behind Airomem as she jogged along the outside wall of the gardens, keeping an eye at her feet where she rushed across measurements made in the earth every ten steps. Behind them, they pulled two carts each, the large wheels leaving trailing grooves in their wake, and the insides empty except for two packed to the brim with supplies from the doctors.

"Here!" she shouted as she came to an arrow that pointed directly into the flat metal wall and came to a stop. "Now, here's the plan. Just on the other side of this wall is where their food is stored – according to Angie, it's piled high and fills nearly the entire room. We only want the food in the back, understood? And just enough to fill those carts, nothing more."

They nodded, and Airomem spoke again. "I'm going to need your help breaking in. I can't do it alone. Get ready, and remember, stay quiet!"

"Can't break the wall," said one of the porters, rolling his eyes. "Manny there has tried many times; had to send him to the doctors after he broke his fist instead over a bet."

"I almost broke through!" exclaimed another porter, presumably Manny, and pointing a suspiciously crooked finger at the first. "And if I did, we wouldn't have to open the door anymore go into the main hall."

"You *dented* it, Manny; there's a difference," smirked the first.

"Well, maybe it's time I tried again and showed you up!" shouted Manny, his face red, but Airomem pushed back against his chest as he tried to move forward, her heels digging into the mud as he looked down in surprise.

"*No*," she said, feeling the suit stiffen as it took on his weight, "I'll be breaking through the wall. All you have to do is help me move it. *Quietly.*"

"Oh, she's going to show you up, Manny!" said the other porter, laughing, until Airomem glared at him.

"Enough," she said. "We don't have time for this."

And taking the Omni-cutter, she started cutting the wall, the porters backing away as the metal fizzed. She made an arc as high as she could reach, then cut straight lines downwards, completing the process with a horizontal line across the bottom. Then she pushed the right side of the arched cutout, the metal grinding as it pivoted on its center, exposing one edge while the other tucked inwards.

"Ready?" she said, the porters transfixed. "Careful, the edges are sharp."

"Told you so, Manny," said the one from earlier and moved forward, grabbing a section of the wall. Manny grasped the bottom and Airomem stepped sideways to let the others through. Together, they wriggled the wall away to expose a foot of space on the inside, then another metal barrier. A few bundles of wire ran bolted to the inner wall, and Airomem pushed them aside as she held her ear to the inner wall, holding her breath as she waited for any noise to break the silence. But none came, and she started cutting again, making the same arcs, though slightly smaller, quicker this time to minimize the amount of white glow showing on the other side of the wall, and taking care to avoid wires.

She stepped back and held a finger to her lips as the porters moved in, twisting the door away to reveal stacks of sacks holding produce piled to the ceiling.

"Remember, only the back layers so they can't tell any is missing," she whispered. "No talking. If the door opens on the other side, stop working until it closes again. When you're finished, take two carts back to Elliott to ration out, then start taking the rest to the bridge. Bring any belongings you want to take on the journey with you. Wait there; we will join you shortly."

She watched them start to load the carts until she was satisfied with their noise level and progress, then turned to leave, running along the edge of the wall. The roar of noise that Elliott had started grew louder with each step, and she skirted the crowd when she arrived, then continued running. Her breath came smoothly – even in running, the suit removed most of the effort.

With a quick gasp of realization, she rushed to the window, flashing her stun gun furiously. But there was no response this time, with the Lear preparing for departure, and she cursed under her breath.

Back in the power room were the other suits just like the one she was wearing, suits that could be invaluable on the new planet. Suits whose abilities had been long forgotten, and now hung on the wall as memories of a past age, and were left untouched out of reverence and preservation.

And now would have been left behind for eternity to continue traveling among the stars.

Chapter 59

"Okay, Tom," said Airomem as she arrived at the section of wall where he waited. "On the other side of this wall is an apartment room. One room over from that is where they are keeping Horatius and Hannah. The problem is, we don't know what is in the first apartment, and we are going to have to move through it. So once we break in, I'm going to need you to guard the door. And if there is anyone inside, you'll need to keep them from getting help."

"You want Tom to hurt them?"

"No, all you have to do is block the door and keep them quiet. As long as it stays shut, we should be okay. Now, ready?"

"Ready."

With a careful hand, she began to slice with the Omni-cutter – here, she was far closer to the windows than she had been earlier, and under no circumstances did she want an accidental gash to expose the entire farmland to space.

Unlike earlier, she cut away a large section of the wall, comprised of rectangles six feet wide and as tall as she could reach, exposing the interior wall. With each completion, Tom helped her lift and set aside the rectangle blocks, their movements considerably more strained than the other porters due to the increase in size.

"You as strong as Tom!" he exclaimed after the second one, when beads of sweat appeared thick on his forehead.

"Yes, but I'm cheating," she said, gesturing at her suit.

Several minutes later, the wall lay bare, and she walked along its edge, searching the metal. Then, she stopped, her fingers parting two bundles of wires, and her expression triumphant.

There, along the smooth metal, were a set of fasteners. A rectangle of them, several feet apart, which would be holding a piece of furniture in place on the other side within the apartment. In this case, a wardrobe or closet, whose back was flush with the inner wall.

"Tom, have you ever heard of the bogeyman?" she asked, clearing away more wires.

"The who?"

"The bogeyman. He hides in closets and comes out at night to scare children. It's just a story."

"No bogeyman on this side of the ship," he answered, his voice resolute.

"That's where you're wrong," she said, and started to cut. "I'm going to need you to be our bogeyman. And this is your closet."

Chapter 60

In all of Dandelion 14's known history on Horatius' side of the ship, no one had jumped between walls. No one had found themselves in a room where they should not physically belong, nor had discovered passageways unknown to the vast majority of the ship. And certainly, no one had ever *created* such a passageway.

Until now.

The three inhabitants of the apartment were playing carrots – a game left over from before the rationing days. The premise was simple – the players gathered in a circle, and the initiator produced a full carrot. He or she then took a single bite from anywhere on the carrot's surface, and then would pass the carrot to their right. The next player would then continue, taking another bite at their own discretion, another piece of the morsel to be eliminated. They too would pass it to their right, and the circle would continue, up until the final play could finish the remainder of the vegetable in one large bite.

It was at the very end of the game when the abnormally large figure slipped from the closet without a sound, like a shadow bouncing along the wall. And it was the player who had just shoved an entire carrot into his mouth whose eyes widened as he saw him, trying to shout in terror as the morsel of food only jammed itself deeper into his throat and caused him to gag.

"Urllllfll!" he shouted as the players around him laughed, and the one closest to him, known as a "shoveler" in cases such as these, whacked him on the back. "Urlllfl!"

"C'mon, Esau, spit it out, spit it out," said the player next to him. "We wouldn't want you to choke now, not at the beginning of the feasts!"

The player raised a hand, gesturing towards the dark figure as the crowd of four laughed again. But they didn't turn around. They didn't have to, because as the figure crossed to the door in two strides, all the clues they needed were provided when it closed with a soft *click*.

"The closet!" Esau finally managed, the chewed bits of carrot exploding from his mouth over the other players as they whipped around, already far too late, their voices stuttering over each other as they jumped backwards.

"Tom is hungry," Tom said, his eyes on them, his voice low and dangerous. "Very hungry."

"W-w-we have plenty of f-f-ood, Tom!" said Esau, his eyes darting to the closet. "W-we can share with you! How did you get in here?"

"Tom so hungry," came the response as he held a clenched hand over his stomach and glared. "That Tom rip the wall in half."

From where she hid in the closet, Airomem suppressed a smile as Esau's and company's faces drained of blood until they reached a white so pale they rivaled the stars.

"We should, we should, ah, probably be fixing –" started Esau, moving towards Tom, but he held up a hand and the smaller man cowered backwards.

"Tom hungry and angry," he said, the muscles in his jaw pronounced. "You play games with Tom's food."

"And I've taught Tom something of the way of my people," announced Airomem, stepping from the closet and flashing her teeth. "You see, on my end of the ship, when we got hungry, there wasn't always food. Sometimes, we had to *improvise*, if you catch my drift. And we taught Tom here a lesson about food. Specifically, how to get more of it when none is around. Just like they did with Segni."

"Oh God, no," they whispered, moving back as Tom nodded, his eyes on the floor. "Please –"

"Oh yes," said Airomem with a low laugh. "But we'll spare you – all you have to do is stay quiet. Not a word. The slightest noise and – *clack*!" She brought her teeth together loud enough to make them jump. "Or, of course, you can leave."

"Of course, we'll be right on our way –" started Esau, edging towards the door, but Tom shook his head as Airomem spoke up.

"No, not by that way," she said, and pointed behind her to the open closet. "*That* way.

"But the others, what're they going to do to us?" he wailed, his face filled with realization.

"That does sound like a problem, one you probably should have considered before stealing the food," replied Airomem, throwing the door open wider so that the hole was fully exposed. "But is that as big as a problem as you staying in here with us?"

They left, quickly and quietly, into the hands of others that intercepted them just outside the wall. And Airomem turned back to Tom, her voice low.

"Well done. And now, for the most important part."

White light flashed as she clicked on the Omni-cutter and started to cut once more, burrowing deeper into the ship.

Chapter 61

My shoulder slammed into the door for the fifteenth time, the blow shaking me to the bone as the metal refused to budge. I stepped back for another charge, feeling the growing bruise on my upper arm groaning in protest, my neck already twisted from nights of improper sleep.

"Help us!" shouted Hannah. "We're so hungry! We need food! And water!" In one hand, she clutched the makeshift weapons, and the other, she clenched into a fist to pound against the wall.

But no help came. And likely, their voices were unheard compared to the uproar outside in the corridor.

"What in the Hand of God," I panted as Hannah drew in another sharp breath, her face blue from the shouting, "is going on out there?"

"No clue," she responded, "but damn I hope Elliott is behind this."

From our position, waves of noise washed over us – shouts combined with falling objects, jeers sloshing back and forth, slews of words completely incomprehensible by the time they were mangled with the other stimuli. Every so often, we would catch a familiar voice or sound – a word from Elliott, a screech from Nean, or the scraping of shovels against the walls.

"What else can we do, what else can we do?" I muttered, racking my brain and coming up with no solution.

"It'll come down to a fight," said Hannah. "Elliott won't leave without me. I know he won't."

"But what good will that do?" I said. "If he loses, that just means none of us escape."

For the fiftieth time, I inspected the walls and doors for weaknesses, and for the fiftieth time, I found none.

"All this way and all this time," I said, staring out the window at the planet. "All to go to waste, from ignorance. Sheer ignorance that will be regretted in a matter of days. But though we may fail, we shall not be forgotten."

Taking the broken metal shard, I walked to the wall and paused. Then I jammed the end in as hard as I possibly could, the tip making a faintly visible scratch on the surface. It screeched as it dragged, and Hannah held up her hands to her ears but uttered no protest.

One by one, the lines and letters came together, forming words. Our own story on the wall, for future generations to see, *if* there were future generations. A monument to our shortcomings.

A story of too few words, a story cut short. Entire lives encapsulated in sentences that could never do them justice.

Horatius and Hannah. Their home turned to prison, their voices silenced. May others survive where they cannot reach.

I swallowed, biting my lip as I finished. My heart knowing that this self-proclaimed prophecy contained what might be our last few hours. That this faint marking might be the extent of the story I would leave behind.

"Oh God," whispered Hannah next to me as a buzzing erupted from nearby, one that made the hairs on the back of my neck stand up. "Is it starting? Is this it, Horatius, is that the ship preparing to leave?"

She clutched my arm as the buzzing grew louder, her eyes shut tight. Mine were wide as my ears were on full alert, trying to determine the source of the sound. To know if the electrical systems were going offline, or if we would soon be losing pressure, or if something worse than I could predict was about to happen.

And there, just below where my shiv etched its last mark on the wall surface in front of me, a bright white light exploded outwards to fill the room.

Chapter 62

The wall bent inwards under Airomem's wrists like a blade of grass dipping under a wind, the suit stiffening from her fingertips to her ankles to apply the load. Her breath fogged on the metal in front of her as she pushed again, the end of her nose brushing against a shelf protruding from the wall, causing her neck to pull away backwards away from the surface at an odd angle. It was an uncomfortable motion, but a necessary one. The cut had to be made here.

The incision itself was like the others she had made, but this time, she had left the bottom of the cutaway intact, such that she could fold the metal upon itself. And as it yielded, the edges grated together like gnashing teeth, releasing a shriek that sent shivers up Airomem's spine and a flinch to flutter across her face.

"Tom thought you wanted quiet," came a voice from behind her, and she grimaced.

"I did," she said and shuffled to her left. "New plan. Help me push!"

Tom's hands appeared alongside her own and the shriek doubled in volume, his grunting doing little to drown it out until a two-foot-wide gap appeared and a head emerged from within.

"Ruth!?" shouted Hannah, reaching a hand through to grasp Airomem's forearm. "Ruth and Elliott, are they safe?"

"They are," Airomem reassured, the words tumbling out of her mouth as fast as possible, "but you are not. Hurry, come through; we're getting you out of here."

"It seems every time I turn around," I mumbled from within, my head shaking as my eyes traced along the incision, "that another impossibility becomes reality. Airomem, how did you do this?"

"Details later, details later," she said, waving her arms forward as Hannah started to step through the hole, her movements slowed due to the constricted space. "*Move!*"

Airomem's head was turned sideways, her ear cocked through the hole, listening as she held her breath. And there, muted but approaching, was Nean, just as Hannah tumbled into the room.

Then it was my turn to jump through the hole, and our turn to flee.

Chapter 63

My hip protested from days of inaction as I raised my knee to enter through the gap Airomem had created, carefully sliding between two sheets of metal. The sharp edges gleamed from both of them, revealing the jagged lines left over from the slag of Airomem's tool that snagged against my shirt when I came too close, leaving stretched ripples that ran down the fabric.

"You'll regret this, Elliott!" I heard from outside the door just as I slipped my back leg free. "I can hear them trying to escape now, and their screams are about to get louder!"

"Tom, help me," said Airomem, stepping forward to grip the shelf that extended out of the cutaway portion of the wall. "Pull!"

Outside the door, there was the sound of scraping furniture as the barricade was cleared, accompanied by the screeching sound of folding metal as Tom and Airomem pulled the gap shut once more, leaving only a thin crack where the hole had once been just as the door on the inside opened and Nean's voice came through clearer.

"You'll wish you had conceded, you'll wish –" he shouted, then choked on his own words. There was the sound of crashing furniture, as well as sheets being pulled from the bed and clothes from the closet in a desperate search. Airomem yanked us backwards into the apartment, gesturing back to the closet, where the hole had been concealed behind a layer of folding clothes.

"In you go," she whispered, sending Hannah through first. "Regroup on the other side. We must act quickly. It will take them some time to find this hidden exit, and we want them to be as confused as long as possible. So long as they think you are still trapped inside the corridor, they won't dare a pursuit. Though with our numbers, they would be little more than a nuisance."

Then Nean's voice sounded once more, this time a shrill scream.

"Search! *Find them* and guard the exits! They cannot have gone far, and they shall know true punishment when they are discovered!"

Airomem smiled and nodded, then pushed Tom and me through the hole. And on the other side, she leaned the metal she had cut away earlier against it to conceal any light coming from the gardens.

I'd always enjoyed working in the gardens to an extent, but never before had I felt the sheer joy of feeling the earth sink beneath my shoes or the smell of compost wafting upwards. I reached a hand down to the earth, touching it as I looked through the window once more, my eyes meeting the visible edge of the planet.

"We made it," I whispered and, above me, Airomem spoke.

"Not yet. We must be moving – I don't know how much time we have left, but it's dwindling."

Ahead, Hannah had already sprinted across the farms and was in the arms of Elliott and Ruth just outside the view of the entryway of the corridor. Beside them, hundreds of people were gathered, holding small bags filled with belongings, far more than I had hoped would ever take the leap to depart.

"Remember this day!" shouted Airomem as she walked before them, "as the day we find new life, as the day your ancestors will thank the heavens that you brought them to their home. Remember this day as the one where you made the right decision, where you chose life and adaptation! Now, take one final look behind you, then do not turn back – keep your eyes on the future, and let us depart!"

Together, the crowd started to move, a long line that passed by the corridor entrance on the way to the bridge. Young and old, with smiles of hope and frowns of worry, packs of families that clustered together and floated downstream. Airomem and I took to the front, while Elliott and Tom held the back.

And together, we walked, leaving behind only footprints on the path.

"We still have the food!" howled Nean from within the barricade, his face splattered with mud, his voice loud enough to be heard along the entire column and Vaca watching idly by his side while chewing. "We'll see who survives!"

Chapter 64

"Prometh, you absolute *genius*," whispered Airomem next to me when we came to the first fork, and a smile broke out on her face. She turned right with confidence, down into a hallway that jutted away from the main at an angle, and had a sharp zigzagging turn near the end.

"What are you doing?" I said at the head of the hallway, my feet planted. "That way is longer; we should turn back!"

But Airomem shook her head, continuing to lead down the side passage, speaking as she walked backwards.

"Before I left, a friend of mine showed me a map of how my people would evacuate. At the time, I thought he needed my help, but now I think he is the one helping us. This map was carefully drawn that, in case the ship were to lose power, there would be the least trouble in still reaching the bridge. And since the ship's sides are symmetrical, I just have to take the mirror image."

"Lose power?" I said, keeping pace beside her as the procession started moving again, "What do you mean by that?"

"I mean it would be as if every knob in the control room was adjusted to its lowest setting. Gravity, lights; both gone."

"*What?*" I said. "Airomem, if that happens, people are going to scatter. It's going to be near impossible to keep them together. They'll head back home!"

"Then send word back along the line that if power is lost, to continue forward," said Airomem, directing her words at the front of the line as they turned to relay the message. I fought the urge to quicken my pace, knowing that there were those who would not be able to keep up. "That no matter what happens, to continue forward! Every one of you, link hands, and *do not* let go! We will make it there together!"

Then she pointed at one of the men at the front, a kitchen cook with no children at his side, and spoke. "We need a count of every person in this line. Be sure to miss *no one*. And quickly! Leave your belongings behind; we will care for them. Go, now!"

He nodded and set off down the line, ducking and weaving to spot the children nestled between parents, disappearing around a bend in moments.

We were close now, mere minutes away, but there were plenty who had only rarely traveled this portion of the ship behind us. The puddles from melted ice were now reduced to tracks of moisture that threatened to trip up every step, and the air had taken on a musky quality from the standing water that caused noses to wrinkle down the line. The slaps of our footsteps rushed ahead, their echoes the only sounds from the front, and the strained hum of quiet conversation the primary sound from the back.

The corridors widened, merging back into the main hallway, and I thought back to the first time that Pliny had shown them to me, about how back then I would never have imagined using them for this purpose. That beside me would be a friend who I would once have considered more alien than anyone on my end of the ship. That together, we would lead the ship on an evacuation from the greatest crisis since The Hand of God.

And with only two more turns, we would have made it unhindered. But then darkness descended upon us like a physical blow.

Screams of shock flew down the line as feet left the ground and the hallway turned pitch black. Beside me, Airomem's stun guns flashed into the air like beacons, illuminating faces flush with fear extending as far as I could see. And my heart skipped as I saw hands that had come unclasped in shock, fragmenting the line, and I shouted, "Rejoin hands! Do not let go of your neighbor! Do not let anyone stray!"

Rapidly, the line repaired itself in my immediate vicinity, but without gravity, the effort of maintaining a straight line was far greater than it had been previously. Twisting torsos combined with loose belongings floating away from owners, the confusion prying hands apart once more, causing panic as the gaps between line segmentations widened.

"We have to get to the control room," I said to Airomem, fighting to remain right-side up, if that still existed. "We'll bring back the gravity, and then we can make it the rest of the way!"

"Without power," she responded, shaking her head, "the control room is useless. We need to regroup – damn, I thought we would have made it. If we had more time, we could have briefed everyone, we could have prepared them better."

"Airomem, this is beyond anything you could have prepared them for," I responded, remembering how well changes as simple as altered gardening methods had been received in the past. "Keep moving forward. I'll run through the line to keep it together. Give me one of your lights. I'll need it."

My hand brushed over hers as I took the stun gun, and her eyes met mine in the blue light.

"Hurry, Horatius," she said, her voice tight. "I didn't come all this way to save you, only to have you be left behind again. There are too many stories left for this to be your last."

I froze, thinking of something to say as her eyes lingered for a moment more. Then she started moving, the blue light bouncing along the hallway as I turned to push off in the other direction.

Chapter 65

"Keep together," I shouted, moving down the line, the retinas of others reflecting my light as I drifted past. "And keep moving. We're almost there!"

Being weightless, especially being weightless in the dark, was far more difficult than I anticipated. Twice, my head slammed against the ceiling or wall after a misjudged kick or a slip against the thin layer of moisture coating present on every surface. Each movement threatened to bring me in a collision course with the fragile thread of people making their way forward, promising to create destructive waves among the already tense crowd. And with each group of people I passed, the fractures grew wider, the panic more palpable, the people clinging more desperately to the sight of my light like a breath of fresh air.

"You, Ben and Asher!" I shouted at a particularly large gap, positioning myself in the center and addressing those on my left and right. "Reach towards me; we need to join your two segments. Ben, slow your side down. Asher, speed up. That's it! Here, take hold!"

Each of them gripped one of my hands, stretching me apart as I tried to pull them together, my chest muscles straining while being careful to keep the draw smooth and continuous. One jerk from the center had the potential to cause fractures on both ends of the line, tripling the problems in my immediate vicinity. But over the course of a minute, the distance closed as we drifted forward. Their fingers fastened, locking together the chain so I could move to the next link. And the next. And the next.

Until after several hundred people, the groups stopped entirely. Individuals peppered the hall, bouncing to wall to wall in lost desperation, their voices crying out as they searched for lost loved ones.

"This way!" I shouted, my light drawing them forward. "Past me and forward! Join the main while you can. You, Dan, how far back were you in the initial line?"

"Slightly past half," replied the former gardener, his body upside down in comparison to my own. "There are many behind us, Horatius. Are you sure, are you sure that what we are seeking exists at the end of this?"

"Positive," I answered, fighting to keep my voice confident. "Absolutely positive. Keep moving and don't let the others stray."

"Will do," he answered. "I'm trusting you, Horatius. I was always among those who adopted your methods. And I can only hope you are right once more."

Then he disappeared, and I dove further into the darkness, searching out movement, tracking down sounds. Looking for life.

"You!" shouted a voice from my right as claw-like fingers dug deep into my forearm and a weight slammed into my side. Yelping, I nearly lost grip of the stun gun as a wrinkled face entered into my vision, and I reeled backwards as it broke into a snarl and released a wailing voice.

"You led us into death, Horatius – at least back home, we had light! What have you done for us, you have manufactured the death of our children. You have sealed our fates!"

Spittle flew into my face with each word as I struggled to recognize the face, eventually realizing it was Granny Vitula, a woman who had spent most of her life in the background of the ship's population. She had been one of the few old enough to escape work, and spending the majority of her days alone, sometimes accompanied by those who wished to consult her memory. A memory that age had started to claim and came in pieces, often recounting past events as far more golden than they had actually been.

"You – you're almost there," I stammered, shocked to see her reduced to this state, wincing as her nails dug deeper.

"Almost to death!" she howled. "Almost to starvation, almost to –"

"No, listen! I can help you get there, I can –" But her wailing cut off my words, and I shook my arm as her nails broke skin, dislodging her, and spoke again, my voice shaking as I pointed and gave her thrashing body a push in the right direction.

"T-that way, go now! Follow the line!" Then I kept moving, trying to clear my head. There were far more others to rescue, others who sought salvation. And with limited time, I could not afford to help her.

But as I found others, and as I searched, her words still echoed in my head. Words I desperately hoped were false.

You led us into death! You sealed our fates!

Chapter 66

"Elliott!" I shouted as he came into view from around a corner, Ruth and Hannah at his side, and Tom behind him. I'd passed through dozens of wanderers before finding him, yet sounds had emanated from each fork I had passed, sounds from people diffusing into every possible direction. And while I knew I had not covered the breadth of the expanding crowd, by finding Elliott, I had reached the deepest end of it.

"Horatius!" he answered, leaping forward. "What's happening? Why did Airomem shut off the power?"

"She didn't do it this time," I answered. "It was bad timing. According to her, we are out of it, like a glass empty of water."

"I didn't realize it would come so soon," responded Elliott, "or at such an inopportune time."

"Neither did we," I said, "or we would have been more prepared. But now we have to herd everyone towards the bridge. We can't leave anyone behind, not after they trusted us."

Elliott shook his head, his eyes sunken.

"We're scattered from end to end, Horatius. Even with hours, there's no way we could find everyone. We've done our best to contain the line ahead of us, but even so, there are those that could have looped behind us."

"Well, we have to try," I said and felt my throat closing. "I can't, I can't lead them to starvation. Not again."

Elliott gripped my arm and spoke, his voice low and steady.

"You did what you thought was right, Horatius. Had we only followed tradition, had we never strayed, we would never have made it this far. Mistakes are impossible to avoid when striking a new path, and we are stepping away from one hundreds of years old. *Leaping* away from it. And we've had our fair share of mistakes. But now, now we have to continue pushing forward. To save who we can and to recognize that those who we can't are those that the mistakes have claimed."

"But –"

"Change cannot happen without resistance. Now, Horatius, you've traveled backwards to find us; let's travel forward to find the bridge. And save who we can before it's too late."

He leapt forward, pulling Hannah and Ruth behind him, and leaving Tom and me to follow. Despite his size, or his lumbering characteristics in normal gravity, Tom exhibited more grace than any of us maneuvering in weightlessness, using light touches against the walls to steady himself and maintain his momentum. The only other place I'd ever seen him so at ease was in the heavy room, back when I had joined him as a porter, back before disaster had struck.

And after a moment of silence, Tom spoke, his eyes straight ahead.

"Tom strongest man on this side of ship," he said, his voice reassuring. "But even Tom cannot carry everything. Horatius can't carry everyone."

Chapter 67

We saw nearly no one as we traveled, but we heard many.

"This way!" shouted Elliott, my voice matching his as we faced down a fork. "Back towards our voices, this way!"

But from within, we heard only shouts too morphed by turns and distance to distinguish words.

"Stop, we can't deviate!" said Elliott as Hannah headed in their direction. "We need to make sure everyone ahead makes it safely first."

"But they'll die," said Hannah, pausing, her body horizontal and five feet off the ground, "You waited for us, you came to save us. What about them?"

"The others first, then we can come back," responded Elliott, his face strained. "We cannot sacrifice those who are almost there for those who are lost. We can save far more with less effort. Then we turn back."

"*If* there's time," I said, drifting between Hannah and Elliott. "With every minute, they drift farther away. Even I haven't explored the full reach of these corridors, Elliott. I don't know where they will be taken."

"All the more reason to regroup," he said. "You'll be just as lost as them in the darkness."

"We could split up –" I answered, but Elliott cut me off.

"*No*, Horatius. We are the leadership of this side of the ship. It is our duty to deliver the survivors to safety – we *must* consider them first."

"Then you're condemning the others to die," said Hannah, her voice borderline accusatory as Ruth looked between her mother and father, and Tom stared into the darkness. "How are we any better than them? How are you going to live with yourself when we arrive at the new planet, and you know that your neighbors, the people you sat next to at meals, the children you saw playing at breaks, the elderly that helped raise you were abandoned here?"

Elliott fell silent, frozen, slowly turning to follow Hannah's gaze. I held my breath as he swallowed. And just as he started to move, the screams began.

At first, it was only a single voice in the distance, a thin reed of sound just barely perceptible, just enough to make me shift my gaze. Then another screech joined in, and another, rapidly increasing in number and volume, reaching a crescendo in mere seconds. And growing closer.

Ruth's head turned as she became the first of us to realize the next quality to the shouts.

That they not only were coming from down the hallway.

But emanated from every direction.

Chapter 68

"My God," whispered Elliott as he took Hannah's and Ruth's hands to pull them closer. "What's happening?"

His head whipped left and right, searching, but found nothing besides the blue light of my stun gun. And as soon as they began, the screams fell away, until only a few solitary new ones popped out of the darkness.

"Are they dying?" asked Hannah. "Why are they stopping?"

And just then, I realized that the blue light from my stun gun had grown brighter. Squinting, I gasped, understanding that the increase in light was not from *my* stun gun.

But rather from others approaching.

"Because they're saved," I breathed, just before three lights appeared down a corner and sped towards us, the wielders far more proficient at weightless travel than we were.

"Let's go, let's go!" shouted the one in the lead, slowing as he reached us and uncoiling a cord. "Grab hold! We're giving you a lift, courtesy of the Lear, your new brothers and sisters!"

"Did Airomem send you?" I asked, reaching out to grip the cable.

"We came as soon as she brought us news of the trouble. She's waiting now, at the departure vehicle. The doors have opened and we've already loaded our tribe – we await only upon the remains of yours!"

"A godsend," said Hannah, tears filling her eyes. "We are more grateful than you will ever know."

"As are we," said the Lear man, "for the return of our princess, for your shared knowledge of farming, and for new friends."

From behind, more bobbing lights appeared, as well as ahead, until nearly the entire area was illuminated as strong as it had been with power. Like us, others were towed behind members of the Lear, their faces alight with amazement as we converged. In minutes, we arrived at the entrance of the bridge, the door thrust open, and the inside glowing so blue that I nearly had to turn my eyes away.

But I couldn't.

The sight ahead was too mesmerizing.

Ranks of the Lear citizens were lined on the left and right of the hallway, ushering our people between them, pushing them along to where a double door had opened at the center of the bridge. And there, just before the entranceway, waited Airomem, personally welcoming each new member through the doors. Her chin high, her smile wide, her hair flowing straight back with no gravity to hold it down.

"Enter and find a seat!" she was saying. "Strap in, strap in! And prepare for the most monumental moment you will ever experience! Remember this to tell your grandchildren, so they may tell their own – today will be a day of legends! Hurry, move on – we are almost there!"

My smile spread to match hers as the Lear pushed me forward through their ranks, moving at the front of our small party, watching as more and more people disappeared within the double door. Then I was at the entranceway, speechless as Airomem pulled me aside for others to enter, my head craning to view the cavernous space within. Thousands of chairs arranged to face forward, crammed together to fit as many as possible into the confined space, with aisles that parted them into sections. And there, painted at the focal point of the room, was a uniformed man who stared at the crowd, waiting for them to settle. On his left pocket was a swirl of blue, green, and white that nearly matched the planet we now approached, and on his right was a bold number sewn on in white.

Fourteen.

"As we speak," said Airomem, beaming, her hand on my shoulder, "the Lear soldiers are combing your hallways, searching for any stragglers that may have become lost. And here, the Lear citizens await, to initiate the bond between our peoples. My father is welcoming them each into the departure vehicle and ensuring each is prepared for the final leg. This is what we were born for, Horatius. *This* is why we are here."

"This is our story," I responded. "The story of our ship, coming to a final end. The longest story I have ever known."

"And the best," she said, shaking Elliott's and Hannah's hands as they reached her. "Elliott, meet my father inside. It's only right that the two chiefs welcome our people together."

"Of course," he said, and Hannah spoke up next to him. "Yet again, Airomem, we owe you our lives."

"If only Pliny were here to see this," I said to myself, my stomach fluttering and heart rising as Ruth rushed forward, forming rapid signs with her hands before barreling into Airomem, who had bent over to respond in their language.

"We're here, we made it, we made it!" Ruth shouted, punching the air with one hand as Airomem laughed.

"You did," Airomem responded. "You are the true hero today, Ruth. The one who connected the ship. Now go on, head inside! We'll be right in to join you."

Then Tom was before Airomem, and he inclined his head in a bow.

"Of the chiefs Tom has known," he said, "you are the one Tom chooses to serve."

"Well, I'm not quite a chief yet – it's still my father – but I am most honored, Tom. Go on inside; we will be there shortly."

He rose his head to meet her eyes, then past her eyes and behind me as his mouth opened.

"No," he said, his voice low, just as I felt something crash against my shoulder and push me into him. I turned, searching, jerking away when I found two wide-open eyes staring back at me. Unblinking. With dried blood matted in the hair above them, and the teeth knocked away under lips that had been carved from the face. And underneath, where the neck and body should have been, there was only a stump with shreds of skin still attached.

The decapitated head bounced away from me and against the wall, and I identified it as one I had only seen once before.

Esuri, chief of the Aquarians.

And from the end of the hall, there was a laugh. A shrill one, coming from a twitching chest, streaking away from a face with a long scar that had just appeared through the door.

"Princess!" shouted Sitient as others crawled through the door behind him. "The reign of the Lear has ended. Your head will join Esuri's!"

Chapter 69

"Soldiers, to me!" shouted Airomem as the swarm around Sitient thickened, bodies already covered in blood and writhing in weightlessness, summoned by his maniacal laughter. She twisted to shout again towards the Lear behind her, and her face fell as she saw the dozen rushing her way, stun guns at the ready.

"The rest are still in the search party," she breathed, eyes widening as she turned back towards the gathering swarm around Sitient. Then she eyed the nearby Lear citizens and spoke quickly.

"Sound the alarm, shout into the tunnels! We'll need as much help as we can get! See if any soldiers are inside the departure vehicle and bring them out, and make sure anyone not in the military is ushered inside."

"Of course," squeaked one and departed, soaring as quickly as she could and narrowly missing the soldiers that had just arrived.

"You twelve," said Airomem, her words coming as quickly as she could think, "we'll need to form a bottleneck defense as best we can, to hold them off. It's just like on our end of the ship – they will only be able to have three abreast to attack. Without gravity, we'll have to defend the top and bottom of the hallway – I want half of you upside down, now, and stay that way. Two rows deep and behind me. When they charge, so do we, and we hold for as long as we can! We cannot let them reach the departure vessel or it will be a massacre."

"Let me help," I said, moving forward, but Airomem held out a hand.

"They'll need you, Horatius, when they reach the planet. We can't afford to risk your life, to lose centuries of culture from your side of the ship, and since you've never fought, you would prove more harm than help. But me – without me, my father can still lead."

I shut my mouth, knowing there was little I could do to refute her statement. Even armed with a stun gun, I knew little of defense, and a hole in their ranks would only leave more area for them to defend.

"Then give me your cutter," I said. "Let me help somehow. I know I can think of something!"

Her eyes on Sitient, her hand went to her belt, and unfastened the Omni-cutter before handing it to me.

"Be careful with it," she said. "What you cut cannot be brought back together. One slice in the wrong place, one opening to the outside, could mean your instant death."

"I will," I replied. "And, Airomem, look at me. You deserve to be on that planet more than any of us. Don't do anything stupid."

"Stupid seems to be working out for me lately," she said, snapping to attention as Sitient and his horde started pushing off the wall towards us. "Think quickly, Horatius. Now, soldiers, for the Lear, for all your ancestors worked for, for your friends and your family – prepare to charge!"

"For the Lear!" the soldiers shouted in unison, then stiffened into formation. Two of them exchanged glances, a young man and woman whose hands were clasped together, stealing a quick hug and kiss. Then the man leaned closer to whisper in the woman's ear, and they shared a bitter smile as well as a small nod. And readied to launch themselves like an arrow into the oncoming horde.

Chapter 70

"Tom, with me!" I shouted as the Lear and Agrarians prepared to accelerate towards each other. "Quick!"

We rushed towards the back of the corridor as I wracked through my thoughts, working for possibilities. There were plenty of tools back near the fields, but those were too far. The battering ram was gone, moved somewhere in the tunnels by the Lear. There was the power room, but without power, there was nothing I could actually *control* with it. But there must be something else, something we could use as a weapon.

And just before we left the bridge, my eyes fell upon the open door that had once sealed away the hallway.

Maybe we didn't need a weapon. Instead, we needed a plug.

"Tom, hold the door open!" I shouted, my voice frantic as I examined the hinges and frame. Without the frame, the door itself was just smaller than the size of the hallway, perhaps giving three inches grace on each side. Around us, Lear citizens shouted into the darkness, their voices shaking my concentration.

"The bridge! To the bridge! Attack on the bridge!"

Just feet away, a boy was zigzagging up and down the hallway, holding a box with a stun gun plugged into it that wailed louder than any human could, interspersing his own shouts in the lulls. And deep in the hallways, blue lights flickered as Lear soldiers rushed back to protect their people.

"Tom," I said, turning back to the door, my hands shaking, "I'm cutting through the hinges. I need you to keep this steady."

"Let Tom cut," he said, holding out his hand.

"No, Tom," I said. "One slip-up with this, if I cut to the exterior, then we are as good as dead."

"Tom didn't die when Airomem cut through," he responded. "Tom saw it."

"That's because the doors automatically seal when the pressure difference is high enough," I said. "We don't have that advantage, especially since we are removing this door."

Biting my lip, I clicked the cutter on, flinching as its white light battled blue for my field of vision. In a single swipe, I cut the top set of hinges, my eyebrows shooting upwards at the complete lack of resistance from the metal.

One down, two more to go.

The middle set was just as easy, and I prepared for the bottom, the only part that still held the door in place, when I heard a shout reverberate down the hallway.

"Charge!"

Five or six more Lear had made it to Airomem before her party drove themselves toward Sitient. Though vastly outnumbered, they filled the gap, their blue lights blazing like a shooting star towards the scattered stun guns, knives, and outstretched hands of the enemy. Screams erupted from the Agrarians, screams of hunger and anger that vibrated in tune with my bones, but failed to falter the Lear as Airomem led the pack, diving with her stun guns to split the assault.

And instants before the sides crashed together, the two soldiers that had nodded at each other before the charge reached forward, each taking hold of one of Airomem's ankles. Together, they ripped her backwards as she screamed with surprise, the group of soldiers forming a small hole for her to pass through as she flew backwards away from the collision to safety.

"For the Lea –" was the last sound the soldiers made, their voices raised in unison, their bodies stretched wide to prevent passage, their weapons bared, their courage forced upon their faces.

Then the Agrarians slammed into them, and the noise of screams and crumpling bodies rifled down the hallway.

I'd seen blood in my life, and injuries. But I've never seen blood spray like a water from a dropped cup, or bodies shredded like cooks pulling apart squash in the kitchen. And despite their bravery and their skill, there was no hope for the Lear as they were torn to shreds.

But that didn't stop them.

Long after their arms should have stopped working, they sliced forward with the stun guns, incapacitating as many of the Agrarians as they could. They formed their bodies into human shields when they could do no more, grasping each other to make passage as difficult as possible. Especially the couple, whose knuckles were white as they clenched each other's hands, both from force and lack of blood.

Tearing my eyes away, I finished the final cut to the door's hinges, and Tom pushed it through into the hallway. Behind us, the blue lights of soldiers had grown so close to hear them buzzing, and ahead, the Agrarians had lost momentum trying to fight through the bodies.

"Incoming, make way!" I shouted, turning the door sideways and pushing it to the left, such that bodies could fit through on the right. And with Tom's steady hand, we raced down the hallway as the blue lights gained on us, and Sitient's bloody head broke through the sacrificed soldiers.

And Airomem alone stood before him.

Chapter 71

Tom pushed off the walls twice, picking up speed as others flew by.

"Help!" I shouted to them, jarring two or three into movement. "Anyone; not just soldiers!"

We whipped past the departure vessel, moving faster than I could run, wind whistling as it passed over the door we held before us. Airomem still faced the Agrarians, her back arched with pride, a stun gun in each hand, hurling threats toward Sitient as he advanced. His eyes widened as he looked past her to Tom and me, and I saw his lips form a curse, a knife appearing in his hand. With all his strength, he threw it towards Airomem, shouting with rage as she deflected it with her two stun guns, the flashing knife spinning past her without injury.

And directly towards me.

I yelped as the blade approached, taking my hands from the door to block my face, my fingers deflecting the edge. I saw blood but felt nothing in those final seconds as we flew past Airomem, her hair billowing forward with the breeze we created. Then Tom and I turned the door horizontal, sealing the hallway, and lowered our shoulders into the metal.

I felt my each of my vertebrae smash into each other as we connected with the Agrarians in a series of racketing thumps, one for each of the bodies that detracted from our momentum. My teeth chattered each time we hit and rapidly decelerated, the back of one of the bottom ones chipping, the shard digging into the back of my throat as we ground to a halt.

"Hold!" I shouted to Tom, and we braced against the walls, keeping the barrier in place. The top began to pivot, dipping downwards as an arm appeared over the top, reaching to push off the ceiling to widen the gap. Just as a snarling face rose over the ledge, the two Lear citizens that I had called out to earlier reached the door at full speed, crashing above Tom's and my grips and forcing the door back to its original angle.

The metal of the door and the ceiling snapped together, severing the arm that stretched through as its owner on the other end screamed, cutting off even the brief flow of blood that showered over us. Then the first of the soldiers arrived, his weight budging the door another three feet forward, followed by another, her sheer speed and fierce momentum driving the door another three feet despite her small stature.

More and more followed, forming a brace, their arms and legs making struts against the ceiling, walls, and floor to keep the door in place. With a new arrival, the door moved forward, but each time the distance was less, decreasing from feet, to inches, then hairs' breadths as the number of Agrarians on the other side grew.

And within minutes, each new soldier no longer moved the door forward. Rather, their momentum only slowed it down as it began to grind backwards in spurts and jolts, as the Agrarians pushed back, and the Lear began to lose ground.

Chapter 72

"Hold!" shouted Praeter, arriving with thirty more of the Lear and bracing himself against the back of the person in front of him. "Hold, and make way! Your new brothers and sisters come to aid!"

Porters leapt forward from behind the Lear, grunting as they positioned their weight and muscles, the Lear organizing them into a structure that spider-webbed back along the length of the corridor, optimizing their strength and the available space. Then the Lear interwove themselves into tighter spaces, giving the porters more room to flex, while helping support them from the walls to prevent slipping.

Lear and Nectians pushed as a single human structure that passed force forwards until those at the front groaned with the pressure. And for a few moments, the door halted, but slowly began to move once more, the porters' breath coming in shallow gasps as their feet dragged across the floor, their heels squeaking with each begrudgingly lost step.

And though it moved slowly, any movement cut down on the remaining space between us and the open entrance to the departure vessel.

"There's too many of them," shouted Prometh from the back, staying clear of the structure, the skin around the severed finger joints pulled tight as he pointed. "Behind that door is a horde, a horde that expands as we deplete our energy. They have no regard for each other. They are a mob, grinding against each other until those at the front die from the force! We must find another way! Airomem, Praeter, to me – we must develop a plan! We cannot beat them through sheer power."

Carefully removing a hand at a time and allowing the Lear to fill in around her to replace her position, Airomem moved backwards, the crowd parting for her to pass.

"Go," said one of the Lear next to me, his eyes on my hands, which were still bleeding too heavily to brace against the door or the configuration the Lear had built. So I followed, careful not to disturb the living struts, ducking underneath shaking elbows and knees that fought for every inch.

"There are no controls within the departure vessel," Prometh was saying once I arrived with Airomem. I'd heard about him from her, and his deformed hand made him immediately recognizable. "The entire system is designed to move autonomously. There is a timer on the inside, one that shows fifty-two minutes remaining – at the pace we are losing ground, we have fifteen at best."

"We can cut away more sections of the ship," I said, stepping forward and gesturing to where I had removed the door. "If we make a barricade, then we can wedge it into the open space of the departure vessel."

Prometh raised an eyebrow, and Airomem spoke up.

"Prometh, this is Horatius. He is the reason why the other side made it here today – without his help, they would never have come of their own will."

"And if he does not exercise more care," said Prometh, looking towards my bleeding fingers, "his hands will mimic mine. I'll take it as a sign of wisdom. Anyways, Horatius, your plan does bear merit, but I fear we will not be able to hold a barricade. And the process of moving our people behind the cut-away metal while refusing to relinquish ground will prove quite difficult. Still, it is a start."

"A start," said Praeter, sweat falling from his temple. "But we cannot afford to let any of them into the vessel. Our bottleneck defense will work for a time, but the entryway is too wide and too shallow to hold for long. All it takes is for a few to slip past to cause havoc. And if our line breaks, it's over. Without gravity, holding together will prove near impossible."

"What if we had everyone out here pushing?" suggested Airomem. "Not just the soldiers and porters, but everyone?"

"It would likely be less effective and more chaotic," answered Prometh, shaking his head. "Too difficult to align the force and we will still be outnumbered."

"Is there any way you can think of, Prometh," said Praeter, "to attach the door permanently in the hallway? To repair it, just as the ship once repaired itself?"

"Not with the time we have left, and not to withstand that magnitude force," replied Prometh, his eyes squinting at the gap between the door and the walls. The back of the human structure reached us, and we moved back a few steps to create more space.

"Barricade, then?" I suggested, and he pursed his lips.

"Barricade it is, for lack of other ideas. I do have some modifications in mind, however, that will help maintain its integrity – sharp strips to ward them off, props to push them away. Airomem and Praeter, stay here. You will be needed to motivate the people. Horatius, you are with me, though with those hands, you will be of little use. You know your side of the ship, and that's where we will cut our material. We'll find helpers on the way."

We turned, preparing to rush to find materials, beelining towards the back of the ship, just when the shouts and groans began. There was a screech as the bottom of the door dug into the floor, skidding forward as the structure of Lear and porters wavered.

"Can't hold!" shouted Tom as the structure shook, quivering in place as it began to slide, no longer slow, but at a near walking pace. And from behind the door, a chorus of guttural sounds exploded forth as the Agrarians gained ground, the anger of hundreds of years manifesting itself in a single drive.

"We're breaking!" snapped one of the back Lear between ragged breaths as the front of the line started to crumple inwards. "Praeter, what do we do here? You have twenty seconds, tops!"

"Cancel the plan," Praeter snapped, pushed backwards by the collapsing structure. "We make our stand at the entranceway of the vessel. It will be costly, but we must make sure it does not extend beyond that – it cannot be fatal."

"Hold, but give ground!" shouted Airomem at the human structure. "Retreat to the vessel and pivot the door sideways to give us some shielding once we arrive. Then bottleneck formation, and prepare for the battle of your lives! For your family, for your friends, for the Lear!"

"For the Lear!" chanted back the soldiers, grunting as they slowly gave way, letting themselves skid across the ground as the Porters shuffled back, their motion clumsy and out of sync compared to the Lear, and I raised my own voice.

"Porters, back through the door first! You're to be the second line; we'll need you as backup." Then, speaking to Airomem, I said, "While they are big, they cannot fight. They would only break your formations. We'll use them to brace your soldiers, but I fear if they took the front, the fight would be over before it began."

Chapter 73

"Slow down!" shouted Airomem as the crowd collapsed in on itself. "Three porters, I need three porters *now*. At the front, we have to decelerate!"

Tom and two others scrambled forward at her call, throwing their weight into the door as the Lear cleared away. There was only ten feet left until the entryway to the departure vessel, and the Lear were flooding into it, waiting just beyond the opening with stun guns at the ready. The hallway beyond was empty – anyone who had yet to leave had now missed their chance.

"Prepare to pivot!" shouted Airomem. "Pivot and turn, keep the door between us, maintain the barrier! We want it sideways across the entrance. Lear soldiers, you must defend above and below the door! We can allow none through. The more you stun, the more bodies will be in their way, and the more difficult it will be for them to advance. Porters in the back, keep pressure on their backs so they can fight. Here it comes!"

Airomem and I slipped within the entranceway, Lear soldiers meshing around us and pushing us backwards. Then the back of the first porters holding the door appeared, and Airomem shouted as loud as her lungs would allow.

"Pivot! Pivot now!"

Tom sidestepped from the far end of the door, releasing it while the other two porters held it in place. It rotated on its axis as hands reached out of the freshly created space, groping and grasping the air, swiping mere inches from his shirt. Then as the door gave way more the first body squeezed through; teeth yellow, eyes wide, and frame bony. He screeched as Tom's free hand caught hold of his neck and threw him down the hallway, cartwheeling end over end until out of sight.

But now that the space was open, others started to flow through.

"Pivot the entire way, now!" commanded Airomem, and Tom completely released the door, allowing it to slam into him and drive him back into the opening of the departure vessel.

"Turn before it is too late!" she yelled, her voice frantic, knowing that unless the door was horizontal, it would be too difficult to defend the hands jabbing from around the outside.

Tom reached a hand above, gripping the top of the door and throwing it downwards, roaring from the bleeding bite marks that had appeared on his fingers after only a moment of exposure. Then he was thrown backwards as the door slammed into the opening at waist height, held there by the struggling mass of Agrarians, and blocking about a third of the bottleneck.

With Tom behind him, the Lear started to jab forward into the Agrarians, flashes of blue intermingling in the mess of flailing limbs and howling faces, striking any movement as fast as possible. The soldiers were six wide on the top and bottom, covering the entire surface area of the opening, each region appearing above and below the split of the door. Twelve moving parts in total, far more than their typical bottleneck, and far more difficult to maintain.

With far more places to break.

And the Agrarians before them far more hideous than last I had seen.

This first wave was weaponless and coated with blood, their own blood, from injuries due to the forward surge of those behind them. Multiple within immediate view had an arm snapped at the elbow, their faces contorted in pain, trying the escape down the hallway rather than attack. Their faces were patterned with black eyes, the bones on their cheeks pinching their taut skin red after rubbing against the door, their clothes ripped from stretching.

They fell over themselves as the electrical shocks fell in, scrambling to avoid the stun guns, yelping as they tumbled down the hallway. With each stun, another body ricocheted away, cast aside by their comrades as more came to fill their places. More that, with each layer, had less injuries. Had more energy. Had watched the Lear defense as they approached.

And then a true bloodbath began when the Agrarians with knives arrived.

Chapter 74

The first of the Lear fell when the timer read twenty-nine minutes. The second fell fifteen seconds later. And the third was down before the second had stopped screaming.

At the onset, the Lear line was taut like a drum, vibrating in and out from the center with each wave, bowing and flexing in more violent motions as the Agrarians gained momentum. It weathered fists and fingernails, bites and kicks, fending away strikes either through electric shocks or by warding the attacker away far enough away that the current of their own people swept them down the hallway towards Nectian territory. Some of the Agrarians waved the stun guns that Praeter had given them in exchange for Airomem, the batteries already worn down to render them useless, a faint crackle of electricity jumping between the prongs at random intervals.

But the first Agrarian with a knife had concealed it well, letting the metal rest under his forearm as he approached, angling it downwards to keep blue light from shining in a telltale signal off its surface. He drifted forward slower than the others, a smile forming across his face as he reached the front lines, his tongue lapping across his lips in anticipation. Pressing backwards, he resisted movement forwards, almost shuffling through space as he arrived at the very center of the Lear line, and waited for the strike to come.

It didn't take long.

With a hoarse shout, the soldier directly in front of him lashed forward, swinging his stun gun in an arc intended to incapacitate multiple Agrarians, his movement lethargic after tiring from holding the door and the start of the fight. Every few minutes, Airomem and Praeter switched out the soldiers fighting to keep the line fresh, themselves stepping forward to take the second shift, and this soldier was only moments away from a transition and ready to be replaced. The Agrarian waited as the stun gun struck the neighbor to his right, then continued towards him, the arc only slightly interrupted by the strike. And with a shrieking laugh, the Agrarian raised the knife and struck.

The soldier stared open mouthed as the edge of the blade embedded itself into his forearm, the blood rushing outwards and spurting onto his shirt in direct contrast to his blonde hair, the surprise turning to horror when a dozen Agrarian hands gripped his still extended arm and wrenched him into the crowd, churning him backwards through their ranks, each layer leaving their own injury upon him. Another Lear soldier fought to fill the open position left behind but was too late, the Agrarians pressing forward into the gap before he had the chance to clog it, splitting the Lear line into two down the center.

Then the Lear soldiers to the right and left of the gap, a man and a woman whose motions were becoming increasingly frantic after seeing their counterpart dragged away, were sucked into the Agrarian vacuum, shrieking as fingernails ripped away any part of them not covered by clothing.

"Fill in, fill in!" shouted Airomem, selecting three of the Lear from behind and pushing them forward, using the porters' strength to restore the line to functionality. For a moment, the Lear line held, until the next Agrarian with a knife struck, taking out two soldiers on the right hand side. This gap repaired itself far quicker, with soldiers ready to jump into position, but their grim expressions told that they knew their coming fate.

"We are rolling dice!" hissed Airomem to Praeter and Prometh, who were bent over the timer with me, searching for any way to accelerate its motion and to close the doors. "Should we lose multiple parts of the line at once, we cannot hold. If we are overrun, this battle is lost."

"Then we will have to hold," said Praeter, steeling his jaw. "But at this rate, it is going to come close. We cannot hold forever."

"And I don't think we can close the doors early," I said, pointing at the timer. Praeter and Prometh had explained its usage to me, saying that they had several like it in their power room, the red numbers flickering back towards zero to indicate time remaining until an event. And if I had the time, I would have admired it for a thing of beauty – it was set into the metal of the wall, a picture of the approaching planet surrounding it, wisps of gold ink depicting two outstretched hands extending away from the orb. More to myself than anyone else, I read the text aloud.

"May all be welcome, and none cast away – our doors are open to all for the journey ahead!"

"Damn," remarked Airomem, shaking her head, "if only the creators knew. There is no way to force it, then?"

"None that I can see," said Prometh as he squinted at the timer. "Unless we try taking it apart. But with the amount of modifications made in repairing this part of the ship after the asteroid, and the systems Necti overrode long ago, I would be hesitant to try."

"Then what do we do?" she demanded. "Wait while our own men die?"

"We stand, and we fight," answered Praeter. "To the last man and woman. Horatius and Prometh, think hard. Every minute fought is more lives lost, more of a chance that *all* the lives will be lost."

I nodded with Praeter, casting my eyes around the inside of the vessel. The citizens not trained to fight were huddled at the far end, a few of the remaining stun guns interspersed for light among them, their eyes darting back towards the opening with every new scream. Elliott and Hannah wove through them, stifling any signs of panic before it could take root, ensuring the group stayed well out of the way of battle. But other than the people and the chairs, there was little else of utility in the room.

In cupboards around the perimeter, there was water along with small packaged clumps of sticky material, marked "RATIONS" on the side. Neither of them had enough weight to be used as a useful projectile or other properties that could be put to use. The chairs themselves were fastened firmly into the ground, no parts removable, except for straps that could be cut away. And besides the timer, and the picture of the uniformed man at the front, the walls were barren and devoid of potential weapons.

"Airomem, Praeter!" came a desperate shout from the front lines, interrupting my line of thought as I scanned the room. "We need you immediately! Hurry!"

Chapter 75

"What is it?" said Airomem, pushing to the middle of the crowd, a sweating Lear soldier with a fresh scratch along his neck waving her over. Praeter, Prometh, and I followed, concern crossing all of our faces.

"Trouble, coming quick," gasped the soldier, his hand to his neck, feeling the shallow cut. "Look for yourselves, approaching down the hallway. Just visible around the corner."

Airomem darted to the front lines, replacing an edge soldier, her stun guns flashing as she stole a glance down at the approaching Agrarians. Her face turned white, and from our position, we heard her curse, taking out two Agrarians with quick jabs before retreating.

"My God," she breathed. "A whole section of knives is coming. There must be forty of them, all armed. There's no way we can hold."

"We'll have to," answered Praeter, just as a voice traveled over the fighting, just loud enough to be heard. Sitient's voice.

"The Lear have always been cowards and have always been cornered! But today, the Lear will be no more; today, we finish them with a final strike! Lear Princess, come out to fight, know that I will carve through the bones of your soldiers for your precious head, and dine upon you tonight in victory!"

"Damn bastard," hissed Airomem, stepping forward, but Praeter put a hand on her arm.

"Wait," he said, but she cut him off.

"No, it's time this ended. It's either we destroy them now or we lose."

"I never said not to fight, daughter," he said, his eyes blurring. "Only to not be rash. Together, we fight – to an end or to a new beginning. We need every capable body."

They moved, sliding to the front of the line, their voices calling to the soldiers, working those not yet at the front into a frenzy. And I moved forward with them, Prometh's voice chasing me.

"Historian, where do you think you're going? You can't fight, not with those hands."

"But I can still push," I answered. "And while I push, I can think!" I took a place next to Tom, helping to brace the line of soldiers. His eyes met mine, and he gave a brief smile.

"Not as strong as used to be," he said, eyeing my attempts to brace myself against the ground and side wall. "Should have gone to heavy room more."

"Maybe if it wasn't destroyed, I would be able to go back," I answered. "But this will have to do."

"Destroyed," he sighed, shaking his head, the smile leaving his face. "Not just heavy room destroyed. All destroyed."

"But soon, when we survive, there will be a new ship, Tom. A better one. We just have to make it there."

The smile did not reappear on his face, but rather the frown deepened as his brow furrowed.

"Tom like old ship," he said, looking ahead to where the Lear soldiers prepared for the onslaught, Airomem and Praeter sharing the center, their voices starting a chant.

"For the Lear!" they shouted, their fighting turning into a dance at the cadence. "For the Lear! For the Lear!"

The soldiers joined in, their voices deafening, their stances in defiance, just as the first of the Agrarians entered their vision, pushing their colleagues away in a rush to attack. They were the biggest I had seen, men laced in scars so thick they could have been clothes, eyes bloodshot with rage, bodies twitching in anticipation.

Sitient was at their center, his mouth opening in a battle cry, launching himself forward into the Lear to spearhead the attack directly at Airomem.

"No!" I shouted, my mind racing, watching as Praeter blocked a blow meant for his daughter by attempting to stun Sitient's attacking arm, but Sitient easily evaded the attack. To their left and right, the Lear fell in a wave, knives cutting down the first layer of defense as more stepped forwards to take their place, only to be cut down themselves.

"Tom like old ship," Tom repeated next to me, his voice shaking as I heard Airomem start the chant once more, the Agrarians returning the noise twice as loud. "Tom like old ship."

"We have to fight, Tom! Don't lose focus!" I shouted, my eyes on Airomem, watching as she narrowly missed another swipe from the side. "Oh God, what can we do? What can we do?"

"This Tom's home," Tom continued, taking a deep breath as his normally deep voice cracked. "Tom's home, only choose one."

"That's right, Tom. We've already chosen one!"

Then Tom gripped me at the hip, his eyes blazing as they looked into mine, his fingers clutched halfway around my torso. His hair was mangled, coming down across his face, strands of grey appearing where they had not before.

"Tom, what are you doing? Stop it, we have to focus. Focus!" I yelled, trying to break his trance.

Even his face appeared muscular from this close, the tissue contorting as he formed the next few words, his grip on me becoming tighter.

"Only absolutely necessary," he said, as if his words made complete sense. "Horatius, make sure I made the right decision."

Then, with a wrenching feeling, his hand left my hip as he launched himself forward, careening into those in front of him.

And Tom broke the Lear line.

Chapter 76

The line shattered before Tom as he swam through it, knocking Lear left and right while using their bodies to increase his own speed. He drove through Airomem and Praeter, splitting them apart with enough force to drive them inside the vessel, then crashed into Sitient as his momentum took them both towards the back wall. His hand twisted around Sitient's shirt before he could cry out, twisting the fabric so tight it cut off all circulation, and hurled Sitient down the hallway to crash through the formation of half a dozen Agrarians.

The other Agrarians turned on Tom as he smashed through them, jabbing through his shirt and pants with knives, shrieking as he continued to move past them and reached the back wall. He fumbled with something in his hands for a moment as another knife plunged into his shoulder blade, grimacing as the wielder pulled it out for another blow.

And Tom turned back towards us, blood streaming down his chest, the Agrarians swarming over his body as the Lear looked on horrified.

"This Tom's home!" he shouted to me as a bright white light exploded out of his hand. He raised the Omni-cutter that he had stolen from my hip high, then faced Airomem, who had just recovered inside the doorway. "For my chief – for the Lear!"

"For the Le –" the soldiers roared back, their voices lost as he slashed the Omni-cutter across the freshly repaired wall, cutting a thin straight line across the metal. In most areas, two layers of metal separated us from the outside – but here, where the ship had brought itself back together, only a thin layer was present. A layer that blasted apart before Tom could complete his stroke, and the inside of the ship met the vacuum of space beyond.

The Agrarians had no time to react as the wall ripped itself apart at the welds – unlike the hole Airomem had cut in the window of the apartment, there was a near unlimited air supply on this end of the ship, since I had cut away the door on one end of the hallway. And this was no pinhole like she had created – rather, this was an uncontrolled opening beyond that screamed at the hungry air to escape at full force, and bring anything it could with it.

Mercifully, the sensors on the doors of the departure vessel registered the pressure differential before Tom's body was sucked through the hole he had created along with the nearest pocket of Agrarians. In a blur, the doors slammed shut, cutting off all visual connection with the bridge as wind roared through the hallway, howling through the now several-foot-wide hole that continued ripping through the crumbling metal, the voices of terrified Agrarians joining its shrieking.

For three seconds, we could hear the screams and sliding as people and objects were grated through the hole and expelled as a gift into the space beyond. Then there was only silence, the supply of air exhausted as pressure doors on the Agrarian end of the hallway and within Nectian territory shut, sealing the already determined fate of the Agrarian hold between them.

And once more, the bridge was broken.

Never to be one again.

Chapter 77

The echoes of the booming door faded away to be replaced by the cries of the fallen, accompanied by shouts of surprise as gravity switched back on, bringing people and objects crashing to the ground. Then Hannah's voice rose above the crowd.

"Leave the injured where they lie! Those who can walk, make your way to a seat near the front. Doctor's apprentices, tend to their wounds, while doctors, come with me to those in most desperate need. Elisha," she shouted and pointed to her personal apprentice far back in the crowd, where she stood with her own family, "bring the medical carts to me, both of them. Let's go, *now!*"

Former members of the school Hippoc darted out from among the crowd, brought to life by Hannah, weaving around chairs to the ranks of Lear that were producing pools of blood near the door. Airomem stood over her father, shouting at Hannah as he clutched a knife that had pierced his shoulder, then shouting at him as he waved the healers away to tend those more wounded. And I stood as the center, my mouth dry, whispering a name in final homage.

"*Tom.*" Perhaps the one among us who most deserved to arrive at the new planet, and who would now never make it. Tom, the true porter, who had carried us upon his shoulder. Tom, who –

"Horatius!" came a small voice by my side, and I looked down, wiping away a forming tear only to smear blood from my hand upon my face, then saw Ruth tugging at my shirt. "Horatius, you have to move! This area is for the injured and the doctors. You can't stay here!"

I blinked, realizing that doctors were actively swerving to avoid me, and let her pull me towards a seat a few dozen feet away. In front of us, Elliott was systematically combing through the crowd, splitting those with minor injuries and those in full health who needed to be seated.

"Let me see your hands," commanded Ruth, and I nearly smiled at the authority in her voice, one that seemed misplaced for one so young. I obliged, holding them outwards, nearly retching as I saw the damage. Two fingers on each hand sliced to the bone, large scabs still oozing blood starting to form over the gashes, while the cut continued in a much more shallow fashion across the remaining fingers.

"There's only so much I can fix," said Ruth, her eyes concerned. She unrolled a bandage from her pocket. "I'm not sure how useful these will be once they've healed."

"You are a gardener; I wouldn't expect much in the way of healing," I said, then stopped, my thoughts spinning, my head tilting, a long overdue thought crossing my mind for the first time. "Wait, Ruth, *why* are you a gardener?"

Maybe it was how preoccupied I had been with the events leading up to Segni's death, or maybe it was my appreciation of having such an astute learner in my classes. But Ruth was the daughter of a cook and a doctor, both the head of their fields, both members of the council. And yet *somehow*, she was a gardener, a position entirely unfit for someone of that status.

Ruth began to wash and wrap my fingers with practiced hands, her eyes on the work, speaking as she applied the bandage.

"You weren't the only one with secrets, Horatius. Not at all, not at all. But I had to promise my parents not to tell, though I still told *her*," she said, and gestured towards Airomem. "Not even my parents knew that, but it felt right."

"Told her what?" I asked, perplexed, biting the inside of my cheek as Ruth tightened the bandage. "And how did you learn to do this?"

"Horatius, my mother is just under the head doctor. She taught me," she said and knotted the bandage before standing up. "I'm still not allowed to say anything, but I can help you think. You are not the only reason Pliny fought for farmer representation in the council all those years ago. And you are not the only one who disapproved of Segni's actions, though our methods would take far slower. I'll answer your question with questions of my own. Who is on the council for head cook? And who for head doctor?"

"Elliott, your father," I said. "And I suppose she started attending meetings prematurely, but your mother was soon to take the role of head doctor."

"Correct. And you, for head gardener. When it came time for you to choose someone to train to be on the council, would I not be in your top prospects?"

"That's rather bold," I said, "but yes, objectively, you would."

"And so it would be a council of Segni's family against a council of my family. And as the years passed, and Segni grew old, the title of chief would come into question. Segni, being childless, would have to pass the responsibility to someone outside his family. And our family just so happens to lead every main class of the ship."

"You," I stuttered, coming to the sudden realization. "You became a gardener, to try to become a chief? By gaining the support of all the people?"

"I said nothing," replied Ruth with a sweet smile, "but I do happen to have a talent for medicine and cooking, which may prove useful in gaining their support. Of course, it just *happened* to be that I took an interest in those things."

"But you're forgetting something," I said, raising a hand. "Segni and Vaca were both young. They could easily marry and have children, and they *would* have had children, had the ship not come back together."

"Oh, Horatius," she uttered and shook her head. "Married or not, there are herbs to prevent such things. As a doctor, my mother would have the knowledge. As a cook, my father could blend them into meals quite nicely. Perhaps this was one time we *were* grateful for Segni's appetite."

Then she squeezed my hand so hard, I yelped, and whispered in my ear, "But remember Horatius, I said *nothing*. Some things are best left secrets."

Letting go, and before I had a chance to comment, she shouted over my head to Airomem where Praeter was still fending away doctors.

"Bring him here; I can help! It's bad, but not so bad! There are others who need the professional help more than him."

"Your family, they planned all this from the start?" I asked as two Lear soldiers carried Praeter with Airomem leading him towards us.

"Planned what?" asked Ruth, a sweet young girl once more, rummaging through a small bag at her side for more medical supplies. "It's all just bizarre happenstance, a lucky combination. Who could have guessed it? *I* certainly never would."

Then Airomem arrived with her father, and Ruth started to inspect the wound as Airomem looked on, her hand on her father's forearm.

"I'll be fine," Praeter protested, but Ruth's small hands pushed him back into his chair.

"I'm just here until one of the experienced doctors is available," she said, "All I'm doing is making sure your condition is stable. Which it is – the knife hasn't hit any arteries, and we'll have it removed soon."

The last few words were directed at Airomem, and the muscles in her neck loosened a fraction as she heard them.

"Is there anything I can do?" I asked Ruth.

"We need more water; find someone who can help you carry it," she responded, and Airomem's attention turned to my hands.

"Horatius!" she exclaimed. "What happened? I never had a chance to ask in the commotion! Your hands; I assumed you would be the one to record this journey. At least, that you would want to."

"I'm no worse than the others, and better than many," I said. "As for recording, it can wait until the story is done."

"Yes, it can," she answered. "And I owe you a thanks, Horatius, a thanks for your quick thinking with the door shield. Without it, we wouldn't be here. Without it, I wouldn't be here."

She wrapped me in a hug, her hair drifting across my cheek. As she pulled away, our eyes met, and her cheeks flushed – and I smiled, realizing that as the Lear princess, nearly all of Airomem's outward actions had to be political. But maybe this one, a rare occurrence among many, was not meant to be.

"Go, help him with the water," said Praeter. "Be seen among your people, old and new. I was chief of the ship, but my hair continues to grey, and new challenges lay ahead. I lie here weak, but it is time for you to be seen in a different light by everyone. Go."

Together, we walked, delegating the task of fetching water to one of the doctor's apprentices, Airomem casting quick looks back towards her father in between settling the general population, helping the injured, and calming those still shaken by the events.

And without you, I wouldn't be here, I thought, looking sideways at Airomem as we worked, helping in any ways I could without my hands. We aided as the doctors rounded up the last of the wounded, transporting them to seats, while forming a small pile of less fortunate near the exit. Three bodies in all, consisting of those claimed by their injuries after the doors shut, the rest of the dead claimed by the Agrarians. Left behind in the void of space.

"Airomem!" came a shout behind us, and we turned to see him and Hannah approach.

"Elliott, Hannah," Airomem exclaimed, breaking into a smile, "you should be proud of your daughter. It's her cry for help that made this possible."

"*No,* Airomem," responded Elliott as Hannah clutched his hand, "it's you who made this possible. As resting chief of our side of the ship, I realize that there is much I do not know. That we do not know. And while I am not willing to give you the same level of authority as Segni, I give you my gratitude. More than that – I give you my allegiance."

"As do I," added Hannah with a nod. "We have observed your character over the past few weeks. So long as we remain on the council, we will ensure you have the full support of our people."

"For a unified ship, and a unified people. I will not betray your trust," said Airomem, inclining her head as they nodded.

Then without my attention on it, the timer reached three minutes, and a short siren played from above.

Chapter 78

"To your seats, to your seats!" shouted Airomem as we walked back to her father, and she stood by his side. "And hold on! This could feel just like the jolt when the bridge opened for the first time, and we want to avoid any additional injuries."

Then she cleared her throat and looked down at her father, waiting.

"Go on," he said, gesturing to his shoulder. "I can't be expected to usher in the new world with an injury like this. And besides," he said, and a darker expression crossed his face, one of regret, and of guilt, "you are the reason the Nectians are here today, Airomem. How can I call myself a leader among them, when I once suggested we leave them behind? While I can call myself the chief of the Lear, I cannot do so for the Nectians. It is not my place to unify the people. It is yours."

"You did what you thought was best," she protested, but he shook his head.

"We will have plenty of time to speak to that later, Airomem," he said, "But now, we have but minutes. Speak. For me, for them, and for those we left behind."

She nodded and turned, surveying the room. My own eyes tracked hers as they flicked over the audience that was now staring at us, as well as the sheer number of empty seats that dwarfed our numbers. For every one occupied, there were at least twenty empty, ones that seemed to stare inwards around us, as if they were filled with the ghosts of those who should have claimed them.

The timer on the wall reached two minutes, and she climbed to stand on her seat, her head the highest in the vessel. And from her pocket, she pulled out a piece of metal, one I recognized from the first time I had visited the bridge. One she must have removed with the Omni-cutter before I had arrived, from the inside of our territory above the door.

A simple square, with *Necti* engraved into it.

"Separate we fly, together we land," she began, holding the square high for all to see. "Many died to give us this moment. Those today, whose memory is still imprinted vividly upon our thoughts, and those long before, so long they may now be nameless."

From her other pocket, she pulled out one of the stun guns and continued to speak.

"Before the Hand of God struck, there were those who numbered far higher than us, our distant grandfathers and grandmothers. We remember them!"

She brought her hands together, striking the metal against the stun gun, the resulting *clang* tolling like a bell.

"We remember those who the Hand of God claimed, those who died in the hours after the tragedy!" *Clang*, rang the metal, calling out to the spirits long before.

"We remember our brothers and sisters who did not die physically, but in their own minds. The Agrarians and Aquarians who lost their way long ago and sealed their own fate." *Clang*, sounded the bell, louder and more aggressive this time, as the volume of her voice continued to rise.

"We remember those who died from hunger and thirst and war in last few centuries. Those who were claimed by hard times, by dwindling resources, and those who are our direct ancestors, and were claimed by age as we too will be." *Clang*.

"And we remember those who fell today! Those who died to directly save us. The Lear soldiers, the porters, and those lost along the way to departure. For Tom. We remember them most of all, and they shall live in our hearts, and their sacrifice shall not go to waste!" Cheers intermingled with sobs among the crowd, whistles with tears as Airomem's own voice broke, and she paused, regaining composure, then holding the writing on the metal for all to see.

"This name on this metal," she continued, her voice now level. "This was carved by Beatrice, the wife of Necti himself, as she waited at the door for him to return. To be reunited with the husband she lost. Today, we are united as brothers and sisters. Today, we cover the gap created long ago, and we become one. On our arrival, *Lear* will be engraved on the back of this metal as our tribes merge, as we are renamed and reformed. As we take those whom we remember and we make them proud of their sacrifice. Together, we share this accomplishment, together, we shall prosper, and together, we will be remembered just as those before us!"

The crowd erupted as she finished, holding the metal rectangle high, leading Nectians and Lear alike in a clamor just as the timer reached zero, and a buzzer sounded, the ship itself joining in the applause. But then the crowd gasped, jerking backwards in shock from something unlike anything they had ever seen.

The uniformed figure on the wall before them moved and spread his arms wide. And above them, a compartment in the ceiling burst open with a *pop*.

Chapter 79

"Congratulations!" exclaimed the figure on the wall, spreading his arms wide as one of the front row children shrieked. "Congratulations upon your arrival, upon your great accomplishment for humanity!"

Above, strips of colored plastic rained down, showering us in a swirling mixture, sticking to freshly applied bandages and forming a small pile atop the dead. The figure opened his mouth once more and raised a hand as the entire front row joined the child in screaming, fighting to back away from the enormous human.

"Hey, *hey*!" shouted Prometh as he walked up to the figure, and turned to face the panicking crowd.

"He's going to eat him!" shouted one of the front children. "Watch out! Watch out! He's dead!"

"You there, quiet," commanded Prometh to the child, and knocked his hand against the figure's waist, the sound of knuckles on something sturdy calming the spectators. "Sit and listen. He isn't real; he's like a memory. Things like this used to be common before the Hand of God. You are in no danger. Sit and listen! We will only hear this once! We are experiencing history and I shan't have your ignorance make me miss it."

Then he leaned back against the speaking figure, his expression calm as the front row's faces turned various shades of red, and the figure continued to speak. Now that the room was calm, I realized that his voice actually came from *behind* me, similar to how the announcement of the ship coming together had come from above.

"Before I begin, ensure you are buckled in. There should be seats enough for everyone, based upon our sustainability calculations, but it will be close! Make sure you make room for your neighbors, and that no one is turned away."

"Not a problem for us," I muttered, looking left and right at the sea of empty seats, and the figure continued.

"Now, for introductions. I am Captain Xavier, the first captain of Dandelion 14. This message has been recorded the day before departure, about one thousand years prior to you hearing it. As you know, each captain since me will have recorded their own messages on their first and final days, messages that many of you have heard repeated in your scholarly studies. Perhaps you have even heard my own – fear not if you have not; these will still be preserved and available after your arrival and stored for access just underneath where I stand now, where as many as a hundred recordings are located in a small cabinet."

I leaned forward in my seat, searching the area he indicated, catching sight of a small recessed handle in the wall. The early captains of the ship recorded just as this one was, true gems of history. Clues about where we were from, and what we had been like before disaster struck! Copies intended just for us, not simply leftovers found among the wreckage.

"But that is the past, and I come to speak to you of the future. The next steps in your journey are crucial – arriving on the planet, surviving on the planet, and thriving on the planet. You have nearly completed arrival – as I speak, the ship has detached, and we are entering into the gravitational field of New Earth 14. The vessel will take you to the designated entry point, which is where the *survive* stage begins."

The figure stepped to the side, and a rotating picture of the planet appeared, a red target mark blinking at a point near its center. The symbol was located on a small splotch of green, much smaller than many of the other masses of green among blue, which mirrored what I had seen of the planet outside the window.

"Here is where the vessel will land and where, when the doors open, you will be. This is an island, meaning it is separated by water from the rest of the land on the planet, a method employed by us to help insulate you from potential dangers and help you become accustomed to your new way of life. The environment has been predicted to be mild, the temperatures advantageous to life, the food and water sources nearby and easily attainable. Furthermore, this is where the supply ship landed several years prior to your own arrival, ensuring that when you arrive, farms have been created, buildings constructed, and infrastructure developed. You'll find when you arrive, you will be mildly busy, as we have based the structure to be maintained by a mere five thousand. Further details of this arrangement have been conveyed to your current captain through instructional logs, and he or she will coordinate arrival activities."

Eyes turned to Airomem and Elliott as they shifted in their seats. "Maintained by five thousand," whispered Airomem next to me. "*Five thousand?*"

"We have hard workers," I responded. "And so long there are farms and water, we can manage."

"What is most important," said the figure, extending an arm and flicking a handful of yellow dots onto the planet, "is that you thrive. These are the locations of technology points, steps that your civilization will take as it matures into adulthood. We have delayed these on purpose, with the reason that many are too risky technologies to share while you are few in number. I urge you to focus upon growing stronger for several decades before attempting to reach these, as there are dangerous obstacles between you and them. Obstacles that were pieces of the original Earth deemed to be preserved, and so they were sent ahead of you."

Things flashed where the man had been, things that stood not on two legs but on four, that bared sharper teeth than I had ever seen, some with long nails extending from their hands. Things I recognized from the descriptions I had read before, maybe not by their particular names, but by their titles. *Animals.*

"Again, beware, as they know no fear of you," he said. "But no danger will befall you unless you travel off the island. Should you come in contact with other creatures on your island, know that they are safe, that they are for your utilization. Further instruction on these shall await you once you have settled in. Now, keep your purpose in mind: arrive, survive, and thrive." Then he raised his hand to his brow in a salute.

"Buckle in, hold on tight. Descent begins soon as the gravity fields initiate. Captain Xavier, wishing you, Dandelion 14, the beacon in the darkness, the hope of humanity, luck."

Chapter 80

A vibrating hum sounded from below, and around the departure vehicle, my hair stood on end. Or rather, straight up, as my stomach lurched into my chest, and our environment transformed from normal gravity to a force pushing straight up. Beside me, Airomem reached up to gather the strands now scattered above her head into a single knot, tightening them with a flick of her wrist. The lights above dimmed as the feeling intensified, and I heard retching from ahead, turning just in time to witness a stream of vomit streak upwards to splatter on the ceiling. Quickly, I averted my gaze as others joined in, and regretted that many of them had sat together in close groups while so many seats had been available.

"Your people," said Airomem, distracting me. "You can start them gardening? You can lead them in that aspect, as well as a portion of my own."

"Maybe not physically," I said, raising my bandaged hands, "but I can instruct. I plan on instructing them in far more than that, however."

"Of course," she responded. "I'm sure Prometh will be happy to assist. But first, critical-to-life skills must be prioritized."

"Agreed," I said. "And we better hope that there is some food available on arrival. What we brought will not last long, and while there appear to be prepackaged rations on this ship, we have yet to take stock of them. Or to see if they are still edible."

"Take however many of my people you need, then," she said, her voice growing strained as the upwards force increased marginally, "except for the soldiers. They'll leave the vessel first, and we'll need to make sure there are no threats ahead."

"Be careful; let's have a better interaction with whatever is down there than we did when we first met," I responded. "*If* there is anything down there."

Then, before she could continue the conversation, the gravity field increased further, making the blood rush to my face, accompanied by a headache. I struggled to grip the edge of my seat, the bandages preventing me from finding a handhold, and Airomem taking hold of my forearm to steady me.

I lost track of time in those moments, the edges of my vision turning red, fighting to keep down the nausea that threatened to make me join the dozens with already empty stomachs. And when I looked up, the vessel was silent. Gravity felt like normal – well, slightly heavier than normal, but not by much. I swallowed to pop my ears and jumped as I heard a sound behind me.

The *whoosh* of two doors opening, accompanied by a bright light that flooded into the back of the ship.

Chapter 81

I will always remember the feeling of sunlight on my skin for the first time. The sensation bearing a warmth that the cold mechanics of the ship could not provide, an experience I never knew existed. Something my imagination could not conjure on its own.

The soldiers had left the open doors first as Airomem instructed, their eyes squinting as they first stepped onto soft grass, whose footprints were the first to ever claim the surface. They fanned out in a semi-circle as the rest of us departed, creating a barrier between us and Earth 14. Airomem, Hannah, Elliott, Ruth, and I led the others, our eyes wide as we stared out before us, taking in the setting.

Gasping.

At the sheer *expanse* of farmland, the absolute lack of any containment making me shiver. The feeling of a breeze with no vents, the smell of what I would later realize was the salt of the sea, the line of tall plants in the distance, their leaves reaching upwards high into the sky, their stems as thick as several torsos. At the blue above us where the black of space should be, tinged with white puffs similar to soup froth. At the earth that rose taller than I, that wasn't *flat*, and hard earth where plants could not grow and I could not smush with my fingers, that I would later know as rock.

And in those beginning weeks, there were many firsts.

There was the first sunburn at the end of the first day, experienced by all.

The first taste of new species of vegetables previously unknown.

The first time entering a building, which we called minor ships.

The first ascension in climbing a tree to view the expanse of the island, the wind drifting through my hair.

The first storm, when lightning split the sky, and we feared for our lives.

The first experience of water up to my waist, wading into the ocean as it sought to drag me deeper, and I retreated back to what I had come to know as sand.

And among all these, there was the first time both Airomem's and my hands clasped together under the stars of night, the first time our lips met as the crickets chirped, and my hand pressed against the small of her back. When we realized that New Earth 14 was not the only new life we were starting, that not only did we depend upon each other for survival, but for something else. Something more.

And that after all this time, our destination had been reached, and a new journey had begun.

Of memories and history wed together, seeking a brighter future.

Epilogue

Ruth sighed from within the departure vessel, glancing outside to see the rain coming down in sheets, and turned back to the captain logs. It had taken her two weeks of recording and interviewing, long afternoons when she wrote down the words of Horatius as his hands recovered, and listened to the experiences of Airomem. Then she brought the pages back to the ship where she had learned how to make a recording alongside the captain's logs, which she and Horatius had been studying at nights.

"So concludes the travels of Dandelion 14, of my family and friends," she finished, staring into the camera, a red light indicating it absorbed her words, "Future updates to arrive as progress is made and new stories created. This is Ruth," she smiled, remembering the words of the captain logs she had watched before her, the next words making her feel official, "signing off!"

Outside, the rain still had not let up, and she remembered how cold she had been the first time she had experienced it. For now, she would stay in the last remaining piece of Dandelion 14 as shelter. And she glanced towards the recordings left by previous captains, ones still unwatched that she had promised Horatius she would wait for him to start.

One couldn't hurt. Besides, she would choose the one at the very end. That way, by the time Horatius and she arrived on it, she would be ready to watch it again.

Selecting it, she pressed the play button and retreated to the front row of seats, feeling only slightly guilty.

Static filled the screen, far more than the other recordings, the image dancing as it came into focus. The background area was not the inside of the departure vehicle like the other logs had been – rather, it was a room she had never seen. Neither was bearded man that stared at her uniformed like the other captains. Red splotches covered the skin on his face, and his hair was missing in tufts, his eyes bloodshot.

With tears upon his cheeks.

"I'm so sorry," he sobbed, his chin shaking, "I – I had no choice. I had to do it. No one else would."

He coughed, wiping his nose on his sleeve, blood showing alongside phlegm on the fabric, his pupils avoiding the camera.

"I had to, you understand. Oh, such a terrible thing, so terrible. But there were no other options. *None*. Oh God, the blood upon my hands. The evil I have wrought upon you, only for a slim hope at the greater good. The slimmest of hopes. I cannot even begin to ask for your forgiveness."

He sniffed again and composed himself, shaking his head and restarting, attempting to control his ranting.

"This is Bobby Cassandra, Scientist of The Well, Earth. Transmitting the message to you, the members of Dandelion 14, should you ever live to find it. If the disaster has not already killed you all. If you survived the asteroid. Oh God, the asteroid. I *had* to, you must understand. I'm so sorry, so very sorry! It was for the good of us all!"

He screamed the last few words into the camera, sobs racking his entire body, his head down so Ruth could only see his hair. Then he stared directly at her, the moisture in his eyes brimming over, his breathing uncontrolled and hyperventilating. And he just managed to force out a whisper, his face so drawn he looked like a living ghost, Ruth leaning forward to catch his next words.

"The asteroid. I sent it."

END OF THE BRIDGE
BOOK 2 COMING SOON
Sign up here for a notification when Book 2 is released:
http://eepurl.com/-j2Oz

Letter to the Reader

Hope you enjoyed *The Bridge!*

I'm an independent author, meaning I have no publisher backing to help my marketing. Instead, I rely upon the **word of mouth** of my fans to help others find my work.

If you enjoy this story, I ask you to please **share** it with a personal recommendation to your friends. It is people like you that help my stories reach the world.

To keep up with my work, follow me in any of these places:

My mailing list for promotions and new releases: http://eepurl.com/-j2Oz

My Facebook page: www.facebook.com/leoduhvinci

My official blog: www.LeonardPetracci.com

Thank you again for your support and your words of kindness. Feel free to drop a line at LeonardPetracci@gmail.com as I read all my fan mail and do my best to reply to everyone.

If you are a school teacher or librarian, I'm sending a few hard copies each week if you want to share with your students. In this world of handheld devices and electronics, let's bring back the paperback.

Don't hesitate to reach out.

Wishing you the best,

-Leonard Petracci

For more works by Leonard Petracci, visit his Amazon page below.
Some of his books are free!
https://www.amazon.com/Leonard-Petracci/e/B00JZC24TO/

Til Death Do Us Part, Science Fiction

Available in Ebook, Paperback, and Audiobook

Frederick Galvanni is the thief of the century, but it's not his first time claiming the title. For Frederick and the inhabitants of his world, reincarnation is real, but people are always reborn in the country in which they died. Now Frederick seeks to pull off his greatest heist yet—enter a maximum security prison, where souls are trapped through reincarnation, and assemble the greatest criminal team that has ever lived.

Allen, The Rogue AI, Science Fiction

Available in Ebook

Humanity cured cancer in 2063. Well, technically humanity didn't do it.
Their Artificial Intelligence did. And it's not finished.

Eden's Eye, Horror/Urban Fantas

Available in Ebook and Paperback

Caleb grew up as anything but special- with a trailer park as his home, a questionable education, and bullies eager to inflict the pain from their own lives upon him, his future looked dim. But when he loses his sight from a horrific accident, Caleb finds that there may be more to the world than most people realize. Stranger yet, being blind, he is the only one who can see the creatures who lurk among the shadows.

Made in the USA
Lexington, KY
03 May 2017